FIRE ON THE FARM

BETTY SHREFFLER

FIRE ON THE FARM

Published By Betty Shreffler

Copyright © 2017 by Betty Shreffler

PROLOGUE

*H*ave you ever been trapped in quicksand? Feeling like you're sinking into a terrifying abyss and there is no one to save you? Neither have I, but it's the best description I can come up with for what it feels like to suffer from depression. That's how you feel when depression hits you—like you're mentally and emotionally sinking into a black hole from which there is no return. No one can save you. No one's cheery smiles, cupcakes, lasagna, or casserole dishes can pull you back from the darkness that consumes you. You lose your sense of self, your self-value, you begin questioning every decision you ever made in your life and how it is you got to this point—feeling as though you have no reason to go on.

You begin feeling like life handed you its best hand and you played it poorly. You lost the pot, and now the game is over. But it doesn't have to end like that. It never has to be the end.

There is always beauty to be found, always love to be

shared. You just have to find the strength to get up each day. To shower and put on clothes. Then the next step, to take one foot out your front door, into the vast world and do the hardest part—trust in your journey. Wherever it may lead.

PART I
PICKING UP THE PIECES

CHAPTER 1

The first time I met my husband, Darrell, it wasn't love at first sight. No, it was a friendship as co-workers. Working as kennel technicians for a veterinary office was not glamorous by any means, but we made the best of it. Darrell had a wonderful attitude; he could find good in anything. It was charming and so was his sense of humor. We became fast friends and that made the job less monotonous.

During down time, we studied for our college mid-term exams in the staff room together. We both were seniors. He planned to graduate with an Agricultural Business degree while I was working toward a B.S. in Equine Management. More than anything, Darrell wanted to move back to his hometown in Kentucky and start a commercial farm. He had his future planned out with certainty and I found that even more charming. I, on the other hand, did not have it all figured out, but Darrell would soon change that for me.

I rubbed at my furrowed brow as the black ink in my textbook blurred my vision. My pencil eraser had been chewed to a nub between my teeth.

"Amy?"

Darrell used his pencil to flick a long, light-brown strand of hair away from my face.

"*Amy?*" he coaxed.

"Hmm?"

I lifted my head from my textbook and caught a glimpse of what seemed like humor in his vivid green eyes. They were the most beautiful eyes I'd ever seen—like soft gems with bits of yellow and brown infused. I could easily get lost in the details of them, but always avoided staring too long. Darrell's messy brown hair, broad shoulders and farm-raised muscles made him incredibly attractive. But he was always off the market, swept up by some pretty thing or another. So, I took Darrell's and my relationship for what it was—a friendship that would end the moment we graduated and went our separate ways.

"Are you still dating that guy? What's his name, Dan?"

"Doug."

"Yeah, Doug. Are you still dating him?"

I tilted my head, surprised by the question. Darrell had never shown much interest in my love life other than to give advice when I'd really needed it.

I leaned against the table, resting my elbow on the textbook and sighed. "No. We broke up a few weeks ago."

He sat back. His jaw twitched. He seemed to be thinking something over. "Why didn't you tell me?"

"Didn't think it mattered."

He gnawed on his lip and then frowned. "It does."

Now, he'd piqued my interest. "Why?"

"I was thinking we could go out tonight, together?"

My heart raced a little. I licked my lips and took a moment

to regain my composure so my voice didn't crack. I didn't need him to see my excitement and get freaked out. He likely was inviting me out with friends of his or playing matchmaker with one of his buddies.

I shrugged. "Sure. Who all will be there and where we headed?"

The corner of his mouth raised. "Just me and you, if that's all right?"

I started to perspire and not in the good way. "What happened to Michelle? I thought you two were doing good."

"We were, until I heard about her panty parade in the dorm."

My lower lip dropped.

"It's the old saying, Ames. Nice guys finish last."

I rolled my eyes. "No, they don't."

He leaned in closer and my stomach did a somersault. His fingertip playfully swiped over mine. Those stunning green eyes watched my reaction.

"So, is that okay? Just me and you?"

Darrell and I had come into physical contact countless times on the job, but now one swipe of his finger and a question leading to time alone with him, romantically, had me giddy as a young school girl.

I caught my breath. "Yeah. So, where to?"

"That's up to you? How dressed up do you want to get?"

I laughed. His cheeks flushed. "What?"

"You know I don't get dressed up. I might be able to dig up a long-forgotten skirt, but that's the best I can do."

His mouth pulled back into a grin. Butterflies swirled in my stomach when his finger swiped over mine once more.

"That's what I like about you, Ames. You're not a girl who requires a lot of make-up and fuss to look good."

I couldn't believe he'd looked at me that way, that he noticed and appreciated my simple style and modest curves.

"In that case, let's go somewhere where you can enjoy a beer and I can wear jeans."

His grin grew wider. "I know the place. Pick you up at seven?"

I started to nibble my lip and released it quickly. I didn't want him to know I was nervous.

"Sounds good."

The rest of our shift, I caught him stealing glances my way. Each time I noticed, it sent those new and unfamiliar butterflies swirling in my gut. I was envious of their dancing. I wanted to participate in the celebration just as much, but I kept my composure and focused on the tasks ahead, hoping the rest of the shift would fly by.

Later, I got my chance to shake my butt as I wiggled with excitement. I was going on a date with Darrell Flanders. My roommate, who I'd shared a dorm with for four years, put her hand to her mouth.

"He's so hot, Ames. You're going to have a great time."

"My hair look okay?"

Heather had helped me put loose waves in it. She was far better at hair styling than I was. My go-to was either long and straight or a ponytail. Not that I didn't think hair styles were pretty. Actually, I admired the women who could imitate hair salon styles in thirty minutes. Unfortunately, I hadn't been blessed with that skill. Heather helped me with some light make-up and lip gloss, then forced me into one of her racier tank tops that I covered with a fitted red flannel.

"You look great. You look like you, but better." I rolled my eyes and she slapped my ass. "You better get going. He'll be waiting."

After a glance at my cell phone, I casually strolled down to the communal area so I didn't seem too eager. When I came down the steps, he turned. His lower lip dropped and he stared gawk-eyed. My stomach knotted, hoping his deer-caught-in-headlights stare was a good thing.

"Ames." My name left his lips on an exhaled breath.

"Yeah?"

"You look great. I think I've only ever seen you in scrubs. I mean, wow..." He lifted his hand, his eyes wide as he motioned it toward me. "I like this look a lot better."

I lowered my head, suddenly embarrassed. His approval of how I looked had never mattered, not until today. I was thrilled with his enthusiasm.

"Ready?"

I snapped my head back up. "Yeah? Where to?"

He bent his arm for me to slide my hand into it. His skin was warm and his t-shirt soft. I could smell his cologne—a mixture of sex appeal and charisma.

"It's a surprise. You up for a surprise?"

A grin spread over my face. "I am."

He opened the passenger side of his Ford truck for me to hop in. When he started the engine, Jason Aldean's voice escaped the radio singing, "Burnin' It Down." Anxious anticipation twirled in my gut. Darrell glanced over, his beautiful green eyes meeting mine. The excitement churning in my stomach was replaced with desire. That may have been the first moment I saw Darrell as something more than just a friend. I didn't know where he was taking me that night, but I didn't care, it felt right just being with him.

As he drove us away from town, a six-pack of beer clinked on the floor behind his seat. He'd glance over every once in a while and wink at me, adding to the cruel anticipation. He wasn't sharing anything. A turn off an old dirt road had the sun setting ahead of us and under the beautiful orange glow, there was a lake sparkling like the stars above. He steered his pickup into high grass and reversed toward the lake. With the truck parked, he grabbed a blanket and the pack of beer out of the back. He pulled down the tailgate, tossed the blanket into the cab, and set the beers aside.

He turned to me and tilted his head toward the tall tailgate. "Let me help you up."

His hands eased over my hips and that fleeting moment of desire I'd felt earlier swam over my entire body. The view in front of me was stunning, but I couldn't take my eyes off Darrell's. His hand grazed my knee, raising goose bumps on my arms. With ease, he hopped up next to me and laid the blanket out behind us. He sat on it and motioned for me to join him, then popped the top of a beer. After handing it to me, he grabbed another for himself.

"Know where I brought you?"

I shook my head.

"It's Heartbreak Lake. The story goes that decades ago, a local man's wife had grown ill. He asked her what she wanted before she died. Anything, he'd said. I'll do it for you. She asked to be brought to this lake, to watch the sunset and sunrise one last time with him by her side. By morning, the woman had passed away. The man's heart was so broken by her loss, he died shortly after, still holding her hand. It's said if you come during sunset, you can see them in the distance, walking together, holding hands."

I placed the beer to my lips and swallowed, easing the sorrow tickling my chest. "Why'd you bring me here?"

His elbow rested on his bent knee, the beer bottle dangling from his hand.

"I knew you'd appreciate this view as much as I do."

He was right, I did. I loved moments like these, where you stopped the busyness of life to appreciate the world's beauty. Apparently, he'd paid attention to the times I'd talked of such things. I assumed he'd thought it was nothing but a woman's romantic fantasies. That wasn't the case. He clearly liked moments like these, too.

The radio hummed out a slow country song behind us. He set his beer down and put out his hand.

"Dance with me?"

For a moment, I felt foolish and then realized what a wasted thought it was. We were out here alone, just the two of us, and I'd never known Darrell to be judgmental.

I took his hand and stood with him. He wrapped an arm around my waist and took my other hand in his. His touch and the smell of his cologne...it was intoxicating. All else in the world faded away as we danced slowly to the music, the sun setting behind us.

CHAPTER 2

 *W*hen darkness came, I was thankful for the bright moon casting light over the lake and truck because I didn't want to leave. Darrell asked if I was hungry. He'd grabbed a couple sandwiches from the pizza shop just outside campus. I ate, but I don't even remember if it was good. My heart had been fluttering too wildly in my chest.

We relaxed, drank, and laid back on the blanket to watch the stars. His hand grazed over mine as we talked about anything and everything. We had more in common than I'd realized.

"What made you ask me out tonight?"

I had to know.

His fingers intertwined with mine. He lifted our combined hands, studying them in the moonlight.

"I've been sweet on you for a while, Ames. I couldn't wait any longer to find out."

A tingling sensation rushed over my shoulders and breasts. My shirt felt tight against my chest.

"Find out what?"

He lowered our hands and leaned over me. "What it would be like to kiss you."

His delicious scent, full lips, and intent stare had desire pumping through my veins. I didn't keep him waiting any longer. I leaned up and he took my face in his hand and pressed his lips over mine. He tasted of beer, unbridled sexual tension, and what I learned to be the arousing and passionate flavor of Darrell. His tongue met mine, driving my desire to the surface.

The kiss lasted for what seemed like an hour. We couldn't stop kissing and apparently didn't need air either, just more of each other's lips. His hand roamed over my side, waist, and thigh, but he never took it further than that. As much as my body yearned for him to take his hands to more intimate places, I also appreciated his respect for me.

When our lips finally did part, we had a moment of silence to catch our breath.

"You can kiss me like that anytime you want to."

His lips pulled back into a devious grin. "Can I? Kiss you whenever I want, wherever I want?"

All I could do was nod and stare into those beautiful green eyes—eyes that had developed a sparkle when they looked at me.

"Yes. I absolutely want more kisses from you."

And he gave just what I'd hoped for. We kissed at work every chance we got. He'd gently push me behind a wall and slip his tongue in between my lips. His warm mouth would caress mine, drawing little breaths of pleasure from me. He'd come to my dorm to study and we'd read over our notes for ten minutes before our lips would lock for hours. He made it a point to walk out of the way to his class just so he could walk with me to mine. His muscular arm either hung around my neck or he had his hand tucked into the pocket of my jeans.

Our lip-locking sessions grew in intensity. The strokes of his hands grew more courageous. The first time his hand slipped into my jeans and caressed me, I nearly came instantly. He groaned beneath the touch of my hand, massaging him. How we managed to keep from having sex is a wonder I'll never know the answer to. Yet, we always managed to stop, breathing hard, our lips swollen and our bodies aching with need. He became a skilled tradesman at giving me orgasms just from his touch alone. Bringing me that kind of pleasure sure did thrill him. Apparently, my body loved him more than any other woman's had.

Three months later, while making out on his bed, his hands caressing my ass, he said the most amazing thing I'd ever heard. Darrell told me he loved me. I popped my head up and stared down at him in amazement. I could see the anxious anticipation creep over his face. He had nothing to worry about.

"I love you, too. I love you so much."

That night, we fulfilled every desire that had been burning inside of us. He held me tenderly as he eased inside. His hand gripped my ass as his passionate thrusts filled me, completing me. My heart swelled with incredible love for him—love I'd never known and never wanted to give up. Neither of us did.

We graduated college and married a year later. I moved with him to his home town where he started the commercial farm he'd always dreamed of.

My life with Darrell couldn't have been better. We made

love often and hardly ever quarreled, and if we did, those nights ended with a passionate trip to bed. It was our rule, after all, to never go to bed angry.

He introduced me to his hometown friends where I met some of the greatest people I've ever known. Our home wasn't gigantic, but it was comfortable and big enough for a small family, which we were anxious to start.

"Would you want a girl or boy?" I asked him, as he laid kisses over my stomach.

"A boy."

I laughed beneath his wet lips.

"Of course you do."

"I'd like him to carry on my name."

Darrell laid flat on the bed. I curled into his chest. He rubbed along my arm and side.

"What do you want?"

"A girl."

He kissed my forehead.

"What would you want to name them?" he asked.

"Devon, if a boy. Kara, if it's a girl."

"I like them both." He turned his body toward me and slipped his hand into my pajama bottoms. "We better get to work, then."

A year went by and we still hadn't conceived. As much as I knew it would be a blow to his ego, I talked him into letting me make an appointment with a fertility doctor. After much chagrin and a couple beers, he agreed.

I made the appointment the next day. We were eager to start a family together and the farm was doing well, but the bad news from the fertility doctor was nothing compared to what I would soon feel.

Darrell came in from work early, leaving his best hand to manage things. We went to the appointment and took their tests. A few days later, results were in and I was incredibly disappointed to find I was the cause for our infertility. We were sent home with fertility options which I began right away.

We didn't stop being hopeful for starting a family and with the added pressure to conceive, we did what we could to keep the intimacy fun. We got creative and found new ways to surprise each other. One night, he left a trail of rose petals through the entry way, up the stairs, and into our room where he had lit candles and purchased a massage lotion. I didn't waste any time letting him undress me and make use of the new sensual product.

I left him notes on the door for when he'd come home from running the farm. They'd give him hints of where to find me or sometimes there would only be a pair of my panties hanging on the knob.

With the farm doing well, I had the opportunity to focus on something I loved—horses. In the midst of our fertility struggle, Darrell bought me my first horse—a gray thoroughbred. I named him Merlin. I instantly fell in love with him. His temperament was like a sweet, old dog. I took him out riding often and even purchased a training pen and jumping blocks.

"You've done well with that horse. I think he's ready for his first competition."

I nibbled on our dinner, pleased with Darrell's approval.

"You think so?"

"Absolutely. There's a champion in that horse."

Pride filled my chest. "I'll look into where the next closest competition is. Would you come with us?"

He came behind me, kissing my cheek before taking my empty plate.

"Of course. I wouldn't miss it."

That night, I fell asleep in his arms, happy with the life we'd created together and hopeful for the family we wanted.

The next morning, Darrell slid my nightgown above my hips as he held my hands over my head, kissing my neck and loving my body with his lips. He slid inside of me and that familiar sensation of arousal swept over me. We laid in bed, kissing like we had in college. When he left, I ached for him to stay with me. Recognizing my agony, he returned to bed for more kisses and cuddling.

He ran his fingers through my hair and stared at me as if I were the most important thing in the world.

"I love you, Ames. If we can't have kids, I want you to know you're enough. You'll always be enough. I don't need anything more."

I laid kisses over his lips until he dragged himself away for a shower and to get ready for work. A while later, he left and I took Merlin out riding. I stopped Merlin at the top of the hill on our property so I could watch the rest of the sunrise. In that moment, I was incredibly happy, content, and loved.

After the bold, yellow sun had climbed its way into the gray-blue sky, I turned Merlin back for the barn. In the distance, I saw unusual activity—people running from the main barn. I sucked in a breath and pulled Merlin's reins when I saw flames explode from the barn. I put my heels into Merlin and forced him into a sprint. I cleared ground in minutes.

Merlin reared up at the exploding debris, nearly knocking me off. I drove him back and tied him down, trying to make sense of the commotion. Darrell's workers were screaming, trying to put fires out; one was calling emergency on their phone. I couldn't see Darrell anywhere. My chest constricted and my eyes frantically searched the crowd. I moved in toward his employees and screamed at them to tell me where Darrell was. They too searched for him. The looks on their faces told me what I dreaded. He was still inside. I sprinted toward the barn, my heart pounding out of my chest. Arms seized me and someone knocked me to the ground as another explosion erupted, sending debris flying past us.

I lifted my head toward the barn. It was completely consumed by flames. The sobs erupted from me. I pounded the ground, screaming for them to let go of me. More hands held tight to my body, pulling me back as tears blurred my vision. I fought to get loose and somehow kicked free. I ran toward the barn, willing to sacrifice my own life to bring him back.

I was tackled, my chin scraping gravel. One of Darrell's employees pinned me down as I wept into my hands.

CHAPTER 3

I remember the next day so vividly. I laid in bed, clutching his pillow, breathing in his scent as tears streamed down my face. I hadn't accepted it. Darrell wasn't gone. He'd walk back in the house any minute, ready to settle down, have a beer and dinner with me. His strong arms would hug me and kiss my forehead and we'd talk about the competition he wanted me to enter. He'd tell me about work and make jokes. It would all be okay. We'd make love and he'd hold me in his arms until we both drifted off to sleep.

I laid like that for hours, unable to move, begging for Darrell to come back to me. The sound of the phone ringing drowned into the background as my sobs filled my ears. Only a day went by before people came knocking on our door. Employees came to check on my well-being and to ask if they still had their jobs. Neighbors and friends stopped by, bringing expressions of sympathy and words I didn't hear because the sound of my shattering heart eclipsed them.

The third day, I didn't answer the door. My phone rang

wildly. I threw it against the wall and collapsed onto the floor, sobbing. I crawled to the closet and pulled his shirts all around me. My tears soaked the fabric until I fell asleep, too exhausted to cry anymore.

A soft hand caressed my cheek, waking me. Opening my swollen eyelids, I glimpsed my mother's round, kind face and blue eyes through blurry vision. She didn't say a word, just cradled me in her arms as I cried again.

What seemed like hours later, she forced me into the shower and made me eat. I couldn't remember the last time I had eaten and the smell of her cooking reminded me it had been a while. I silently nibbled on the food, pushing it around my plate as I tried to wrap my mind around the fact Darrell would never walk through the front door of our home again, never hold me in his arms, whisper in my ear, touch his lips against mine. I dropped the fork and pushed the plate away as tears rolled down my cheeks.

My mother silently rubbed my back and ran her fingers through my hair. An hour or maybe two later, I woke from where I sat at the table. My mother had cleared it, cleaned the kitchen, thrown out the neighbors' casseroles I'd left on the counter. She'd called the funeral home and made arrangements for me to go there and pick out Darrell's coffin.

His coffin. I wept as soon as the words escaped her lips.

"Amy, darling, there aren't words for a tragedy like this. And I won't lie to you, it's not going to be easy. Darrell's affairs need taken care of, though. You'll need to sign paperwork, prepare his funeral, and decide what happens to the farm. I'll be by your side every step of the way."

"Why, Mom? Why was he taken from me? He loved me so much. I can't bear to go on without him."

The hole in my chest was a crater. I was empty. All I could do was cry and sleep. I couldn't fathom all the things that needed to be done.

"Honey, I don't know why terrible things like this happen. Darrell was an incredible man. He was taken far too soon."

I nodded as slow tears streamed down my cheeks. "He was incredible. He was my world."

My mother's hand took hold of mine. "You'll see him again and when you do, he'll be waiting with open arms."

I made my way through the next several days as a walking corpse. I hardly ate and when I did, it was very little and tear-soaked. My mom walked me through the insurance paperwork, buying a coffin, and scheduling the funeral date with the funeral home. With Darrell no longer here to run the farm, I gave each employee a severance check and apologized for having to close down. Most understood and only a couple left angry.

I told my mom I didn't want visitors and she followed those instructions except for one—my grandmother. She arrived with three full luggage bags. After piling them in the guest room, she started some tea. I was lying in bed when she brought it to me. She sat at the end of it, her familiar blue eyes stared at me, but not with pity, with empathy. My grandfather had died when I was in junior high. Grams had taken it hard. I remember Mom and me going over to her house often to spend time with her and to cook dinner.

"The moments when it's the hardest, you need to remember how much he loved you and how much he would want you to live."

I set the tea mug on the nightstand and crawled into her arms as the tears poured out of me.

"Grams, I can't do it. I can't do it without him."

She wrapped her little arms around me and rubbed my back. "I know, baby. Learning to live without him will take time, but it is possible."

CHAPTER 4

*E*ach day, my mother and grandmother dragged me out of bed, made me shower and eat. My depression had worsened as the funeral neared. I'd lost hair, lost weight, and had permanent bags under my eyes. I didn't even recognize myself in the mirror. The day of the funeral came and I moved through the events, completely unaware of anyone around me. With slow, painful steps, I walked to Darrell's coffin and ran my trembling fingers along the smooth finish. It wasn't real. It couldn't be real. He wasn't gone. He wasn't lying inside this box. My knees buckled beneath me. I collapsed over the coffin, sobbing hysterically. Hands took hold of my arms and assisted me out of the room.

I curled into a ball along the wall, heaving short breaths, trying to compose myself. My grandmother fanned me as my mother brought me water.

"You have to calm down, sweetheart. You need to speak with family and friends."

"Why?" I bit back. "So I can hear over and over how sorry

they are for my loss? It means nothing to me. I just want him back."

My grandmother's sad eyes met mine. "Do it for Darrell. Let others have peace with his death."

With those words and my mother and grandmother's arms tucked into mine, I walked back into the room and stood numb as one person after another gave me expressions of sympathy and words that meant very little to me.

After the funeral, my mother, father, and grandmother returned to my house with me. My father took a walk out to the farm and returned in time for dinner.

"When is the last time you rode Merlin?" he asked.

"The day of Darrell's death. I think I'm going to sell him."

My father shook his head. "Don't. You'll regret it. You should go out and see him. I think he misses you."

Hearing those words sent something other than sorrow and depression through me. I felt guilt. After dinner, I walked out to Merlin's barn and he huffed and stomped his feet as though he were angry with me for not having come to see him for a week. Thankfully, Mom had taken care of him after the employees had left. I opened the barn door and his gate and let him out to pasture. He ran, grateful for the long-awaited freedom. I watched his graceful stride and the evening sun cast over his shiny, gray coat.

I didn't understand how I could even think of getting rid of him. He was a gift from Darrell and something that brought me joy as I thought of him. He returned to me, nudging his muzzle against my shoulder. I rubbed his face, cheek, and neck. I picked up a brush from inside the barn and eased into mindless strokes over his shoulders and back.

Merlin drew in a breath and let it out slowly, sighing. He'd clearly missed this simple grooming activity and it offered me a brief reprieve from my sorrow. After a clean coat and a treat, I returned him to his stall. Dad walked up behind me and outstretched his long arms. I collapsed into them.

"Amy, I know my words may not soothe you like your mother's can, but I'm here for you, pumpkin. Whatever you need."

His embrace and long strokes over my head and hair were all I needed. I sobbed into his chest as he silently held onto me, giving me the fatherly affection I needed. Moments later, he eased me out of his arms and held onto my shoulders.

"Amy, this farm...it's too much for you to take on. Why don't you move back home with us?"

I shook my head. There was no way I could leave. Everything about Darrell was still here. As long as I stayed, I still had a piece of him with me.

"I can't, Daddy. I don't want to leave."

He didn't argue, simply nodded as though he understood. "All right, but you'll need to downsize and sell all the equipment. You could sell a couple of the fields. After that, you could probably stay here comfortably. The insurance will be enough to pay off the house."

My father stepped in when I needed him most. He helped me through all the deals and when the insurance check arrived I used it to pay off the house. The rest I put away in savings while I figured out what was next.

That wasn't easy. I still struggled to make it out of bed every morning. I refused to wash the bed sheets because they still smelled like Darrell. Every day, I'd walk into the closet and pull his shirts in close, just to have his scent around me. Then, the nightmares came. I'd wake, drenched in sweat, with a deep ache throughout my muscles. Each one was as terrible as the last. I'd see him in the fire and I could never reach him; I could never stop the flames from consuming him. I cried myself back to sleep and sometimes my grandmother would hear me sobbing. She'd boil tea and bring it to me and rub my back as I swallowed my breaths, gasping for air.

When the nightmares began, my depression slid further into darkness. I'd walk out to the burned and crumpled barn and I'd wish I had been taken instead. I'd collapse into the ash and broken debris, sobbing into my shirt.

My grandmother brought food out to me one evening as I sat, staring over the burned barn, into the falling sun. She wrapped a blanket around me and handed me a warm mug of tea. She sat next to me and then asked a question I hadn't expected.

"What's next, Amy?"

I turned my swollen, tired eyes to look into the same blue eyes I saw in the mirror.

"What do you mean?"

"You'll be twenty-four soon. You have many more years to live. I'm asking you, what's next? It's time for you to start thinking about it."

I shook my head, half-angry, half-shocked. I couldn't believe she was telling me to move on already.

"Grams, you don't understand. I don't have interest in anything. I wish it was me that had died instead."

My grandmother wrapped her arm around me. "The pain you feel when you think of him, it will never go away. He will always own your heart, but you must live, Amy. It's what Darrell would want. He would not want you wasting away.

He'd want you to find something that brings you joy. He'd want you to live."

I lowered my head as tears slowly trickled down my cheeks. As much as it pained me to even think about what I would possibly do with my life now that Darrell was gone, I also knew she was right. If Darrell could speak to me, he'd caress me tenderly, tell me he loved me and that I must carry on, if not for myself, then for him.

Clutching the warm tea in my hands, I watched the purple and pink sunset fall below the horizon.

The next day, I woke from my usual nightmare, but successfully managed to drag myself to the shower. I even opened the fridge for the first time in three weeks and made eggs for breakfast. My mother and father had returned home to their jobs and their lives, but Grams had remained behind. She put on a pot of tea while I ate.

"I'm going to call a contractor today to remove what's left of the barn."

She nodded as she read through the morning paper. "I think that's a good idea." She folded the newspaper and slid it toward me and pointed out a particular section. "It's a shame, that this horse should die because of its wound. I'm sure it still has life left in it."

Staring down at the black and white picture of the horse drew me to the sale blurb at the bottom, as well as the contact. I didn't know why, but I felt an immediate connection to the horse in the picture. I desperately wanted to save it. Was it an effort to save myself? Probably. But it was my first step towards Grams' question of "what's next?"

I called the owner of the horse before the contractor. He invited me over to look at the gelding. I brought my trailer with me, because I knew if the man said yes, I'd be taking him home with me.

After some negotiating, I exchanged several bales of hay, feed, and a few thousand dollars for the horse. It was a small price to pay to have him in my life. Ransom, a stunning black and white Gypsy Vanner, was a show horse and had taken a severe injury to his leg. He was then sold and used as a trail horse. Arthritis and a re-injury had made him no longer valuable to the owner. Without the money or time to nurse him back to health, the owner felt he had no choice but to either sell him or put him down.

As the contractor removed what was left of the commercial barn, I distracted myself by brushing out Ransom's coat and making sure he got a healthy mix of feed. I wrapped his leg and made a trip to the vet. I picked up supplements I knew would give his body the boost it needed and scheduled a physical for both horses. The vet was more than happy to come out to my property, especially when I told her I'd just purchased a Gypsy Vanner.

Andrea, the veterinarian, was a kind woman a few years older than me with a short and robust stature. She had shoulder length, dark-brown hair she always kept tied back. The day she came over to meet Ransom and Merlin, she was ecstatic about their beauty.

"You've taken good care of Merlin. He's sturdy and his coat is stunning." She moved over to Ransom. "Wow, Mrs. Flanders, he's a beaut. Is he putting on weight with the mix you're feeding?"

"He is, but he could use a teeth floating? Do you offer that?"

"I do. I offer power floating. I can schedule a time to do both of them."

"Let's do that."

"How's his leg?"

"The supplements are helping, but the floating will ensure he gets more feed into him. He needs more strength. He favors it in the pasture but is getting around. I think Merlin motivates him."

"I can see the connection between them."

Merlin held his neck over Ransom's as if to protect him from any impending doom.

Andrea bent Ransom's knee and he let out a breathy groan. "The wrap and supplements seem to help?"

"Yes."

"Good. Keep up the supplements. I'm going to prescribe you a topical ointment called surpass. It will help with his joint pain. As well as firocoxib. It will help with range of motion." She lowered Ransom's leg and removed her gloves. "I can come by Wednesday next week for the floating, if that's good for you."

"Yeah, that will work fine."

She smiled proudly at me. "I'm glad you brought Ransom home with you." She patted his neck and forehead. "He's got a spirit that wants to live. You saved this beautiful horse's life."

Andrea left me with an emotion I hadn't felt in over a month—joy. I'd done something good, saved a life. I clung to that sensation as I brushed both their coats and gave them their evening feeding.

After dinner, I returned to the horse barn. On my way, I stopped and stared at the vacant and dark brown ground where the commercial barn had once been. I walked onto the dirt and something caught my attention. A tiny purple flower had popped up from the devastation and burned earth. It was fighting to live among death and destruction. I reached down and grazed my finger over its soft petals as a tear rolled down my cheek.

The message came across clear. I could feel Darrell as if his warms hands were holding my shoulders. The breeze swept over my skin and his lips grazed my cheek. The breeze faded, as did the warmth of his embrace. I collapsed to the ground, holding my hands over my shoulders.

"Please stay," I whispered to the wind.

The air around me stilled and so did my heart. I knew then Darrell would always be with me.

CHAPTER 5

The first day I put a saddle on Merlin, he startled. It had been so long since we'd gone riding, he'd lost the familiarity of it. I stroked his neck and mane and eased into the saddle. I took him on a slow walk through the pasture because Ransom insisted on following, tagging a couple strides behind. Merlin let out a confident neigh as though the feel of the ride was coming back to him. I guided him to the gate and Ransom snorted when I left him behind. His body leaned against the gate, already upset about the separation.

"We'll be back. I promise."

Ransom snorted again as if to say, *you better.* I coaxed Merlin into a trot, cantor, and then gallop. Soon after, I let him run free with the wind as I held steady in the saddle. The evening sun was lowering and I took us to the top of the hill to look over my property behind us. When we reached the top, I dismounted and laid in the grass. Merlin laid beside me and huffed. He was clearly out of shape.

I rubbed his neck before resting on my elbows to watch the sun sink below the horizon. The memory of Darrell's and my first date at Heartbreak Lake came back to me. I leaned up, hugging my arms around my knees. This time, I cried tears of joy as I remembered that beautiful night. It was then I realized I could have Darrell close to me in moments like these—when I appreciated the beauty the world had. He was now a part of that beauty and I wanted more than anything to appreciate these moments, just so I could have him with me.

After the sun was gone, I took Merlin back to the barn. We reached it as the night sky had turned dark gray. Ransom snorted and nickered at us as if we'd kept him waiting too long.

"I know, boy. It's not fun staying behind. I'll get you out. I promise."

I led them to the barn and gave them their feed. I heard Grams entering the barn behind me.

"I'm leaving, dear."

"Where are you going at this hour?"

She shook her head. "No, I'm going home. You don't need me here anymore."

Tears welled up in my eyes and my chest ached. "Who will I eat breakfast with? Who will I talk to? I'll be alone."

My grandmother waved her tiny, soft hand in the air. "Amy dear, as much as I want to stay, I can't. I don't want to be your crutch. It's time I go home. I have my own affairs to tend to."

I gathered my grandmother in my arms. "Is there anything I can say to make you change your mind?"

She patted my head and then held my arms in her hands as her soft, blue eyes looked into mine. "You have a strong spirit, Amy. It's fighting to live, just like that beautiful horse behind you. Your journey isn't over yet. It's time for you to embrace what's next. You don't need me for that."

I pulled her in for a long, tight hug. She eased out of my arms and left the barn for her car. I watched the dust clouds erupt as her car rambled down the long drive and out of sight.

That night, I had my worst nightmare yet. Trembling and soaking wet with sweat, I ambled to the bath and ran warm water and added soap. I laid in the tub and remembered the last time Darrell and I had bathed together. He'd washed my hair and palmed water over my shoulders. He'd kissed me and touched me intimately, readying me for more between the sheets.

I lifted his bottle of soap and washed my whole body in it, needing the scent of him close to me. Afterwards, I put on one of his flannels and his pajama pants and grabbed one of our sleeping bags from the basement. I traipsed out to the barn and curled up outside Merlin and Ransom's stalls. The sounds of their snorts and nickers distracted my mind and gave me the restful sleep I needed.

When morning came, I woke to their eager noises, excited for food and attention. I fed them and let them out to the pasture. With sorrow in my chest, I dragged my legs up the steps and entered our bedroom. I slowly and reluctantly pulled the sheets from our bed. I placed them in the washer as tears streamed down my face. I wiped them away and forced myself to eat.

After breakfast, I saddled Merlin and took him for a morning ride. We came along the creek where he drank water and the morning birds chirped. I took in a deep breath and listened to the water bubble over the rocks. Closing my eyes, I imagined Darrell there with me, laying kisses over my lips, cheeks, and eyelids. The sun broke through the gap in the trees, and it warmed my skin. I felt him then in that moment. His kiss came and went with the breeze.

I brought Merlin back to the pasture and checked Ransom's leg. He didn't groan when I bent it and the scab looked like it was healing well. I gave them both a bath and re-bandaged Ransom's leg.

That night, I opened a book and read by the bay window. I fell asleep on the window seat and woke with the moon high and bright in the sky. Looking up at it, I admired its magnificence and the bluish-gray glow it cast over the trees and ground. After gathering my shoes, I took a long walk under the moon. The warm summer breeze swept over me, giving comfort as I wished Darrell was here, walking with me.

An owl whooed in the distance and critters scurried away in the night. I placed the blanket I carried in my arm on the ground. I laid there, looking up at the ocean of stars, wondering if Darrell was looking down on me, thinking of me, as I thought of him.

I closed my eyes and I imagined him lying next to me, holding my hand.

CHAPTER 6

J woke to the sun warm on my face and my back stiff from the uneven ground beneath me. I hurried back to the house and showered and ate breakfast. Andrea was coming by today for the teeth floating. I'd just finished brushing their coats when she and her assistant arrived.

The process took an hour for each horse and it would be a while for them to rouse from the anesthesia. I stroked their necks and then left them in their stalls to thank Andrea before helping both women carry their gear back to the truck.

"I have an odd question for you, Mrs. Flanders."

"Please, call me Amy."

Andrea smiled. "Amy, what I'm about to ask, please don't feel obligated to say yes. If you want to say no, I'll understand."

My brows pinched inward at my curiosity. "What is it?" I lifted a box into her tailgate.

"There's a client of mine. His daughter and her horse got injured in a barrel racing competition. Mr. Owens has a few other horses and with the daughter always there, treatment is difficult for the horse. Mr. Owens is willing to pay if you agree. Would you be willing to let their horse be boarded here? There's a lot more room, and I'd have the freedom from his other horses and his daughter to do what I need to. I also have this gut feeling the horse would recuperate better here. You clearly have experience with training and tending to a horse's injury."

I was flattered and wasn't sure what to say.

"I know it's a lot to ask. I understand if you're not willing to take on the responsibility. I just had to ask, you know? For the horse and for Sarah."

A sharp pain surged through my belly. I'd never been given the chance to have a daughter and probably never would. I was envious of this man I didn't know. I'm not sure the exact reason I agreed to help, but I felt compelled to—as though this act of kindness may bring me more peace in my lonely life.

"Yes." I nodded. "I'd be happy to help them."

Andrea's lips pulled back into a smile. "I knew you'd say yes. Thank you, Amy. I'll make arrangements with Mr. Owens and contact you to finalize them."

Later that day, Andrea called to check on Merlin and Ransom. Understandably, they were a bit fatigued from the dental procedure but overall doing well. She asked if it would be all right to bring Mr. Owens horse, Daisy, over tomorrow. I agreed. Andrea said she'd be there for Daisy's delivery, set up and that Mr. Owens would have a check for me.

After the call, I took Merlin out riding and then came back and tied Ransom's lead to the saddle and let him join us on a casual stroll. I guided them down to the creek and let them drink and lay in the sun. When I returned, I talked with my parents, letting them know I was doing okay and taking on a horse that needed boarding and care. They were happy to hear from me and hoped to come over for dinner later in the week.

Lunch came and went, Andrea and Mr. Owens arrived with Daisy in the trailer. She limped out, her front left leg wrapped in a cast. She'd suffered a broken leg and she was tender and jumpy. I soothed her with my words and stroked her face and neck. Before I guided her into the barn, I gave her one of Merlin and Ransom's treats. She settled and slowly followed. Once in the barn, I wrapped a blanket around her and placed her several stalls away from Merlin and Ransom until her stress level went down and she could get used to them being near.

I put out water and feed for her and returned to Andrea and Mr. Owens. The tall, middle-aged man with tan skin and soft brown eyes tipped his hat at me.

"I appreciate what you're doing for us, Mrs. Flanders." He outstretched his hand for me to shake. His demeanor was kind and friendly, yet there were signs of fatigue under his eyes. A warm sensation filled my chest. I knew by doing this I was taking some stress off this man and his family.

"I'm happy to help and you're welcome to check in on her anytime."

Mr. Owens pulled a check out of his wallet and handed it to me. "This is for the boarding, care, and feed. Andrea said Daisy would need to be here for sixteen weeks. I'll bring you another check in a couple months, if that's all right?"

I took the check from him and glanced at the amount. It was written for twenty-five hundred dollars.

"This is enough for the whole sixteen weeks. Please, no other checks are necessary."

I pocketed the check and Mr. Owens lips curved upward into an appreciative smile.

"It was a pleasure meeting you, Mrs. Flanders, and thank you again."

Mr. Owens left and Andrea and I walked toward the barn. "I'll check on her to make sure she's doing all right but won't administer any treatment today. She's been through enough stress with the move. She's on antibiotics to ensure an infection doesn't form and will need to be given the antibiotic daily along with a fresh cast change and her temperature taken. I can show you how to change the cast." Andrea stopped and looked at me, worried. "Is this too much?"

I gave her a comforting smile. "Not at all. I was raised with horses and have a bachelor's in equine management. I know a thing or two." I winked at her, hoping to ease her worry.

Andrea smiled. "I knew I was right about you." We walked into the barn and Daisy's ears perked up as we approached. She seemed relaxed enough to lay down in her stall. Behind me, Merlin and Ransom nickered and snorted, clearly interested in the new arrival.

"She looks comfortable. I'll come by tomorrow to show you the cast change and bring her medications."

The next morning, I looked in the mirror, giving myself a good once-over. I'd gained weight back and my hair was fuller. I was starting to look like myself again. Andrea arrived shortly after I completed my jumps with Merlin. I put feed out for the horses and greeted her as she approached the barn.

"How's our girl doing?"

I took off my gloves and shoved them into my pocket. "She's good. Eating well. Seems to be in high spirits. Merlin wanted to visit her this morning, but I didn't let him. It's too soon."

With my assistance, Andrea and I administered the antibiotics, checked her temperature, and put on a new cast.

"I can come by and check on her tomorrow if you'd like?"

I shook my head. "No, need. We'll be fine. Won't we, Daisy?" I stroked her muzzle and she snorted as though she were content.

After ten weeks of working with Daisy, Mr. Owens and Andrea stopped by for one of their usual visits to check on her progress. They were impressed to see her standing on all four legs out in the pasture.

Mr. Owens, who I'd learned was named Mark, owned a ranch with cattle and horses. He leaned his arms over the fence. "She's looking fine, Amy. You think she'd be willing to see Sarah? Sarah asks about her on nearly a daily basis. We keep her away so Daisy can heal."

"She's not quite ready. A few more weeks and then we'll start with some easy trust exercises."

I'd been spending my time gardening, working with the horses and studying up on my horse training and therapy. The time was well-spent. Ransom was now used to being saddled and could take longer, easy rides, Merlin was jumping on higher jumps with confidence, and Daisy had lost her jittery nervousness and was gaining strength in her leg. Her fracture was healing well and Andrea expected her to make a full recovery. After Mark left, Andrea lingered.

"You ever think about doing this for a living, running a horse therapy ranch? Mr. Owens isn't the only client with a horse that needs medical care or training."

I gnawed on a piece of straw grass. The cooler breeze of

the oncoming winter sent a chill over my shoulders. It was a thought that had crossed my mind, but I hadn't entertained it too much.

Merlin came to the fence and nuzzled my shoulder as I scratched behind his jaw. I pulled the grass from my mouth.

"If I bring in more horses, I'll need to hire an extra hand or two," I said aloud, more to myself. "Go ahead and give them my name and number. I'll see what I can do."

Five weeks later, two new horses and two employees joined my crew. Jared was a college student at the local community college. He was eager to learn and already had skills working with horses. My second hire was one of Darrell's old employees, Rick. He heard I was looking for an extra hand with the horses and stopped by in person to let me know he was interested in working with me. I remembered him being a good employee for Darrell and hired him on the spot.

Jared helped clean stalls, bathe and brush the horses, and worked with leading and training. Rick helped with medical care, training, and night shifts. We made a good team and with their help, I was able to focus on rebuilding Sarah and Daisy's bond.

Sarah arrived with a small, mobile black boot. It took coaxing and many trust exercises, but the day Daisy let Sarah up on her back to ride across the pasture was a tear-filled one at the Flanders Ranch.

That's what I decided to name it. I did the official paperwork and opened for business. I offered boarding, training, and horse therapy. I named it after the incredible man who'd made it all possible for me.

PART II
WHAT'S NEXT

wo Years Later…

Grams washed the fresh-picked blackberries as I stirred the fried potatoes, and Mom set the dining table. The summer breeze lifted the kitchen curtains, bringing with it the scent of horse and hay.

"Why is it you haven't tried to date?"

The laughter rolled up from my belly and out of my mouth. "Grams, you know why. I'm married to this ranch. I don't have time to date."

She clicked her tongue against her cheek. "Nonsense. You're a beautiful, successful young woman." She gave me a pointed look. "*Make* time to date."

I grabbed four plates and divvied up the potatoes and meatloaf. Dad came in just as we were setting the plates on the table.

"The ranch is full and looking good, Amy. You've done well."

My father was right. My horse therapy ranch had become well-known across the state and into the surrounding ones. I had gained something of a horse whisperer reputation and hadn't had an unhappy client or horse we couldn't work with. Jared had graduated from college and chose to continue working at the ranch full-time. He'd become an asset with training. His calm demeanor earned him easy trust with the horses. Rick had turned out to be a great employee and we'd become good friends over the last couple of years.

With the ranch doing well, I was even able to offer health benefits for all of us. Jared and Rick were still my only employees. I'd chosen to place a limit on the number of horses we'd take in at a time to avoid overcrowding and to ensure each horse got the best care they could.

After dinner, my parents helped me care for the six horses I had boarding or under therapy. We returned to find Grams asleep in the chair with a book in her lap. Mom and Dad took Grams up to the second guest room and then settled themselves in for the night. I started upstairs and then an itch to go back outside to enjoy the cool night motivated my feet the opposite direction. I walked toward the barn and heard Merlin and the other horses snorting and whinnying. I shined my flashlight around the outside of the barn.

The light caught two silver eyes and I swam the flashlight through the air and landed the beam on a coyote. If his intentions were to get in to feed or attack one of the horses, he'd never succeed. The barn was locked, secured, and I'd always made sure there were no holes or broken boards.

The coyote's eyes remained fixed on me, as if evaluating

whether or not I was predator or prey and whether it wanted to run or fight. Then, I heard several whimpers behind her. A couple pups hid in the high grass. I lowered the flashlight and she and the pups kept on their way to wherever they were headed.

I watched them huddle close to her as she led them through the high grass. I observed the family disappear into the darkness and the same feeling I'd had in the last several weeks nagged at me. The feeling that I'd never know what it was like to have a family of my own, to hold my own baby in my arms and know a mother's love.

I entered the barn and soothed the horses' nerves. A pregnant mare named Bella whinnied behind me. She was due any day. The owners had brought her here because of behavioral issues. She was purchased as a riding horse for their two kids, but her moody and unruly behavior baffled them. Shortly after arriving here, I let them know she was pregnant and that was why she didn't want to be handled or ridden. They'd asked if she could stay and be worked with up to and after the foal was born.

Of course, I agreed. The ranch would be a more suitable place for her to give birth and it would also be my first foal. I offered to purchase the foal from the owners and they agreed. I approached her stall and scratched her neck, jaw, and forehead. My hand came back from her hair damp. She was visibly uncomfortable. I glanced down to see her udder was enlarged. She whinnied again, swished her tail and kicked at her abdomen.

I rushed to the house and called Andrea. My mother and father heard me on the phone and came rushing downstairs. I handed my phone to Dad and told him to call Rick and Jared then ran back to the barn. I returned to find Bella moving about the stall restlessly. I'd carefully placed her into the double-sized stall specifically for this event, giving her plenty of room to labor her foal.

I didn't want to linger, knowing human presence stresses mares in labor. I grabbed a grooming stool and awaited the others to arrive. By the time they joined me, Bella was lying on her side in the stall. I'd never seen Jared's eyes so wide and filled with excitement.

"You can take a peek, but make it quick. We need to stay out of her way during labor."

The corner of Jared's mouth creased. He crept along the stalls and peered his head down into Bella's. He returned with an equal level of excitement.

"She's crowning or whatever it's called. I saw a hoof."

"How did she look?" I asked, concerned.

Rick leaned his arm against the barn. He and my parents stared at Jared expectantly.

"She's sweaty and her eyes are bulging, otherwise, she seems fine."

I breathed a sigh of relief.

Truck tires spun gravel as they raced up my driveway. Andrea parked outside the barn and grabbed her vet equipment out of the back.

"How's she doin'?"

"Jared says she looks good. She's already in the second stage of labor," I told her.

We all remained at the edge of the barn while Andrea joined Bella to assist her if needed. Andrea returned an hour later, messy and smiling.

"She's a beaut, Amy. Go in and see her."

I rushed through the barn to find Bella's foal—a peach-colored, blond-kissed, beautiful, tiny, palomino thoroughbred. I fell in love with her the moment her tail flicked and her scrawny legs wobbled to stay standing. Her eyes met mine and I was sure I experienced the same imprinting sensation that Bella felt.

Bella, being the good mother, licked and nuzzled her. Yes, her. I had to decide a name. But nothing came to mind that matched her sweet, innocent beauty. I looked at the others. The same expression of awe filled their faces.

"Jared."

He peeled his eyes away to look at me. "Yeah?"

"What would you name her?"

He seemed surprised by the question, then he turned to her, tilted his head and said, "Honey."

I smiled. It was perfect.

"Honey it is."

We all lingered for a while, chatting and watching mom and foal before we slowly trickled out of the barn and made our way back to our homes. I was the only one who remained behind. I did one last walk through the barn, checking all the horses and saved Bella and Honey for last. I leaned against the gate of her stall, watching them bond over soft nuzzling, snorting, and cuddling against each other.

As I watched, an ache developed in my chest and spread, giving awareness to an empty cavern inside my heart where love for a husband and child should have been.

I turned away as tears welled up in my eyes. I slowly trudged back to the house and eased that ache with a warm shower before crawling into bed.

The next morning, Grams and my parents paid a visit to

the new foal before heading home. I did my usual work alongside Jared and Rick. At the end of the day, I shoved my dusty gloves in my back pocket and told the guys to call it a day.

Rick nibbled on grass as he leaned against the wall of the barn.

"You wanna go out for a beer? You look like you could use it."

I glanced over at him as I put the grooming gear away. Perhaps it was loneliness or the restless night of sleep, but I agreed.

"Where should I meet you?"

"Stonie's Bar and Grill."

CHAPTER 8

I looked in the mirror. I'd done a decent job of cleaning up. I showered, actually blow-dried my long, sun-kissed hair, put on a little gloss and mascara, a newer pair of jeans with only slight wear, and a fitted red flannel over a cream camisole. I didn't get out much these days with all the work on the ranch and thought it might feel good to get out of my everyday work clothes. It did. I actually felt pretty.

I walked into the bar and scanned the area, looking for Rick. He hadn't arrived yet, so I pulled up a stool by the bar and ordered my first draft.

Halfway through it, I checked my phone and then the entrance of the bar for the umpteenth time. Still no sign of Rick. I figured he was running late or had to bail for some reason.

The tall bartender with a kind smile and large hands asked if I wanted to order anything. I did. I was plenty hungry, but I wanted to wait for Rick. I glanced at the door again, and my tongue stuck in my throat.

A tall, broad-shouldered man with a narrow waist and round thighs strolled through the entrance. He flicked his cowboy hat and I got a glimpse of the short, dark hair underneath. His shirt appeared too thin to cover the bulging muscles of his chest and arms. A hefty breeze looked like it would blow it off him, and well, I wouldn't have minded seeing it do just that, just so I could have a peek at what laid beneath.

I giggled at my own girlish thoughts. It'd been far too long since I'd had a man's touch and apparently, the added beer on an empty stomach was fueling the sexual tension warming between my thighs.

I turned away so I didn't get caught staring. I tipped my beer toward the bartender.

"Larry, I'll take another. I'll take a menu, too."

The air around me suddenly grew thick, and my body warmed with electric heat as the man from the entrance neared my stool and took the one right next to me. I stared at him like he'd just caught my hand in a cookie jar. He winked at me and smiled and, good grief, his smile was beautiful and so were his stunning hazel-green eyes.

"All right if I sit here?"

Words, what were those things, something starting with a letter, a vowel or two, along with some syllables. Oh, yes. I knew those words.

"Yeah, that's fine," I stammered.

Yeah, it had been too long since I'd seen an attractive male. No, not attractive, this man was carved from some kind of toned, golden-skinned statue and magically given life. There were no words for how gorgeous he was. As sparks went off like the Fourth of July from my hips down, I turned to my beer and swallowed with great enthusiasm.

I set down the empty beer. From the corner of my eye, I could see him staring at me.

"Rough night?"

I turned and looked at him. It was almost painful to stare too long. Not because I found him so ridiculously handsome, but because the longer he stared at me, the more intense the heat between my thighs burned.

"No, I'm actually waiting for a friend, but I don't think he's coming."

The stunning male sculpture next to me seemed disappointed. The corner of his mouth creased into almost a frown. Seeing it made me want to do anything to make it go away. I needed that smile back.

"It's his loss. You're a gorgeous woman. He's a fool for not being here."

He nodded to the bartender, and I adjusted to stay upright in the stool. His words hit me like a freight train. Was I in that much need of a man's affectionate words?

He glanced back at me, and I dug a smile out from somewhere.

"Not a date. He's my employee. We were meeting here for a drink."

My phone buzzed in my pocket. "Speaking of..."

I pulled it out and glanced at the screen. Sure enough, Rick had canceled on me. My shoulders dropped.

"He just canceled."

A beer was slid into this mystery man's hand. "I'll take his place, if you'll let me."

I looked up at him, surprised. Was he hitting on me? A little shiver of excitement trolled over my skin.

"Well, I was about to order food. I suppose some attractive company alongside it wouldn't be so bad."

Even after a beer, I was still rusty, yet his lips curved upward into that infectious smile.

"My name's Brock." He tipped his hat at me, and that slight gesture tickled from my sex to my toes. Brock. Even his name was sexy.

"Amy."

His smile widened. He grabbed the menu. "What are you gonna have?"

"Probably burger and fries."

He closed the menu. "I'll have the same." Larry took our orders and brought two more beers on Brock's request.

He handed me one.

"Thanks." I seized the beer and brought it to my lips. His eyes clung to the bottle, and his jaw flexed.

FROM THE MOMENT I WALKED IN, she caught my attention. Her golden brown hair glowed like a halo around her thin, fit frame. When I caught the attraction in her eyes, I couldn't stop myself from hoping she was here alone. I filled the stool next to her before any other man could. When her eyes did a strip-search over my body, my cock jumped inside my thankfully loose jeans. My gaze swept over her, too. She had soft baby-blues under thick long lashes, sun loved skin, and curves I was sure would fit perfectly in my hands.

I could tell right away she was down to earth, not a lot of fuss and make-up. Shy eyes, worn jeans, and her tight flannel over a toned frame told me she worked hard for that body but didn't know just how beautiful she was.

Only a few minutes in and I was already dying to know more about her. Relief filled me when she let me join her for dinner. Even her attempt to flirt was cute. As was her smile. It seemed she wasn't used to wearing a smile, and beneath those shy eyes, I sensed something more.

A bit of pride filled me when she ordered a burger and fries. She was my kind of girl already. I watched her nervously take the beer I ordered for her. Her attraction to me was apparent, and the sweet way she avoided staring at me too long made my mind fill with thoughts I tried hard to suppress. Her breasts clung to her tank top as the beer bottle met those full, pink lips. It was all over for me then. I had never wanted to be a beer bottle so badly in my life. She licked those perfectly plump lips, and my groin ached. I had to adjust in the stool so she didn't see the semi growing in my jeans.

I couldn't stop wondering what the ass in that stool looked like in her tight, worn jeans either. I took another swig, eyeing her sideways. Her eyes simmered a slow burn over my back and arms. I adjusted again, swigging more beer and hoping the food would arrive soon to keep my hands busy instead of putting them where I really wanted to. Even though my mind was working like a teenage boy, I needed to keep the rest of me acting like the gentlemen I could be.

"You said you were meeting your employee. What is it you do?"

"I run a horse therapy ranch, Flanders Ranch."

A sudden familiarity hit me. I had to pull it out of a distant memory cabinet, but I remembered the whole town talking about it a couple years ago. I was away on a contract job building a new house, but the news still reached me via the gossip train of women in my family. There'd been an explosion, some kind of machine overheating on the Flanders Farm, and the woman left behind had started a horse ranch. Now, I understood what I saw behind those baby-blues. She'd known the kind of loss that no one should have to suffer, especially not this young and sweet.

"Amy Flanders?" I asked, confirming my suspicion.

Her proud smile spread wide. "Yes. That's me." She took another sip of her beer, and her eyes lingered over me a little longer this time. I gnawed on my lip to control the tension building in my lower abdomen. Finally, the food arrived, and I peeled my eyes off her rosy cheeks and kiss-me lips.

"What's your last name?"

"Baisdin."

"What do you do?"

"I own a contracting company. I build houses all over Kentucky and surrounding states."

"Are you from here?"

I nodded, swallowing down a mouthful. "Yeah. Grew up here. When I'm not working, I've got a little place of comfort I like to call home. Nothing special, but it sits on a lake and it's just far enough outside of town to enjoy the woods."

"Sounds nice."

"It is. Maybe you could come by sometime."

She seemed to clam up at the suggestion. Damn, I was coming on too strong. There was no backing out of that one.

"How's your burger?" I tried to change the subject.

Her shoulders lowered, and my chest loosened.

"It's good."

"Want another beer? You're almost dry."

She nodded, and I waved the bartender over and ordered us a couple more.

As INSANELY GORGEOUS AND KIND as Brock was, I couldn't help the nerves that bunched when he'd mentioned seeing his place. That meant he wouldn't mind seeing me after this encounter, and I wasn't sure how I felt about that. Actually, it made me sweat and an uncomfortable knot to form in my gut.

Thankfully, he'd changed the subject and ordered me another beer because I needed it to shake off this strange sensation running through me. The beers came, and I tugged a little too heavily on mine. His hand came up and lowered my bottle.

"Slow down, gorgeous. I don't want to have to carry you out of here."

I should've been embarrassed, but his joking tone made me smile.

"Don't worry. It takes five to plaster my face to the floor."

He let out a light, airy laugh that rolled across his stomach and chest and escaped his full, kissable lips. I glanced away as my cheeks grew warm.

He pushed our finished plates away and left cash on the bar, paying for both of us.

"Want to play some pool?"

He pointed to the corner of the bar behind me.

"As long as you're prepared for how terrible of a player I am. Haven't played since college."

He slid off his stool and nodded toward the pool tables. "I'll help you out. C'mon."

I stood in front of the pool cues, eyeing them unskillfully, then settled on one that seemed like it would work for me. I turned and caught Brock eyeing my ass. An unfamiliar sensation of flapping butterflies danced in my belly. The corner of his mouth tilted into a mischievous grin. He clearly wasn't ashamed I'd just caught him ogling me.

With three beers and good food warming my body, I didn't mind the attention. With ease, he racked and shot, dispersing the balls across the felt and sinking two stripes in.

"You can be stripes."

I laughed and shook my head. "No way. No special treatment. I want to try my best to beat you."

He grinned. "All right, gorgeous. Let's see what you can do."

He leaned over the table, and I took a step back—not only giving him more room to sink another ball in, but to admire the way his jeans fit him. Oh and they hugged him like they loved him. His ass was as firm, toned, and gorgeous as the front. As he leaned over, a tattoo peeked out under his shirt. The dark ink on toned, solid muscles sent heat shooting right between my thighs. I let out a breath.

He turned too soon and caught me admiring him. That same mischievous grin spread over his face.

"Come here." He nodded for me to come to him, and my legs followed his command as easily as my horses follow mine.

His hand gently took a hold of my hip, and that light, sensual touch electrified me. Thankfully, my bra covered how hard my nipples had become. With his large hand, he tucked me into him and bent me over the table with ease. My breath caught when my ass grazed over his package. Against my ear, a low grumble escaped his lips.

His hot breath teased my sensitive skin, and I bit down hard on my lip, fighting the fire scorching between my legs. It'd been so long since a man had touched me intimately, and it seemed my body was desperate for the contact.

His hand left my hip and showed me where to place my arms and hands on the cue.

"Like this…" he whispered in my ear.

The stick slid through our joined hands, and the ball slammed into the pocket. I didn't even see it sink in. I stood, inches from his chest—my breath heavy and arousal aching in my sex.

He bent his knee, and with one swift motion, he turned my ass against the pool table, pinning me between him and it. His hands gripped me fiercely with shocking control, and then those kiss-me lips landed on mine.

EVEN WHEN WE WERE CLOSE to finishing dinner, I knew I had to have more time with Amy. I had to explore the desire that simmered just beneath those hungry, shy eyes of hers. To keep the night fun and lasting, I stopped her from drinking too much too fast. A little body like hers could only take so much beer.

When her ass left the stool, I watched it walk the whole way to the pool tables. It was incredible—the best ass I'd ever laid eyes on—and I didn't want to stop staring at the perfect round curves tucked into a jean cloth platter. When she caught me staring and gave me a look that begged for me to bend her over this pool table and take her here and now, my cock jumped to life. I tried to ignore the thoughts swimming through my head and focused on the balls on the pool table instead of the blue ones in my jeans.

I made the mistake of showing her what to do, and when her ass grazed my growing hard-on, I nearly lost it right there. She stood and those lusty blue eyes and plump lips begged for me to claim them. So, I did.

HIS KISS WAS ELECTRIC. SPARKS detonated from every nerve in my body, and he was the power source. My hands fisted his shirt, pulling him into me, devouring his lips, his kiss, his touch. My body charged to life. It vibrated with thunderous need. His tongue slipped in between my lips, and I couldn't get enough. I moaned into his mouth and lost all sense of where the hell I was.

He eased off our kiss and I fell forward, pulled by his magnetism.

His hand gripped mine as his gorgeous hazel-green eyes stared down at me, a fierce hunger in them that left me wet and starving for his lips to claim mine again.

"I'm taking you home with me. I want more of you, so much more." His hunger vibrated out of his chest and lips. I didn't respond. My brain was mush, and my body had taken over for me.

He held my hand tightly, nearly putting us into a run out of the bar.

Every red light we stopped at, his lips ravaged mine, pulling me further into a lust-filled coma. When we reached his house, he came to the passenger side of his sleek, Chevy Nova SS and yanked me out of it. He lifted me off the ground, cradling me against him and carried me into his home like he'd just claimed a prize.

The interior of his house whizzed by as he carried me into a bedroom. It smelled of wood, masculinity, and the bed he placed me on smelled of his cologne. The scent surrounded me, complementing my reeling desire and the beer still warming my body.

Having left his hat in the car, I now saw his short, trimmed, dark brown hair and it contrasted his beautiful face and eyes perfectly. He took tall, dark, and handsome to a new level. When his shirt went over his head, my eyes glued to his toned, rock-hard chest. He'd obviously earned his body through blessed family genes and working hard on the job. I couldn't wait to see what the rest of him had to offer, and he didn't disappoint.

He pulled off his leather belt, unzipped his jeans, revealing the black briefs below, and then kicked off his cowboy boots. My eyes bounced between the two tattoos on his arms, his rippled abs, and the lines that made an arrow sign to paradise.

The jeans hit the floor, and he eyed me with a grin. The briefs followed, and my mouth dropped. Colossal was an appropriate word. My body shook with anticipation.

His work of undressing me went slowly. He seemed to be savoring every detail of my body. His eyes roamed over me as my hands eagerly palmed his tight abs, and then his ass. I gave it a squeeze, and a growl escaped his lips.

SHE WAS STUNNING. EVERY CURVE was perfect, her skin soft, her body tight. Her eyes were already devouring me, just as I wanted to devour her. Her hands traced over me, learning me and then, when she squeezed my ass, that was it. I couldn't hold back any longer. I needed to be inside of her. I needed to feel her body wrapped around mine. I wanted to discover what she liked and how she liked it and then, I wanted to do it all over again.

I crawled over her beautiful, naked body, and I spread her legs wide for me. A breath of surprise escaped her when I claimed her with my mouth. She was already incredibly wet for me, and she tasted perfect. I dove and swirled my tongue, lapping all that she had to give. I held her legs firm in my grasp as she bobbed her hips, desperate needy moans escaping her.

I slid a finger in and lost my shit at how tight she was.

A DEEP, GUTTURAL GROWL ESCAPED his lips, and it drove my desire wild. His skilled fingers ventured farther in, stroking me with his expert touch. His other hand held my gyrating hips. I wanted this man so badly, my body ached with need. He climbed up, took my hardened nipple into his mouth and sucked it before pulling it between his teeth.

The orgasm rippled over my body like a shockwave. I poured over his hand, and he continued his strokes, milking every last bit of my release.

"That was beautiful, Amy. I want you to come for me again."

My head arched back as he slid in between my wet folds. He filled me to the brim.

I EASED IN SLOWLY, MOVED my hips against her with gentle strokes, letting her body stretch over me. The moans escaping her lips tempted the hunger inside of me. When her hips sped up, wanting more of me, I held tight to her thighs, lifting her ass off the bed, and I claimed the beautiful body beneath me, taking her over the edge with me.

Her orgasm poured over me once and then again. Her body trembled beneath me. I laid above her, holding her close to me, kissing those sweet lips 'til they were swollen. I pulled her bottom lip gently between my teeth, and she let out a desperate whimper. I loved the sound of it. I loved every sound she made. I loved the way her body responded to me, how hard she made me and how much I wanted her again already.

I buried my face into her neck and hair, sucking the scent of her into my memory. Her shallow, calm breaths told me she was drifting off to sleep. I laid there, tracing my finger over her curves, admiring her beautiful body. It fit perfectly inside mine, and I couldn't help pulling her in close to me. I didn't want morning to come. I didn't want her to have a reason to go. After only one night of having her, I knew I wanted more of her...much more.

$\mathcal{I}$ ignored my dry mouth, awful breath, and aching head as I scrambled quietly around the room gathering my clothes. I glanced up to ensure Brock was still asleep. He was beautiful in his relaxed state, but my eyes darted away as the waves of betrayal, shame, and discomfort washed over me. I found a pen and a half-torn envelope to write a note for him, then I dashed out of his house and called Rick to pick me up along the road.

He handed me coffee as I tucked my behind into his truck seat. I leaned my head back against the rest as the coffee soothed my throat and calmed my nerves.

"What happened last night? Whose house did I just pick you up from?"

"Rick, I will give you a raise if you never speak of this again."

His lips remained sealed shut the rest of the way to the ranch. He went to work while I trudged up my steps and doused myself with a hot shower. The shower and my citrus soap washed away the scent of Brock and my out of control lust, but the memories were still there. The thought of him hardened my nipples and caused me to ache with unwanted need.

I shook the thoughts from my mind, angry with myself and my total loss of control. Just in one night, after three beers and one insanely hot guy, I'd turned into a bar slut. It wasn't like me to do something like that. I'd never had a one-night stand—*ever*. I'd only been with two men: Darrell and the young man I'd lost my virginity to.

I stumbled out of the shower and dressed quickly, anxious to get to work and make the night before a distant memory.

I WOKE TO AN EMPTY BED, and my chest ached from the realization she was gone. Her clothes had been picked up. I looked around and found the note.

Thanks for everything last night. See you around.
~Amy

I scrunched the note in my fist and tossed it, then landed my head into the pillow. Apparently, she didn't have an interest in seeing me again. She probably regretted how far things had gone. Maybe she was embarrassed and didn't want me to think poorly of her decision. Either way, I wouldn't be satisfied until I saw her again.

My bed still held the lingering scent of citrus and sex. I grew hard instantly thinking of her. If she hadn't scurried out while I was still sleeping this morning, I would've loved that body again, discovered what she liked for breakfast, and tried my damndest to make it for her.

Instead, I climbed out of bed, pulled on briefs, and traipsed into the kitchen—alone. I dug out the O.J., dumped some into a mason jar, and threw some stuff together and called it breakfast. After a shower, I got to work checking emails and making sure all checks had been paid out to my staff. I walked out to the garage and pulled the cover off my baby—a black steel horse—a heritage softail classic Harley.

I'd always had a thing for anything with a classic, sleek design and enough power to make my chest rumble. Being a big guy, I could never fit into a bright-colored compact car nor would I dare to. It had to be American muscle for me.

I slid onto the smooth leather seat and backed her out. I had a house I needed to check the progress on today and wouldn't mind putting some work into it myself. Anything to get Amy off my mind. The woman had somehow latched onto my brain and cock, and both couldn't forget her.

I parked the softail by my Nova and grabbed my hat—my newest one—couldn't go without it. The memory of the long legs, tight ass, and sweet lips of the woman who'd filled the seat next to mine tightened my jeans. Her kisses had been wrought with desire. The woman under those shy eyes knew how to take pleasure as much as she knew how to give it and damn, I longed to have more of it.

I took a bite out of my cheek and fought to get my head straight. I straddled my softail and fired her up. Beneath my thighs, a high output twin cam engine came to life, rumbling beneath me. It vibrated through my body and eased the tension in my muscles. I put wheels to pavement, letting the cool breeze and sun on my skin carry away any remaining thoughts.

I FINISHED MY TRAINING SESSION with Maisie in the round pen and put her out to pasture with the rest of the horses. I leaned against the fence with my boot tucked into a rail, watching Honey's tail flick as she hung close to Bella. Only one day old and she was already showing strength and spirit. I looked forward to getting to know her personality as she grew.

Merlin, Ransom, and the others seemed equally interested in the new arrival. They all reached their heads over the fence that held Bella and Honey on the other side. They'd likely never seen a foal before or were simply interested in the tiny filly. They nickered at Bella and Honey. Bella ignored them, nibbling on grass to fill her belly while Honey perked her ears, looked at them curiously, and then swished her tail.

I patted Ransom on his face and neck when he left his post to visit me.

"Lookin' good, ole boy."

Jared came up behind me and set his boots on the fence to lean over it.

"Wanna take Merlin and Dixon out for a ride? Dixon needs some exercise."

I definitely needed a ride. My thoughts had slipped toward the night before too many times throughout the day. No matter how hard I tried, I couldn't forget the memories of Brock's roped muscles, his body covering mine, and the incredible pleasure he'd given me.

Every time the thoughts snuck in, my body responded instantly, warming and then clenching with need.

I dropped my boot and whistled for Merlin.

"Get the saddles ready."

I led both horses to the barn. Jared and I saddled them and headed toward the hill and high sun.

"You doin' all right?" Jared asked amid my silence. "You seem distracted today."

I chuckled. Jared and Rick knew me too well.

"I have a lot on my mind is all."

"Anything to do with last night?"

My eyes bulged when I looked at him. Disappointment and anger filled me that Rick would say anything. It wasn't like him.

"What do you mean?"

"You and Rick went out for a beer last night. Your truck isn't here and you arrived in Rick's truck this morning. I know nothing happened between you and him, but something happened."

Relief filled me that Rick hadn't said anything.

I glanced over at Jared's shaggy, light-brown hair and his stocky, toned physique, sitting atop the black thoroughbred. "You're too observant."

Laughter escaped his chest. "You're like a big sister to me. Of course I'm going to notice you rolling in late after a night out at a bar. You know you can talk to me about anything, right?"

My heart warmed. Jared had become like family. He and Rick both had.

"I know I can, but not about this."

"You embarrassed?"

I let out a breath. "No. Guilty."

"You shouldn't be."

I couldn't explain it to him. He wouldn't understand if I did. "Thanks, Jared."

We reached the top of the hill and stopped the horses, giving them a rest while the sun warmed our faces.

"Let's run 'em back. They need it."

We raced horse against horse, driving their own competitive instinct out of them. Merlin's long, lean legs carried him faster. I reached the barn before Jared to find a silver, sporty SUV coming up my drive.

I hopped off Merlin and gave the reigns to Jared for him to unsaddle them while I approached the parked vehicle.

A shorter woman with full curves stepped out of the SUV. Her curly hair was much blonder than it used to be, but I recognized her instantly.

"Heather!"

I pulled her right into my arms and squeezed her tightly.

"What are you doing here?"

"I should've been here sooner, but I took a job in Florida and I could never find the time to visit. I'm so sorry. I'm a terrible friend."

"No, no, it's so good to see you now. I'm glad you're here. What are you doing here and how long can you stay?"

"I've moved back to Tennessee. Last I knew, you lived in Kentucky, so I looked you up and drove to see you. I can stay the night as long as I'm not a burden."

Our conversation was easy as if we hadn't gone over two years without seeing each other.

"Absolutely, you can stay here. Let me tell the guys I'm taking the rest of the day off. I'll get cleaned up and then we can catch up."

Her eyes scanned the area. I could see her interest.

"Want a tour?"

She nodded with enthusiasm. I glanced down at her cute, strappy sandals. "Got any other shoes with you?"

She looked down at my boots and then her shoes. "No." She frowned. "But it's all right. Show me around."

She followed me into the barn. I introduced her to Jared and Rick and then walked her by the stalls, showing her the different horses and explaining their reason for being at the ranch. I ended with introducing her to Merlin and Ransom and then proudly showing my newest addition, Honey.

"She's adorable!" she squeaked. "This place is amazing! You have a great set up. You run this whole place yourself?"

"Yeah, with help from Jared and Rick. I wouldn't be nearly as successful without them. They're great guys. Hard workers too."

We went inside and she poked around while I showered and changed. I came down the stairs to find her looking at a photo of Darrell and me. My gut wrenched. Guilt and sorrow struck me simultaneously.

"I'm so sorry I wasn't here for you when he passed."

I took the photo from her hand as tears welled up in my eyes. She pulled me in, holding me tightly.

"I'm so sorry."

I pulled away before I lost it entirely. I set the photo back on the bookshelf and turned away. She followed me to the couch and I tucked my body into the cushions.

"I miss him every day."

A tear streamed down my face, and I wiped it away, holding my composure together the best I could. I didn't want to break down in front of her. I didn't want to start her visit out this way.

Heather tucked herself in next to me and pulled me against her. The tears unleashed, and I sobbed into her shoulder. I hadn't cried over Darrell like this in two years, but my guilty conscience only made the pain of missing him and talking about him worse.

Between sobs, I blurted it out. "I slept with a complete stranger, Heather. I don't even know him."

She took hold of my shoulders and wiped away a fresh tear. "When?"

"Last night. It's the first I've been with a man since Darrell." I wiped my tear-stained face and sniffled, trying to collect myself. Having said it out loud eased some of the guilt. "His name is Brock. He's from here. Lives nearby. I was very attracted to him, and we had a few beers. He bought my dinner, then we played pool together, and before I knew it, he was kissing me, and I wanted his kisses. I wanted him so much, I couldn't control myself. I slept with him without even knowing him, and this morning, I ran. I ran from a guy who was clearly interested in me because I still love Darrell and what I did feels like betrayal."

Heather pulled me in for another hug. Her comfort was exactly what I needed. She couldn't have arrived at a better time.

"I'm so glad you came to see me." I pulled away from her shoulder. "If you had come before, I wouldn't have wanted to see you. I was an empty person. I didn't want to be around anyone. The only thing that moved me forward were the horses. You came now, when I needed you most and I'm so glad you're here."

Tears welled up in Heather's eyes. "I missed you so much. I thought about you often, but life has a way of keeping us busy. And you're not the only one with guilt." She lowered her head. Grief filled her eyes. "I'm getting divorced."

I rubbed along her shoulder, remaining silent so she could continue if she wanted to.

"He's never home and when he is, we fight all the time. I didn't understand why we had changed so much, and I tried to figure out what I had done wrong, but it wasn't me after all. He's seeing someone else. I looked in his phone while he was sleeping and saw the text messages and photos. The hard part is, our little girl is two. I'm going to take her away from her daddy, and it kills me."

"Does he know that you know?"

She nodded. "We got in a huge fight. He tried to blame me, but I knew better. A wife doesn't drive her husband to cheat. He's an asshole, and I'm ready to move on, but I know my baby girl is going to have a hard time with it. She loves her daddy so much."

Tears welled up in Heather's eyes. I put my arm around her and leaned my head against hers. "We're a mess."

Heather laughed. "Yes, we are." She leaned back to look at me. "This Brock guy. Would you want to see him again?"

I shook my head.

"How come?"

"I'm not ready." I grabbed the pillow next to me and put it on my lap and ran my finger over the embroidery on it, distracting me from my confused emotions. "I'll probably never be ready. Darrell was my person."

"You're okay with spending the rest of your life alone?"

I couldn't answer. I had accepted long ago that I would spend my life alone until Brock awakened a need in me I didn't know I had.

"I don't know."

"I don't think you want to spend your life alone. I think you accepted being alone as your new life. It doesn't have to be. I could have stayed with Andrew and been miserable, but I'm not going to. I'm not going to accept a cheating husband or forgive him. At least, not anytime soon. I'm going to make a new life. You can too."

I glanced up at her. "I have made a new life. It doesn't have to have a man in it."

She rolled her eyes. "That's bull. Every woman wants a man. You aren't open to one because of your love for Darrell, but that heart of yours," she pointed to my chest, "has room enough for two."

Was she right? Did I have enough love to give to someone else or would I always see it as a betrayal to Darrell? I didn't know the answer to that question, but I did know my night with Brock wouldn't be forgotten anytime soon, and that if I were honest with myself, I wanted to feel his touch again.

I grabbed her hand and pulled her from the couch. "Now that we've shared what a hot mess we both are, let's spend the rest of our time together having fun. Do you still ride?"

She nodded. "It's been a few years, but I'm sure it'll be like riding a bike."

The corner of my mouth raised into a smile. "Grab some jeans. I'll lend you a pair of my boots and we'll go riding. Then, we'll go out for dinner and drinks after."

"I love those ideas."

CHAPTER 10

*H*eather pulled up to Stonie's and parked next to my truck.

"All right, don't get too excited about this place. It's literally the only place to go for probably twenty-five miles, but rest assured, the food is good. Plus, I needed to pick up my truck." I gave her a playful wink.

"Ah, so this is where you met the hunk?"

"Yes."

I hopped out and gave a once over on my truck. Everything looked fine. We headed in and filled a booth, then ordered a couple beers while we perused the menu. I glanced over at the pool table and tried to ignore the rising heat swirling like a hurricane all over my body.

"What's good here?"

Her voice pulled me back from my sinful thoughts.

"Oh, the burgers, wings, taco salad. The owner gets all the meat from a local butcher shop, so you really can't go wrong with anything you choose."

"I'll get the wings."

I chose the same. After the waitress took our menus, I caught myself glancing toward the pool table again.

"So, what's he look like?"

"Hmm?" My attention returned to Heather.

"The guy you can't stop thinking about. What's he look like?"

"A hot, ripped, tatted cowboy. Tall, dark-haired, and yummy."

Heather laughed, almost spitting out her beer. "Christ, Ames. He sounds hot. You absolutely should see him again. Was he a nice guy?"

I let out a breath. "Yes. He was. At least, he seemed to be."

"So, was it at your house or his?"

I bit my lip as my body warmed. "His house."

"Got his number?"

I laughed, embarrassed. "No."

She tugged on her beer as they delivered our wings.

"Remember where he lives?"

"Yes." I poured some ranch and dug into my wings. "But there's no way I'm stopping by his house so you can forget that idea."

KICKING OFF MY DIRTY BOOTS, I landed on my bed in a thump. I was exhausted. I'd worked hard on the house, using physical labor to keep her off my mind and yet, on my way home, the thought of stopping by her ranch crept right in. Unfortunately, I couldn't come up with one damn good reason, other than I simply wanted to see her again.

I dragged myself to the shower and let the cool water wash the day's sweat and dirt off my sore muscles. Afterwards, I thought about lounging on the couch with a beer and trying to find something entertaining on TV, but that wouldn't last long. Watching TV wasn't something I did a lot and I wasn't in the mood to sit at home, alone.

I'd had enough of being alone for quite some time, but dating was rough with my lifestyle. I was gone often and for lengthy amounts of time working on jobs and even worse, I had a tendency to be very picky about women. I'd learned from my mistake, one big mistake—Cassandra Levreau.

I'd put my heart out on the line for her and she ripped it out and stomped on it. Being the daughter of a prominent race horse owner and the beautiful woman she was, I'd thought I'd landed on a gold mine when she set her sights on me. Unfortunately, she'd been more interested in using me as her current play thing and my young, foolish heart fell for every red-lipped lie that spilled out of her mouth.

When it ended, it crushed me. I'd fallen hard for the woman and had even planned an engagement. I'd asked her father for her hand in marriage, and two weeks before I planned to ask her to be my wife, I found her humping one of her father's employees. The only good thing is I was still within the return date for the ring and that was the first place I went. I returned the ring, slammed the door in her face when she showed up at my house, and then drank myself into a stupor for a week.

After Cassandra, I became very picky about who I dated and more recently, I'd become too busy to date at all. Running a business took a lot of my time and at thirty years old, it was getting harder to find single women who were worth my time. Then last night, when I'd decided to stop at Stonie's for a beer and some food, I'd met Amy—an independent woman who had to be equipped with a good heart to run a business like hers—who was sweet, funny, beautiful, great in bed, and who understood love and loss. When I looked into those baby-blues, I could see there was a genuinely good woman underneath them.

The day had left me wondering what made her take off like she did. I wanted to know the answer, but I wasn't going to find out tonight, and I wasn't going to lay here all night thinking about it, either. I called up my buddy, John, and asked him to meet me for a beer.

I LEANED OVER THE POOL TABLE and tried to do what Brock had showed me the night before. The seven ball almost made it into the pocket but bounced off the corner just before.

"You know you're really bad at this."

I looked at all the colorful balls scattered on the felt and laughed. "And you're not much better."

Heather smirked. "Didn't say I was, but at least one of us should be 'cause this game is going to take forever to finish."

I leaned over the table and aimed for the four ball. That one actually made it in. I wiggled my butt in a happy dance. I stopped dancing when I saw Heather looking intently behind me.

"What's wrong?"

"Uh, I think your cowboy just walked in. He's staring right at you."

My whole body let off little sparks of electricity. I turned around to see Brock's eyes locked on me from across the bar. My cheeks grew warm instantly. He headed right toward me and I froze, feeling as though I was trapped in thick, heavy tar. When he came closer, the memory of his lips touching mine the night before swam through my head, leaving me light-headed.

Goodness, he was handsome. I'd forgotten how good-looking he really was. His blue flannel with folded sleeves, worn jeans, and his dark hat had my knees about to buckle. A beautiful smile spread across his face as he approached. He came in close. Close enough that I wanted to lean forward and fall right into his arms.

"I hoped I'd get to see you again. You left too soon." He sounded disappointed.

I hated seeing him disappointed.

"I'm sorry. I had to get to work early."

His shoulders seemed to relax, and I was relieved to see the disappointment fading from his face. Heather bumped into my side.

"Brock, this is my friend, Heather. We went to college together. She's visiting for a couple days."

Brock tipped his head and hat. "Nice to meet you, Heather."

Heather's eyes sparkled when she looked at him, and a tickle of possessiveness formed in my belly. He didn't seem to notice, though. His eyes went right back to mine. We stared at each other for a moment, apparently admiring one another and figuring out what to say next. What did you say to the person you just shared the most intimate human experience with and yet you barely knew each other?

"Do you mind if my buddy, John, and I join you?"

Heather spoke up for us.

"Sure," she replied, bright-eyed and smiling.

Yet, Brock's eyes still remained locked on mine. To my surprise, he leaned in and kissed my cheek and whispered before he pulled away, "You look gorgeous." He grazed his hand through mine, and with the simplest words and touch, my sex burned with arousal.

He walked away to find his friend, and I turned to Heather and began breathing again.

"Damn, Ames, he's super hot. If you don't want him, I do. Although, he seems pretty smitten with you."

I stared at his delicious backside walking through the bar. "He takes my breath away."

THE MOMENT I WALKED INTO Stonie's, I saw her in the corner, playing pool with another woman. Didn't matter I could only see her ass, I'd recognize her from anywhere. Her long, light-brown hair hung loose and she wore a pair of ass-hugging jeans with a couple rips in them that gave a glimpse of her smooth, peach-colored legs. As I neared, I saw the cowgirl boots beneath the jeans, and it made me smile, so did seeing her again.

I was happier than I thought I'd be. When she turned and looked at me, I saw that same attraction I did the night before, and then, her cheeks flushed. I knew she was thinking about us, and my body responded, equally aroused.

I wanted to pull her right into my arms and kiss those lips until she moaned beneath me, begging to have me inside her again, but this woman seemed skittish, so I had to force myself to take it slow. She left me wanting to peel back the layers and discover all there was to her.

When I neared, I saw the gloss on her lips and smelled her citrus scent. It took all of my self-control not to kiss her right then. Instead, I said the first thing that came to mind. Her explanation of why'd she rushed out this morning was reasonable. Perhaps I'd put too much thought into why she'd left so abruptly, so I asked to join her, hoping to spend more time with her. And end the night the same way—with her in my bed.

BY THE TIME BROCK AND his friend, John, arrived with food, I'd nervously guzzled my beer, anticipating his return. Brock handed me and Heather both a fresh one from the bucket he'd purchased. After introductions, Brock racked the billiard balls and then scattered them across the table for me and Heather to start a new game. He and John—a toned, tall guy with dirty blond hair and brown eyes—ate their dinner and watched as Heather and I attempted to hit balls into pockets.

Pool balls skittered across the table, right in front of where the two men sat. I could feel Brock's eyes burning holes in my jeans as I bent over to take the shot. His presence filled the space behind me, and his hardening erection stole the breath from my lungs. He leaned over me, sliding his hands on top of mine.

"You're beautiful, Amy. I can't keep my hands off you," his hot breath whispered in my ear.

Pulling my hand and the pool cue back, he knocked the ball right into the pocket. I leaned up, and his hand took hold of my hip. Slipping his thumb into the waist of my jeans, he rubbed across my skin, enticing me with his touch. His eyes glossed over, filled with desire. Heated need vibrated just beneath his skin. I braced my hand on his arm to keep from falling over. Slowly, I stepped back before we embarrassed ourselves with the thoughts I knew were in both our minds.

I turned out of his grasp, and his hand grazed my ass. I glanced back to see his hungry eyes stripping my clothes off my body. I winked, and a grin spread across his face. He went back to the table, watching me as he chatted with John.

Heather came up to me, and we looked at the table, pretending to talk about our next shot.

"You need to stop with the eye-fucking and just get it over with."

I bit my lip and tried not to laugh. "I'm not going home with him again. You're staying at my house tonight. I'm going home with *you*, to my house."

"You should give me your keys."

I glanced at her, red-faced. "No."

"Then, I'm inviting them back to your house."

"What? No, you're not."

"Uh, bet your ass I will. I'm separated, and I haven't had sex in six months, and John's a hottie."

"Don't you dare invite them to my house. I'm not ready for that."

Heather reached over and handed me my beer. "Drink up."

I rolled my eyes at her and took a swig.

After a painful game of chasing balls around the table, John and Brock finished eating and grabbed their own pool cues to join us. Each time it was my turn, Brock tucked me into him and helped me make my shot. He kept it sweet, not coming on too strong, and I liked it. I liked having his warm body covering mine and his whispers in my ear and soft kisses on my cheek. Each time I picked up my cue, anticipation of his touch tingled all through my body.

When John was making his shot, Brock stepped up next to me and moved my hair off my shoulder and brushed his hand over my back. The affectionate touch warmed my body. I found myself craving more of his affection as the night went on. On Heather's next turn, John leaned over her, helping her get her angle right. She smiled and laughed at whatever he said to her. Brock surprised me by coming up behind me and wrapping his arms around my waist. I fit perfectly inside his strong arms, and the heat of his body against my back warmed me from head to toe.

His hot breath tickled my ear. He didn't say anything, just held me close against him, rubbing his thumb across my belly. When it was my turn, he wouldn't let me go. I giggled, and he pulled me tighter against him.

"I need a kiss before I let you go."

With several beers in and the tenderness of his touch, I was more than happy to praise him with a kiss. I turned in his arms and leaned up, pressing my lips against his. His body tightened around mine. He slid his tongue between my lips, and arousal trickled from my mouth to my sex. When our lips parted, I swam sideways, dizzy with desire. He held me steady and grinned at me.

"I've been waiting all night for that."

His fingers intertwined with mine. He raised my hand up and kissed it before letting me go. For the second time, I knocked a ball into the pocket on my own. I wiggled and danced with excitement. Brock took off his hat and put it on my head and pulled me in for another kiss.

"Nicely done."

FROM THE FIRST TIME SHE bent over to take a shot, I was hopeless. My cock grew hard watching her ass in those tight jeans. I had to touch her. I needed her to know how aroused she made me. After the shot, when she stood and looked at me with those lust-filled baby-blues, I knew she wanted me as much as I wanted her.

She winked at me as she swayed her hips around the table. I was ready to take her home immediately, but I was determined to take it slow and show her another side of me. I wanted to give her affection. I wanted her to melt under my touch and throughout the night, I was pleased to see her eyes light up and her body lean into mine. Her first layer was coming down. I started to doubt taking her home again. She'd finally warmed up to me, and I didn't want to come on too strong by asking her to come home with me, but I ached to have her beneath me. I swelled from the thought of it.

When I bribed her for a kiss, it made my internal struggle a war. Brain versus cock and I wasn't sure who was going to win. Then, I saw her wiggle that ass, and her smile lit up her face. Feeling proud and possessive of her, I put her in my hat. Damn if she didn't look gorgeous in it. I desperately wanted to see her in nothing *but* my hat. I decided I was going to spend the night with her, even if I had to keep my clothes on all night long.

I pulled her in for a kiss and praised her. She kept my hat on and went for her next shot. She got it too and did another wiggle. I gnawed on my lip, keeping things down south under control. She tried for her third shot but hit a little too far on the right of the cue ball. She came to me with a pouty lip, and I bit it between my teeth. She giggled, and I pulled her in close to me.

She turned in my arms and watched John take his shot as she leaned into me. I lowered my chin, breathing in her incredible citrus scent.

I whispered into her ear, "I want to be with you tonight."

Her body tightened, and I held her steady.

"Not what you're thinking, Amy. I want to stay with you and hold you. I want to fall asleep with you in my arms."

Her body relaxed and so did mine.

She tilted her head toward me, looking up at me with those shy baby-blues. She gave one simple nod. I kissed her cheek, appreciative she'd said yes.

It was my turn to take a shot. I was ready to end the game and take her home. Her hand reluctantly left mine. I winked at her, then leaned over the table and put the last three balls in. I went back to her and claimed a kiss before taking her pool cue and putting it away with mine. I walked over to John and let him know I was going home with her. To my surprise, John was joining Heather. We all were going to her house.

I grabbed her hand and pulled her into me and gave her a kiss. "C'mon gorgeous. You're riding with me."

When we exited the bar, hand in hand, I walked her to my

bike. Her eyes widened and filled with a glimmer of excitement.

"This yours?"

I nodded.

"I've never been on a motorcycle before."

"Hop on. I'm gonna show you what it feels like to have hard steel and horsepower between your thighs."

She fearlessly slid in behind me and wrapped her arms around me. She leaned in close to my ear.

"I think you've already shown me."

My cock hardened instantly. I bit into my cheek as I glanced back at her sexy grin. Damn, it was going to be excruciatingly difficult not to have her tonight.

Having her on the back of my bike, her breasts against me, her arms firmly around my waist just above my package, had me in a little space of paradise. I knew she was enjoying it too. Her thumbs rubbed along my waist, and when I glanced back at her, she was smiling. I drove up her drive and parked it outside her house. Heather's SUV pulled in behind me.

"How'd you like it?"

Her giant smile already told me what I knew.

"I loved it! I want to go riding again."

I put my hand on her lower back and kissed her.

"I'll take you anytime you want to go, anywhere you want to go."

She moved into my arms and stared up at me. I could see affection in her eyes. I'd no doubt brought down another wall, and man, did I enjoy seeing them fall.

She took my hand in hers and led us into the house. John and Heather had lips locked before they even made it into the room Heather was staying in. No doubt John would be thanking me in the morning.

I followed Amy into her room. When she glanced back at me, her eyes betrayed her. I could see she was nervous. I pulled her into me and kissed her gently.

"I promise all I'll do is hold you *and* kiss you." I couldn't forget that. There was no way I would be able to keep from kissing those full, soft lips.

"I'm going to the bathroom to change."

I pulled her chin up to me and kissed her again. "How comfortable are you with me sleeping in my briefs?"

She nodded reluctantly. "That's fine."

"I'll keep my jeans on."

She smiled, and beneath it, there was a mixture of relief and disappointment. She left my arms to gather clothes and went into the bathroom. I took my hat, flannel, undershirt, belt, and boots off and set my phone and wallet on the night stand. I crawled into her bed and waited anxiously for her to get back to me. When she came out of the bathroom, I was glad I'd kept my jeans on. Her hair was wound into a sexy mess above her head, all make-up was gone, and she'd slipped into a tank top without a bra and little shorts that barely covered anything.

I bit into my cheek, trying to control my growing erection. She slid under her comforter, joining me in her bed. She tucked herself into my chest and stared up at me. I ran my hand across her cheek and leaned in and kissed her. She clung to me, and I held her tight, kissing her until her lips were swollen. I desperately wanted to place my hands all over her body, but I kept to my promise and rubbed along her back and waist.

When I felt myself losing control, I pried my lips away from hers and tucked her into my chest as I laid on my back. She curled herself over me, one leg between mine and her arm around my chest. I ran my fingers along the side of her arm and before long, I could hear her calm, rhythmic breathing indicating she'd fallen asleep.

Having her in my arms felt incredibly right. I wanted her there every night and I still barely knew her, but I hoped it wouldn't stay that way.

CHAPTER 11

I woke to Brock's solid arm tucked around my waist and his warm body at my back. Guilt instantly seized my stomach at the fact I'd brought another man into the bed I'd shared with Darrell. Yet, it had been one of the better night's sleep I'd had in a while, and Brock held me all night long, keeping to his promise. I needed his affection. I needed to just be held. He gave me just what I needed and didn't ask for more. It created a tenderness toward him I couldn't deny.

I turned my body to face him. His eyes slowly opened and locked with mine. He seemed so happy. A smile spread over his face, and he leaned in to kiss me. Warm, soft and affectionate, it soothed the stress in my head and heart.

"What do you like for breakfast?" he asked.

I smiled wide. "I think that's what I should be asking you."

He chuckled. "In that case, I like anything you're willing to make."

"You want to make breakfast with me?"

He kissed me and smiled. "Yeah, I do."

He pulled me from the bed and grabbed his flannel. "Here, gorgeous." He held his flannel out for me to put on.

"What's this for?"

"I don't want John to see you in this sexy little outfit."

I slid his shirt on and leaned against his chest. His possessive gesture warmed me and took me by surprise. He buttoned one of the buttons and pressed his lips against mine.

"Let's see how good of a cook you are."

We moseyed downstairs and I dug out sausage, hash browns, and eggs while Brock found his way around the kitchen and got out pans. He cooked the sausage while I did the rest. As I flipped the last of the eggs, he came up behind me and wrapped his arms around me and kissed my shoulder, then neck, then cheek.

"I like this—waking up with you and cooking with you. Can we do this again?"

My stomach knotted from fear of saying yes or no. Thankfully, I didn't have to answer. We heard footsteps coming down the stairs. Brock let go of me, and I slid the last of the eggs onto plates. Heather and John joined us in the kitchen. They both looked tired and happy.

"Grab a plate and head to the table."

All four of us chatted about our jobs. Both guys asked several questions about the ranch.

"How many horses do you have?" John asked.

"Nine, including three of mine. My newest addition is palomino filly named Honey. She's a sweet girl. I can show you all around after breakfast, if you want."

I glanced at Brock, who had a big smile on his face.

"Yeah, that'd be great. Can't stay too long, though. Have to get to work," John said.

"All right, toss your plates in the sink. I'll get dressed."

I LOVED THE WAY HER face lit up when I watched her talk about her ranch and horses. I could tell she was passionate about her work and loved working with them. It made me like her even more, and honestly, *like* wasn't a strong enough word. I was coming to care for her.

Following her up the stairs, I gave her butt a squeeze when she reached the top. She giggled, and I chased her into her room. She wrapped her arms around my neck, and I kissed her, putting my tongue in to meet hers, and steered the kiss with more passion. She moaned beneath my lips and I couldn't stop my hands from cupping her ass and pulling her into me.

"You didn't answer me downstairs."

I could feel her clam up. I held her close to me, running my hands over her back. "We'll take this as slow as you want." I kissed her, and her head lifted, following my lips when we parted. "But I want to see you again, and soon, tonight, if you'll let me."

I hoped she'd let me. It felt amazing having her in my

arms. Her scent, her soft skin, her sweet and sexy personality. I was already addicted, and my only satisfaction would be to have more of her.

Her head lowered. I could see she was struggling with something. I lifted her chin to me. "You don't have to answer now. Think about it. I'll leave you my number."

She left me to go into the bathroom and get ready. I put on the rest of my clothes, my chest tight from the unknown, from the potential she might say no, that she didn't want to see me again. If only I could figure out why she was struggling with spending time with me when I knew she wanted to.

I left her room and met John downstairs.

He patted my shoulder. "Thanks for asking me to come out last night. That Heather is a fox in the bedroom. How was your night?"

I leaned against the back of the couch.

"Great. I'm hoping to see her again."

"She's a tight package. I can see why you'd want to see her again. I'm guessing last night wasn't the first time you've hung out. You two seemed pretty infatuated with one another."

John's words trailed off. A bookshelf with a photo caught my attention. I walked over to it and lifted the photo from it. It was of her and a good lookin' guy in their early twenties. She looked incredibly happy. The frame said Darrell and Amy and the year they were married. My chest tightened as I stared at the photo. John looked over my shoulder.

"She married?"

"No. Her husband died in a fire a couple years ago."

The stairs creaked, and I lifted my head. Amy stood there, staring at me, looking at her photo. Tears welled up in her eyes. I could see her trying hard to keep her emotions in control. One tear streamed down her cheek. This was it. This was why she wouldn't open up to me, why she took off our first night together. She still loved the man in the photo, and he was keeping her from me. I set the photo down and came toward her. She put up her hand to stop me from touching her. My jaw and chest tightened. I wanted to hold her, but she didn't want me.

"I can't. Please. I need to get to work. You both should go."

She turned her head from me. If John weren't here, I would've pulled her into my arms and made her talk to me, but I couldn't ask her to do that in front of John. Not something so close to her heart. I turned away and nodded for John to follow.

"My truck's at Stonie's," he said.

All I had outside was my bike. "We'll figure it out."

Heather came down the stairs behind us.

"Where you guys goin'?"

She took one look at Amy crying and pulled Amy into her arms just like I had wanted to. The ache in my chest worsened. I swallowed the lump in my throat and walked out her door. The moment it closed behind me, I was afraid that was the last time I'd see her and I couldn't accept that.

"Wait here," I told John.

I walked back in. They were gone. I heard her sobbing upstairs. I walked up the steps and opened the door to her room. She and Heather were sitting on her bed. Heather was holding her as she sobbed into her shoulder. She lifted her head, shock filling her face.

"Heather, can you take John back to his truck?"

She glanced at Amy and then back at me. She nodded. Heather left her side and I took it.

Amy fell into my chest, and I held her in my arms, letting her sob against my shirt until she quieted and her breathing calmed. I rubbed her back and kissed her forehead.

"I can't do this. I can't do this with you."

I didn't say anything. My chest had tightened so severely at her words that I couldn't bring myself to speak. I couldn't understand exactly how she felt because I hadn't gone through what she had, but I knew loss and the thought of not seeing her again pained me.

"Please say something."

She pulled away from my chest. I looked at her sad, tear-stained face and puffy, red eyes.

"What do you want me to say? I don't know the kind of pain you've suffered from your loss, but I can see it affecting you now and all I want to do is fix it. I want to do anything I can to stop those tears from streaming down your face. I want to come back to you after work, and I want to hold you, hell, I'll stay here all day and hold you if you'll let me, but you don't want me, so I'm not sure there is anything I can say."

She fell into my chest, tears coming heavily down her cheeks. "I do want you. That's the problem."

It was starting to make sense now. I pulled her into my lap. She cried into my shoulder. I rubbed along her back, trying to soothe her.

"Am I the first man you've been intimate with since your husband?"

"Yes," she cried quietly.

Damn, her reaction made perfect sense now. She was dealing with feelings she hadn't had since her husband. She'd gone two years without the touch of a man and I'd taken her to bed the first night we'd met. Great job, Brock.

"Amy, look at me."

I held an arm around her back and wiped away her tears with my hand. I looked into her soft, sad blue eyes. "I'm not going anywhere. I'm staying right here with you, and you're going to stay in my arms until your tears have dried and still after that. I'm sorry we started off as strong as we did. I can tell you weren't ready for that, but I think you still want me around. There's something between us. We both know it, and I want to explore more of it, but I understand if you need to take it slow. I'll go as slow as you need, but please Amy, don't shut me out."

Her hand reached up and stroked my cheek and jaw. I gave her what she wanted. I leaned in and kissed her as tenderly as I could. She melted under my kiss—a broken angel in my lap. I laid her on her bed, still kissing her. She clung to me, as though my kiss was her lifeline. I didn't stop kissing her. I held her close to me and rubbed my hand along her side.

She pulled away for a breath and buried her face into my chest.

"I'd like it if you came back tonight."

I kissed her forehead and rubbed her back. "I'll be here. Whatever time you want."

She held onto me. Her breathing became calm and rhythmic. She fell asleep in my arms. I caressed her cheek, watching her sleep peacefully beneath me. As I watched her, pride filled my chest that I'd been the only man since her husband. She'd chosen me out of any man she could've had.

Heather cracked the door.

"She okay?"

I gently slid my arm out from beneath her. "She's sleeping."

"I'll take it from here. I'm sure you need to get to work too."

"I do. I have a few things I need to take care of, but I'll be back later."

I looked around for her phone. I grabbed it off the nightstand and put my number into it and then texted my phone.

Heather walked out with me. We reached the bottom of the stairs and she turned to me.

"I knew her husband. We all went to college together. He was an incredible guy who truly loved her. They had the kind of love that others envy. When he died, she lost it. She didn't want visitors, and she shut everyone out. She and I lost contact after that. But then the ranch gave her a reason to go on. I don't think she allowed herself to date or even consider another man out of respect and love for Darrell. I can see the way she is with you, though. It reminds me of how she and Darrell were, but I think it scares her. She accepted she'd be alone the rest of her life. You've changed that. Blown up her plans and made her feel things she didn't think she'd ever get to feel again. Be patient with her and don't break her heart. I don't think she could handle another heartbreak."

I swallowed the tennis ball in my throat. That was a lot of pressure Heather just put on one man.

"Thank you. Take care of her until I can get back here."

"Don't worry. She'll be fine. She needs some time to work through her emotions is all."

I nodded, understanding what she meant.

I walked out of the house to the sun bright on my face. I headed toward my bike. A tall, dark-haired man in his late thirties or early forties waved a hand to get my attention. I stopped by my bike and waited for him to catch up with me.

"Nice ride," he praised.

"Appreciate it. She's my baby. Twin cam engine, three-thousand torque."

He nodded. His expression lacked the usual spark most bike enthusiasts had. I got the impression he didn't come to talk about the bike.

"You the guy whose house I picked her up from?"

My chest tightened. Who was this guy to her?

"Sorry pal, not sure that's your business."

He chuckled. "It is my business. I'm Rick. An employee and close friend of hers. Amy's a great woman, deserves nothing but the best. You better treat her right and if you can't, don't come back around."

I liked the guy already. It took balls to tell a complete stranger, much bigger than him, to hit the road if he wasn't here for the right reasons. He obviously cared for her and knew her better than I did.

"I respect that you want to protect her. You're clearly a decent man and so am I. I know what she's been through. I wouldn't do anything to hurt her. I'm here because I care for her. I hope to keep seeing her, if she'll let me."

Rick looked me up and down. "All right. We'll see about that."

I outstretched my hand for Rick to shake. He took it.

"I'm Brock Baisdin. I hope to see you around, Rick."

The corner of Rick's mouth pulled back into a bit of a smile. "See you around."

HEATHER HANDED ME AN ASPIRIN and a glass of water. My head throbbed from crying, from drinking, from too much thinking, and from the embarrassment of breaking down in front of Brock. Surely, he thought I was nuts at this point. I wouldn't be surprised if I never heard from him again. That thought stung my chest. I did want to see him again.

"You ready to talk?" Heather asked carefully.

"I blew it, Heather. I'm sure I won't hear from him again. I kicked him out and then lost it in front of him. He probably thinks I'm crazy."

Heather shook her head. "He still wants to see you. I think he understands what you're struggling with. He seems very understanding and the chemistry between you two. Phew!" She put her hand to her head. "It's off the charts!"

I smiled at her dramatic emphasis. My emotions were settling as Heather and I talked and mostly from knowing that Brock didn't think I was insane.

"What about you and John? How was your night last night?"

"Oh gosh, Ames. I needed that. I needed one night of a man wanting me and giving me pleasure. It felt good to be wanted again."

My cheeks warmed. I knew how she was feeling. It was incredible being wanted by Brock.

I put my hand on her knee. "I'm so glad you came to visit me. You're only four hours away. We need to get together more often."

"You have no idea how much I needed this get-away. I'm glad I came to see you, too."

"Want to have one last ride before you go?"

"Yeah, I do." She patted my leg. "Come on, sister. Let's get you feeling better so when Brock comes to see you again, you're not a hot mess."

CHAPTER 12

*W*orking on the new house on a warm day had sweat beading and trickling over my arms and chest. Grabbing a cool cloth, I put it around my neck to lower my rising body heat. I chugged water and sat down on the cement blocks. I pulled my phone from my back pocket. She hadn't texted or called. It was well into the afternoon, and I'd hoped she would've contacted me by now.

I didn't like having to leave her in the morning, not with the emotional state she was in. I understood things had happened more quickly than she was ready for. She'd gone a long time without a man's touch and now, clearly she was overwhelmed with emotions. I was sure she felt guilty about her actions. I wanted to soothe all her troubling thoughts. I wanted to hold her, kiss her, make love to her. I wanted to see her every day if she'd let me.

She was the first woman in years who had made me feel anything this incredible, and I wasn't about to lose it. Even if it took time, I didn't care how much. I wanted to know everything there was to know about her. I wanted to be the one to put a smile on her face, soothe her fears, and warm her bed.

My cell phone buzzed in my hand. I glanced down to see her name. I swallowed the lump in my throat and opened the message.

I'm sorry for how I acted this morning. I hope you'll give me a chance to explain. If I haven't scared you off, I'd like to see you again.

No need to explain. I'll come over tonight if you'll let me.

Yes. Come over whenever you'd like. I'll be here.

Getting her text gave me a renewed energy. I finished helping the guys put up the final wall, and I headed home to take care of the administrative business side of things. After a shower, shave, and clean clothes, I went to the store to buy her flowers. If I was going to make her mine, I needed to start over and do it right.

I PULLED BACK INTO MY driveway with my truck after Heather and I picked it up from Stonie's.

She hopped out of her SUV and joined me as we walked back into the house.

"You need to get ready for him to arrive and I need to hit the road. You going to be okay?"

"Yeah, the ride and your talk this morning helped. You're right that I'm thinking about things too much. I do want to give Brock a chance, and I need to have an open heart to do it."

Heather hugged me on the stairs in front of the door. "You're going to be okay, Ames. I truly believe Brock could make you happy. You deserve to be happy, *with a man.*"

I pulled back from her hug and smiled. "So do you. You deserve so much more than Andrew. He's an idiot for not knowing how good he had it."

Her eyes filled with tears. "I'll miss you."

I scrunched my face. "We're going to visit more often so don't say I'll miss you like we aren't going to see each other for another two years. So, I'll say, see you later."

We walked in and the scent of the roast I had put in the slow-cooker had filled the whole house. We both stopped and breathed it in.

"He's going to be hooked after dinner tonight."

A smile spread across my face as a bit of excitement danced in belly from the thought of Brock arriving in the evening. I walked out with Heather, carrying one of her bags. We hugged again, and I waved good-bye as her SUV kicked up dirt down my driveway. A knot developed in my stomach now that I was alone again. My eyes started to tear up from missing her already. I distracted myself by checking on Rick and the horses.

Rick was getting the evening feed ready when I walked in.

"I'm going to bring the horses in early. I have someone coming over tonight."

"Would it happen to be that man with the bike?"

I helped him fill the second feed bucket.

"You saw him?"

"Yep, had a chat with him this morning before he took off."

He stopped and looked at me with his dark eyes and usual serious expression. "He seems decent, but be careful, Amy. I don't want to see you get hurt."

"I have to let him in to get hurt, and I'm having a tough time with that."

I didn't even mean to be so honest and bare my heart in front of him, but it slipped right out. He leaned against the wall and clicked his tongue against his cheek.

"Yeah, I figure that's not easy for you to do, but it's been a long while now, Amy. There's nothing wrong with you having feelings for a man."

Rick knew Darrell well and hearing him say that gave me relief. Rick was my connection to my past life and having his permission made me feel like maybe it was okay to have feelings for someone other than Darrell.

"I needed to hear that. I've been struggling with my emotions."

He poured the last of the feed into the bucket. "I can't help you with those womanly emotions, but I do think you spending time with a man is good for you. Like I said, just be careful."

The smile on my face was probably huge. Rick glanced

over at me and chuckled. "Get the horses in here so you can get ready for your date."

I rounded them up and brought them to their stalls, saving Bella and Honey for last. I hadn't spent much time with Honey, but I could see she was doing well. In a couple weeks, I planned on starting her on her training early while she was still curious and fearless of humans.

After the horses were fed, in their stalls, and the barn locked up, I put on a pair of shorts and went out to the garden to pick vegetables to put in with the roast. A motorcycle engine rumbled down the road. It slowed and turned into my drive. Excitement somersaulted in my belly. I hadn't expected him to arrive this early in the evening.

I DIDN'T WASTE TIME GETTING ready and getting to the store. I found a bouquet of orange and yellow carnations I thought suited her and grabbed a six-pack from the coolers. I put them in the saddlebags and got my ass moving to her place.

As I came up the drive, I saw her across from the house, knees-deep in the garden. She stood, and I nearly wrecked my bike. Her hair cascaded from a tight ponytail down over the back of her white tank top and her legs extended from her cut-off shorts, glistening in the sun. I parked the bike and grabbed the flowers out of the bag. I walked to her, and she set down the basket of vegetables. She took the flowers, her smile wide and her eyes sparkling. I pulled her chin up to me and kissed the lips I'd thought one too many times about throughout the day.

Her warm lips pressed against mine as the scent of horses, sun, and citrus enveloped me. Good God, she was beautiful.

"Thank you for the flowers." She closed her eyes, breathing them in. "Carnations are my favorite."

That was a good start. "I'll remember that."

Her cheeks flushed, and her eyes sparkled as she looked at me. I leaned down and grabbed the basket and stepped in line with her toward the house.

"You're earlier than I expected. Dinner isn't ready yet, and I need a shower."

I put my hand on her lower back. "You look damn good to me, and I'll help you with dinner."

She bit her lip and glanced over at me. Every time I saw that look, it hinted to a more seductive side of her—a side that I wholeheartedly wanted to discover.

I left her to grab the six-pack from the saddlebag. I joined her as we walked into the house.

The scent of home-cooked meat and spices assaulted my nostrils. My stomach grumbled. I couldn't wait to eat whatever she had cooking. It smelled delicious.

"Whatever you're cooking, I'm looking forward to trying."

I followed her into the kitchen and put the six-pack in the fridge. I set the basket of vegetables on the counter as she placed the flowers in the sink. She stretched to a higher cabinet for a vase, and her shirt lifted, revealing her toned stomach. My groin ached at the sight of her in those cut-offs and tank. I slid behind her and reached for the vase above her. Her hand gently took it from my mine as she turned toward me. I rested my hand on her hip and pulled her close. She stared at me, lust and affection filling her eyes. I claimed those lips that were begging to be kissed.

She set the vase in the sink as my lips devoured hers. Her tongue met mine, and my body grew hungry with need. I cupped her cheeks just below her shorts and lifted her firm ass onto the counter. She clung to my shoulders as I pressed my growing erection into her warmth. She was on fire, enticing my hunger further. I moaned into her mouth. I wanted to be inside her, feel her orgasm pouring over me. My hands claimed her body, touching everywhere she let me. She responded eagerly, moaning and tightening around me.

I moved my hips against her, thrusting into her, letting her know how much I wanted to have her.

"Brock."

My name escaped her lips as a whisper between kisses. My brain snapped back, regaining control over my stiff cock. She needed me to take things slow and this wasn't slow, but damn she didn't know how difficult she made it for me.

I eased off my kisses and held her against me.

"I'm sorry, gorgeous. You're like a drug. I can't get enough."

I eased her out of my arms and set her feet back on the floor.

She smiled up at me. There was no fear in her eyes and that gave me relief.

"I like your touch." She laughed and widened her eyes.

"Maybe a little too much." She let out a breath. "I just need to go slow. Baby steps."

Yep, I needed to get acquainted with my blue balls. We were going to be friends all night. I held her face in my hand and kissed her forehead. "What do you need me to do in the kitchen?"

She turned on country music, and I opened a couple beers. We drank, talked, and I watched her sexy body as she cut up vegetables. She tossed them into the cooker and then came to me and nuzzled right into my arms. Dan and Shay, "From the Ground Up" came on the radio and I placed my hand in hers, wrapped my other around her waist, and pulled her to the middle of the kitchen floor.

"Dance with me, gorgeous."

Tears welled up in her eyes as she stared up at me. There was sorrow and tenderness in her eyes. I held her in my arms, doing everything I could to drive away the pain I saw. I kissed her cheek, held her against me, and sang to her as I danced her around her kitchen.

When the song ended, tears were streaming down her cheeks. I kissed her tears and then her lips. She clung to my chest, and I could feel the weight of her emotions. Lifting her up and holding her against my chest, I carried her upstairs. I laid her on the bed and caressed along her arm and waist as I continued to give her tender kisses. The tears stopped and I looked down at her beautiful face. Bringing her hand to my lips, I kissed along her fingertips.

"I know you want to go slow, but I want to soothe the ache that's here." I pointed to her heart. Another tear slid down the side of her face. "Will you let me take the pain away?"

She closed her eyes and let out a breath. "Yes," she whispered between tears.

Putting my hands in hers, I raised her arms above her head. I laid above her, kissing her as tenderly as I could. I lifted her shirt and placed kisses across her stomach. Undressing her slowly, I eased her out of each piece of fabric. She laid beneath me—bare, beautiful, and broken hearted. I undressed and laid above her, tucking her under the comforter with me. I held her face in my hands as I gave her soft kisses.

She wrapped her leg around mine, and I lowered my hand to find her warm and wet. I slid my fingers inside of her and slowly worked the moans from her lips. She leaned into my touch, and my cock ached to be inside of her. I removed my hand and lowered her hip. Slowly, I eased inside of her and that fire and warmth spread around me like a glove. I took it easy and offered her the tender love she needed. I kissed her over and over as I thrust deep inside her, filling her, giving her all of me.

I LAID MY HEAD IN the crook of his neck, running my fingers over his hard chest. He'd given me incredible tenderness, soothed the heartache burning my chest. He'd made love to me, and I wanted to cry because it meant the world to me, but I refused to shed any more tears. If I didn't stop, he'd think I was a fragile, unstable female.

I leaned up and kissed his delectable lips. He held my face in his hand and turned onto his side, still kissing me.

He pointed to my chest. "Did I take away the pain?" His hand caressed along my arm.

He had. He'd taken it away and filled it with something stronger—love and affection.

I nodded. "Will you stay the night with me, so if it comes back, you'll be here to take it away again?"

He leaned forward and kissed me, bringing his tongue between my lips and driving more passion into his kiss. Our lips parted and my sex ached with arousal.

"I'll stay every night, if you'll let me."

I WAS GRATEFUL I'D BEEN able to soothe her troubled mind and aching heart, but I wasn't done loving her yet. I watched her start to dress, and I couldn't stop myself from touching her again. I came behind her and wrapped my arms around her. My growing erection slid between her thighs and feeling her warmth on it deepened my arousal. I licked her ear and slid it between my teeth before kissing along her neck.

"Would you like to shower with me?"

A breathy moan escaped her lips before she said, "yes."

"C'mon gorgeous. I'm going to clean you so I can make you dirty again."

She started the shower, and as soon as it warmed, she stepped in. I joined her, tucking her ass into me. I reached around her and grabbed the bottle of her citrus soap. Pouring some into my hands, I slowly lathered her body. My hands worked in circles across her stomach and up to her breasts, massaging them and lingering over her hardened nipples. Her breathy moans stiffened my growing erection.

I slid it between her warm, wet thighs and continued to rub my hands over her arms and down to her abdomen. Rinsing my hand, I lowered it, stroking against her clit. She pushed her ass into me and leaned her head against my chest. I kissed along her neck as I massaged her. She wrapped her arm around my neck as my strokes grew in intensity. She held me tight, legs weakening as her body convulsed through her orgasm.

I took her hands in mine and placed them on the wall of the shower. Stepping back, I tugged her ass to me. I eased in and held my hands tight to her hips as I thrust deep within her. She clenched around me. Her tight, wet folds and her eager, breathy moans fulfilled the hunger inside of me.

HE HELD MY TREMBLING LEGS steady. The warm water trickled over my sensitive body. His beautiful hazel-green eyes stared down at me, piercing mine, making my heart beat faster.

"I can't get enough of you, Amy."

My breath was heavy and all I could do was remind myself to breathe as he kissed me. When he let go, I gathered my soap, filled my hands, and then worked it over his solid muscles.

He closed his eyes as he breathed in the scent of my body wash and took pleasure in my hands massaging him.

"You're not allowed to ever buy another soap. Your scent is forever branded into my mind by this body wash."

I laughed and praised him with a kiss. I stroked my hand over his lower abs then over him, cleaning him from base to tip. He opened his eyes, pulled me close, and then placed his lips on mine.

"I don't know how it's possible to feel this strongly for you already."

Butterflies flapped in my stomach. I had already grown strong feelings for him too. His beautiful smile spread wide.

"Turn around, gorgeous. I'll wash your hair."

His strong hands were like heaven on my scalp. I leaned into his touch, taking pleasure from every stroke of his large, calloused hands. I moaned beneath his ministrations. I could hear him smile. He leaned in and kissed my collarbone before turning me around so the water could rinse out my hair. As the water streamed down over my hair and face, his lips touched mine. He kissed me as the water flowed over both of us. I leaned forward and his tongue slipped in to meet mine.

He pulled me out of the water and wrapped his arms around me. "We should get out of this shower or we never will."

He stepped out and wrapped a towel around me and dried me before himself. I tossed my hair into a wet bun above my head and walked into my bedroom. I put on a pair of pajama shorts and also slipped into his flannel.

I was downstairs in the kitchen, getting two plates ready, when he walked in. He leaned against the archway and admired me in his shirt. A satisfied, possessive look filled his eyes as he watched me move around the kitchen. He stepped in and grabbed the plates I'd prepared and took them into the dining room.

When I walked in, the plates were right next to each other. I moved over to them and he pulled me into his lap. Apparently, that's where I was eating.

He fed me a bite and then moaned when he took a bite himself.

"Amy, this is amazing."

"I'm guessing you don't get home-cooked meals often."

He caressed his thumb over my thigh.

"No, I can't call my throwing of food together home-cooked. I can get home-cooked if I dare step over the threshold of my mother's house, but I do that sparingly."

"Why's that?"

"Don't misunderstand, I love my mother, but she's a nagger

and a gossiper, and I can only take so much."

I laughed at his wide eyes and the expression on his face. "My mother is the opposite. She's very quiet. My grandmother is much more outgoing, but neither are gossipers."

"You were blessed, then. I was the only male in a house full of loud-mouthed women. Luckily, I had my grandfather, or I would have lost my mind."

"Where was your dad?"

"He left after my younger sister was born. Took off and didn't leave a way to find him. My mom raised me and my sister and then, after my grandfather died, my grandmother moved in with my mom. My baby sister, Bethany, is actually getting married in a couple weeks."

"That's wonderful. Have you met her fiancé?"

"Yes, and I approve. He's prepared to take care of her. Has a good job, a level head, and I know he loves her. They've been together for four years."

"How old is she?"

"Twenty-four."

The thought crossed my mind that Bethany was now the same age as when I lost Darrell. It left an ache in my chest.

"You should come with me to the wedding."

My body tightened and nerves bunched in my stomach. Brock set his fork down, wrapped his arm around me and rubbed his thumb over my lower back.

"Don't do that. Don't get freaked out and clam up. We would have a good time. I want to take you. I want you to meet my family, as nuts as they are."

He rubbed his hand along my back and looked at me expectantly with those stunning hazel-green eyes that were becoming too good at reading me. Even though the thought terrified me, I couldn't bring myself to say no to him. I knew if I did, it would hurt him.

"All right. I don't have a dress, though. I'll have to go shopping."

His tense muscles relaxed. "I'm glad you said yes." He kissed my cheek and then picked up his fork and dove into the remaining roast and vegetables.

After dinner, he helped me clean up, then responded to a few emails on his phone. I slipped into my boots, still wearing his flannel and my shorts, and walked out to the barn.

WHEN I FOUND HER IN the barn, she was wearing cowgirl boots with her tiny shorts and my flannel. It was the prettiest sight I'd ever seen. I watched her nuzzle and talk to each horse. Her love for them was apparent, and they responded eagerly to the sound of her voice and the touch of her hand. I knew the excitement they felt when she neared. It was a feeling I was becoming familiar with myself.

I leaned against the wall, watching her, and as I did, I recognized the sensation warming my chest. I was already falling for this woman. Some might think emotions have timelines, but they don't. They develop at their own pace and she had my heart on full-speed. It would have taken an incredible woman to build what she did and to overcome the loss she suffered. I understood why it was hard for her to let me in, why it was difficult for her to make plans. Every step forward was a risk she'd suffer the same fate of a broken heart.

As strong as she was, she was equally vulnerable. She opened her heart to me, but that meant opening wounds from her past as well, yet she'd done it. She let me in, and I knew I'd do anything to stay with her, to have all of her.

I walked up behind her and covered her body with mine as I reached up and stroked the face of the horse she lingered over.

"This is Merlin. He's my baby, my first horse. Darrell bought him for me."

It was the first she'd mentioned her late husband. I knew it was a difficult step forward for her. I tucked my arm around her and rubbed along her waist as we both stroked Merlin's soft coat.

"He picked a beautiful horse."

One tear slid down her cheek, yet she remained calm. "He did."

I took hold of her hand and held her close to me. I leaned against her ear. "I don't feel like I need to replace him in your heart, because I know it's big enough for both of us."

She lowered her head. I turned her in my arms and wiped away the single tear running down her cheek. "Amy, I'm not going anywhere. I want you in my life."

Her soft, blue eyes looked up at me, and I could see the grief and adoration in them. "I want you in my life, too."

CHAPTER 13

*I*t had been two days since I'd seen her and I was already going through withdrawals. She was busy with work. One of her client's horses had gone home and the very next day, a horse on the waiting list arrived and it needed a lot of care. I knew how important her work was to her and wasn't going to get in the way. On the third day, I received a text from her that she was free.

I planned the whole evening. Dinner at a nice restaurant and then I was taking her to a country music bar where a popular new band was playing. I fully intended to wine and dine her and make love to her before the night was through. I couldn't wait to have her in my arms and to kiss those full, soft lips. I pulled up to her house and saw a bag sitting on the steps. She'd packed an overnight bag and that small gesture pleased me. I looked around and didn't see her nearby. I knew where she was, though.

I walked into the barn and she was standing outside the stall of her new arrival. Of course, she was checking on him and giving him attention. I came behind her and wrapped my arms around her.

"Hello, beautiful." I kissed her neck and she giggled beneath me. "Who's the newcomer?"

She stroked the face of the brown thoroughbred in front of us.

"This is Catapult." She moved us to the left. "See his hind end?"

The horse had a large gash on his upper hind leg.

"What happened?"

"Got stuck and freaked out, put a broken chunk of wood right through his hind leg. Now he's skittish and won't go near the owner."

"He seems fine around you."

"Well, you know, I have a knack for working with horses who have suffered from trauma *and* Andrea may have given him a light sedative."

She gave me a coy smile, and I chuckled at her. "C'mon, gorgeous. I'm ready to take you out and have you all to myself for the night and hopefully morning."

Her cheeks flushed, and I knew she was looking forward to this night as well. I took her hand as we walked out of the barn. As she locked up, I grabbed her overnight bag and placed it in my saddle bag.

She held tight against me as I drove her to the steakhouse in the city a few miles from town. She filled me in on everything she'd done the last two days. I watched her light up as she discussed the progress with the horses. Damn, she was beautiful. Her blue eyes radiated with life when she talked about the horses. I knew I needed to get out and ride with her the first chance we got.

I didn't have much to share. I told her about the current house my staff and I were building. It was half-finished at this point. After full stomachs, I paid for dinner and gave her a long awaited kiss before letting her get back on my bike. I squeezed her tight ass as she turned to step onto the back and she smiled and eyed me with those sweet, seductive eyes. I grew hard just thinking about being inside of her.

When we arrived at the country bar, music flowed out each time the door opened. I took her hand and led us to the bar. After ordering a couple beers, we found a high-top table to sit at and listen to the music. I rubbed along her back, wanting to feel her in my hands. She leaned toward me, and I claimed her lips and slid my tongue in to meet hers. I grazed her cheek and held her face in my hands. I was falling hard for this woman.

My eyes shifted to the dance floor. "C'mon." I nodded toward it as I took her hand and pulled her onto it with me.

I'D MISSED HIM, REALLY MISSED him. I was anxious all day hoping I could see him tonight. When I texted that I was free and he told me he was taking me out, I spent the rest of the day as giddy as a school girl. When he arrived, the butterflies I'd become familiar with flapped in my stomach, and my entire body warmed at the simplest touch of his hand.

I laid my head against his chest as we danced to the slow song. He held me tightly against him and I realized I didn't want to be anywhere else in the world, but right here with him, in his arms. He was incredible. He made me *feel* incredible. He made me feel wanted and sexy, and, even in the moments where it was painful to look forward without looking back, he'd comforted me. He'd been patient with me. I wanted more of him. As scared as I still was, I wanted more of him.

He kissed my forehead, and I stared up at him, knowing he'd planted a seed in my heart and it was growing.

The music switched to a more upbeat tune and several other dancers joined the crowd. It turned into several rows of line dancers. I laughed and smiled at the big, handsome cowboy kicking his boots and turning next to me. He winked and smiled and kept to the beat. After the dance, I fell into his arms, giggling and smiling. We walked to the bar, and I squeezed his sexy backside. He grabbed my side and pulled me into him.

"I loved watching your sexy ass dance out there."

He kissed my cheek and held me close at the bar as he ordered more drinks.

"Couple shots of whiskey." He leaned into my ear and squeezed my ass. "My girl's feelin' a little frisky." He licked and nipped at my ear and sparks of electricity shot through me. I looked up at his beautiful hazel-green eyes. The heat of his stare warmed between my thighs. He reach his hand up and grazed my bottom lip.

"I love when you look at me that way."

I grinned. "What way?"

He leaned in close. "The way that tells me you want me deep inside of you, claiming that beautiful body."

The shots were set on the bar. I peeled my eyes and steaming hot body away from his hungry gaze. I downed the shot, and he chuckled next to me.

"Guess I was right." He took his shot and kissed my cheek. His hand grazed my backside.

"I'll be back, gorgeous."

He left, headed for the restroom.

I ordered another beer for each of us. A tall, brown-haired man appeared next to me, startling me. I looked over at his glossy brown eyes. He looked like he'd had a few too many drinks and smelled like it, too.

"Hey beautiful, wanna drink?"

"I'm with someone. Already ordered a drink."

He glanced around the bar and waved the beer in his hand. "I don't see him around."

SHE MADE ME SO AROUSED, I could hardly get the piss out. I walked back out to the bar, ready to take her home and love her into the night. My chest tightened when I saw another man talking with her. I waited a moment, watching the encounter, figuring out if she knew him or not. She took a step back and looked around. She seemed uncomfortable. Whether she knew him or not, she clearly didn't want his company. He was probably some tool trying to make a move on her.

I slid in behind her and put my arm around her waist. Her body instantly relaxed.

The tall guy with decent muscles glared at me with irritation in his glossy, drunk eyes. Yeah, he was trying to make a move on her.

"Sorry bud, she's taken."

Drunk arrogance dripped from his mouth. "She doesn't look taken to me. I don't see a ring on it."

She moved farther into my chest and arm. I rubbed my thumb along her waist. My patience was quickly waning.

"Look bud, you're drunk. Take a walk before this gets ugly."

"Ugly? I don't see why this needs to get ugly. I was trying to have a chat with the pretty lady here and you interrupted us."

The douchebag was starting to piss me off. "She's not interested." I leaned into her ear. It was time to go before this ass made any more of a fool of himself. "C'mon, gorgeous. Time to go." I turned her body with mine and then pain rippled across my cheek and jaw. I stumbled back a step, more out of surprise than the throbbing in my face. Amy squealed next to me, her body going tight against mine. The asshole's fist just barely missed her. I moved her out of the way and slammed my fist into the guy's face. Blood splattered out of his nose.

The guy clutched his face and stumbled sideways against the bar counter. I nodded to the bartender.

"He needs cut off."

The bartender nodded. "I saw what happened. We'll get him out of here."

Wrapping my arm around Amy's shaking body, I kissed her cheek and led her out of the bar with me. Outside, she turned to me and examined my face.

My swollen cheek was tender to her touch. I held her hand in mine and kissed it as concern filled her eyes. "It's okay, baby. I'm fine. Not the first time I've had to deal with an asshole like that. You okay?"

She was slowly gathering her composure. "Yeah, I'm okay. I don't like that he hit you."

I smiled at how sweet her concern was and then kissed her softly. It warmed my chest to see how much she cared.

After helping her onto my bike, I drove us back to my place. She laid her head against my shoulder and hugged me tight the whole way home.

I grabbed her bag and walked her into my house. After she got a look around at my remodeled ranch, she went to the kitchen and dug out a bag of frozen peas. She pulled me to the couch and made me lay down as she held the frozen bag to my cheek.

"Your home is beautiful. Did you remodel it yourself?"

I rubbed my hand over hers. "Yeah, I redid the kitchen cabinets, flooring, counters. Remodeled the bathroom, painted and put down hardwood floors in the rest of the house. Added the French doors out to the deck and built the deck, too. Had some help with the deck, but everything else I did."

Her eyes roamed over the house, bright with intrigue. I could see she was impressed.

"You're incredibly talented."

I pulled her down onto the couch with me and grinned.

"I like to work with my hands."

Reaching over my head, I set the frozen bag onto my wooden end table and then wrapped my arms around her and slid my hands over her ass. I pulled her against me as I kissed her deep with the fire burning inside of me. I lifted her tight little body over mine, setting her on my hardened erection. She wiggled over it, pressing against me.

Arousal rumbled out of my chest and lips at her warmth. "Amy, you don't know what you do to me."

Her eyes fixed on mine as she unbuttoned my flannel shirt. I leaned forward, helping her take it off. Raising my under shirt over my head, she let it fall next to the couch. She pressed her warm hand against my chest and lowered me.

As she lifted her shirt and bra over her head, my tongue caught in my throat. I admired her beautiful breasts as she leaned down and undid my belt and opened my jeans. I raised my hips, and she pulled my jeans and briefs lower over my hips. My erection sprung free, and her eyes widened as she admired it.

Arousal swept over her face, and she licked her lips. My cock jumped at the sight of it, and she glanced at me. Her eyes stayed glued to mine as she took hold of me in her warm hand and stroked me in her fist, before filling what she could in her mouth. Her warm, wet tongue touched my head, and I nearly came right then.

I couldn't stay focused on her eyes. My head rolled back, and my hips raised instinctively, trying to put as much of me in her mouth as she could take. Her mouth was cruel and delightful, sucking me hard and pulling the orgasm from my abdomen into my groin. The blood left my brain, and all I could do was feel. Feel her mouth and tongue working its way over me, thickening me and making me helpless with aching need.

My orgasm came, strong and fierce. I fisted her soft hair and held tight as it burst out of me. Her mouth clung to me, taking it all. She licked the tip clean and pulled back and looked up at me with sweet, curious eyes. I knew she wondered how she did. She had no idea how fantastic that had been. I was putty in her hands. I'd do anything for this woman, anything to keep getting loved like that.

I pulled her half-naked body over mine and held her close to me. I tucked a loose strand of hair behind her ear and stroked her soft cheek.

"That was incredible." I kissed her softly and rubbed my hand along her back as I stared into those tender baby-blues. "You're so beautiful."

I claimed her mouth with mine and squeezed her ass, pulling her tight against me, letting her feel the heat building. Now, it was my turn to love her. I lowered her onto her back and leaned one leg over the couch as I brought my head down and licked and sucked at her nipple. It hardened in my mouth. The way her body responded to me, thrilled me, arousing me further.

I leaned back and watched her eager, lust-filled eyes follow me as I unbuttoned her jeans, slid them off her hips, and tossed them to the floor. Lowering myself, I kissed over the tiny, satin fabric covering her. Her head arched back as the heat of her sex warmed beneath me. I pushed aside the fabric and felt the hot wetness below. She was soaked and swollen and I loved it. I teased her, swirling my finger in circles around her clit. A needy breath escaped her lips.

Pulling my hand away, I used it and my other to pull the satin from her hips. A hungry growl escaped my mouth when I looked down and saw she'd trimmed her delicate folds. I grabbed her hips and yanked her toward me. A sinful smile spread over her lips. I leaned down and claimed her, licking and twirling and suckling at the sweet nectar that was Amy.

HIS MOUTH WAS MAGIC. HIS lips devices for cruel and erotic pleasure. His tongue ravaged me, and all I could do was fist the couch and cry out his name as my orgasm swept over me. I lay there on his couch dizzy, light-headed, and grinning from ear to ear. His mouth left me and trailed kisses up my inner thigh and then across my stomach, to my breasts until he was lying above me, tucking me into his arms.

I touched the cheek that was red and slightly swollen from the hit he'd taken to protect me. He gazed down at me. I could see it in his eyes, a mixture of satisfaction and affection. It left me feeling my own mixture of adoration and trepidation. I wanted this man—wholly—heart, body, and mind, but fear kept me from giving into it entirely. What if I lost him, too? I couldn't bear it. Brock had brought incredible pleasure, love, and happiness back into my life. The harder I fell for him, the worse the fear of losing him consumed me.

The last two days, I had struggled with letting things go any further at all, but the need to see him and have his touch snuffed out my thoughts. Now, having him lay above me after giving each other the intimacy we had, my heart and mind were on a battlefield, both willing to fight to the death. I wished I could shut off my mind and aid my heart, but it wasn't possible. I had to face my fears if I was going to move forward with him.

LOOKING DOWN AT HER LOVING, tender eyes, I wanted to tell her I was falling in love with her, that whatever shell of a man I was before her was nothing compared to what I was now with her. But like the horses she trained, she was skittish and had been traumatized. The last thing I wanted to do was push too hard, too soon. I could see it in her eyes. She still held fear in her heart. The only way I knew how to drive away that fear was to give her undeniable love.

I WRAPPED HIS FLANNEL AROUND me as I watched his naked backside walk to the fireplace and put logs into it. His body was firm, solid, hard muscle. As he worked, his back muscles flexed. I had to close my mouth before the drool started to seep out. The ink on his arm added to his already enticing sex appeal.

"What's the tattoos?"

"This one here," he pointed to it, "I got after my grandfather passed. He taught me to always be the best man I can be, to leave behind a legacy and to take care of the ones I love. The tattoo was for him."

I couldn't deny he just kept getting better. I was right all along when I'd thought he was carved from a golden skinned statue and that magic had brought him to life.

"This one," he pointed to the other that crawled over his

arm and shoulder, "was an idea I had after my fresh start from a bad breakup."

My stomach coiled. "What happened?"

"I caught her sleeping with another man."

I was relieved to see no emotion filled his face when he spoke of the tramp who'd cheated on him. He stood from the now burning fire and my eyes fell to his torso and admired the flickering light of the fireplace dance over the indentations of his abs and delectable package. He grinned at me as he passed by. I leaned over the couch and watched him walk to his room. He returned with a blanket and stopped by the fridge and grabbed a bottle of wine and two mason jars.

He laid the blanket by the fire and set the wine and jars on the floor next to it. He glanced over at me and curled his finger for me to come to him. I didn't waste time. My legs scrambled to get off the couch and take me back to his waiting arms. He laid me down beneath him and slowly unbuttoned his shirt, trailing his fingers over my skin. Sparks of warmth filled me everywhere his fingers caressed.

"Tell me about how you met Darrell."

His question surprised me. I tightened and then relaxed as his fingers continued to rub along my sides. I leaned into his chest and I shared the story of Darrell's and my relationship. The memories I hadn't thought about in a long time brought back painful emotions. My voice lowered as I worked to get the words out. Tears welled up in the corner of my eyes. Brock kissed my cheek and continued rubbing his hand affectionately over my body.

More tears streamed down my face as the story reached Darrell's accident. My whole body ached from the memories.

Brock pulled me closer to him, comforting me with his warm touch.

"The morning I took Merlin out riding, I saw the fire at the bottom of the hill. I ran Merlin as fast as his legs would take him and I searched for Darrell among the chaos. I realized he was still inside the barn. I wanted to go in and get him. His employees tackled me and stopped me from entering before an explosion made it impossible to enter."

I turned into his arms and buried my face into his chest. The tears poured out of me. I hadn't spoken about it in two years, not to anyone. The pain came flooding over me as if the accident had happened all over again. Brock wrapped his arm around me and held me close, stroking his hand through my hair and over my back.

He kissed my head and soothed my tears with his affection. "My sweet, Amy." He pulled my chin up to him and wiped my tear-streaked cheek with his thumb. He pressed his lips against mine, and my shaking body started to ease. I clung to him as he rolled over me, giving me the tenderness I needed.

CHAPTER 14

The previous night's fire smoldered next to us. Beside me, her body smelled of wine, citrus, and sex. I'd made love to her twice throughout the night, and if she didn't look so peaceful in her rest now, I'd have her again. She had the ability to turn me into a witless bull in rut. I couldn't think of anything else other than being inside of her. When her tears came, all I wanted to do was soothe her, take away the pain and sorrow. Her body clung to me, taking every bit of what I had to give and she wanted more of it. Each time I touched her intimately, she moaned with pleasure and gave equal passion in her touch.

With it being Sunday morning, it was my day off and I had no intention of leaving her side. I let her sleep while I started breakfast. She stirred and woke just as I put eggs and toast on two plates. I set them on the table and came to her as she sat up and pulled my shirt over her naked body.

I slipped my hands beneath my shirt, feeling her soft skin and warm body in my hands. I lifted her, and she nuzzled my face and kissed my cheek.

"Bathroom."

She joined me at the table a few minutes later with her hair tied into a ponytail and her mouth minty fresh. She slid into my lap and we devoured breakfast, water, and orange juice, making up for all the lost energy. I leaned back and held her waist.

"I was thinking I could come to work with you today. I'd like to see all you do and help if I can."

Her face lit up, and she smiled. "Absolutely. I can always use an extra set of hands. Especially today. I'm the only one working."

"Good. Let's get a shower and head over to your place."

I CHANGED INTO WORK CLOTHES as soon as we arrived back at my ranch. I found Brock in the barn getting acquainted with Ransom.

"He's a beautiful horse. Yours?"

"Yes, actually, he is. He was my first purchase a couple years ago. He had an injured leg, and the owner was going to put him down if someone didn't buy him. He's good for short rides and company for the other horses. Because of his arthritis and weak leg, he can't do anything too strenuous."

"He's stunning. Has a great temperament too."

"You know much about horses?"

I pulled the feed buckets out and Brock lifted one after I did. He followed me to the first couple stalls.

"Yeah. Worked at a racetrack for a few years."

"That must've been fun."

"It had its pros and cons like anything else, but I did enjoy working with the horses."

We moved onto the next stalls.

"I need to exercise and do some training drills with a few horses today. Want to ride?"

He winked at me. "Of course."

Brock helped me move all the horses out to pasture except the two under medical watch and Merlin and Ranger, the ones we were riding.

He saddled Ranger without any problems, moved into it with ease, and joined me outside.

"My property ends on the other side of the hill there," I pointed west, "and on the other side of the creek there." I pointed east.

"How many acres?"

"Twenty-three. Used to be more, but I had to sell some of it to pay off expenses."

I moved Merlin forward into a trot as the memories tightened my chest.

"Ranger can be temperamental. Keep his reigns tight or he'll try to bully you."

Brock nodded. "Thanks for the heads-up."

He kicked his heels and moved Ranger into a gallop. I pushed Merlin into a run and passed Brock and Ranger. It didn't take much for Brock and me to race our horses against each other. Merlin and I only beat them to the top of the hill by one stride. Ranger had improved significantly and would be going home soon. I always felt a mixture of pride and melancholy when each horse left. It meant they were ready to go back to their homes and a better life, but it also meant I'd never see them again.

"Ranger's owners will be coming to get him in a couple days. His fetlock fully recovered and his training lessons are finished."

"He's got a smooth stride. You did well with him."

"Thank you."

We stopped at the top of the hill and I tilted my head toward the sun, letting it warm my face. I closed my eyes and let the breeze sweep over me. When I opened my eyes, I caught Brock watching me. My cheeks warmed.

I turned Merlin east. "Let's head down to the creek and let the horses get a drink."

We walked the horses side by side, down through the field of high grass and yellow flowers.

"What was her name? The woman you mentioned last night."

He let out a small sigh as if I'd ruined the moment by mentioning her. "Cassandra Levreau. Her father owned a race horse. She came from big money. I thought we were in love, but I was nothing more than her current play toy."

"She broke your heart, didn't she?"

"That she did."

"Is that why you stopped working at the racetrack?"

"Yeah. Starting working with my grandfather and ended up starting my own business."

"Do you like what you do?"

"I like it enough. I enjoy working with my hands and seeing something I built from the ground up. I do miss working with horses."

"You're welcome to join me anytime you need a fix."

"Is that an invitation for the horses or you?" A lascivious smile spread across his face.

I bit my lip as my body warmed. "Both."

His lips pulled back into grin. "I accept."

I tied the reins around the horn and stripped out of my flannel. Brock lifted his hat and wiped his brow. The sun had reached high noon. It was time for lunch and the training lessons to begin. I moved Merlin into a gallop. Brock and Ranger came up next to us as I was stepping out of the saddle. Taking my hand cloth from my back pocket, I doused it in the creek. I wrung out the excess water and came up to Brock and put it around his neck. I used it to pull him into me. His eyes brightened with appreciation.

He leaned in, wrapped his arms around my waist and pressed his lips against mine. "Thank you. Just what I needed."

As soon as our lips touched, little sparks of electricity filled me, warming me below. "We should ride back up here before dinner. Have a picnic and maybe…" I eyed him playfully.

His eyes widened. He squeezed my ass and pulled me into him. "Yes. We're doing that…all of that."

I giggled and stroked my hands over his sun-beaten, sweat-covered arms.

"I thought you might like that idea."

"Damn straight, I do."

SHE CONTINUED TO SURPRISE ME—from the way she knew her way around horses, to moments she took to enjoy the simplest comforts like a breeze sweeping across her face and the little hints of pleasure she wanted to share.

I loved the idea of having her outside beneath the stars. I was disappointed I hadn't thought of it first. After the horses got their rest and water, we ran them back to the barn. Running in the breeze cleared the high sun's heat from my body and eased the arousal teasing my groin. I unsaddled the horses while she took a horse named Maisie into the training pen.

I put the horses out to pasture with the rest and strolled over to the training pen. I leaned against the fence, watching her careful gestures and sweet words used to build trust with the horse. She responded eagerly to her call. There was no fear in this horse's eyes when it looked at Amy.

She gently tied the horse to the fence and easily lifted a saddle to its back. After securing all buckles, she raised her boot into the stirrup and gracefully put herself atop the saddle. Taking wide circles, she guided the horse until they both seemed confident.

With a trot to the fence, Amy kicked the lever up. The gate opened and she and the horse galloped into the next pen. She walked Maisie over ground bars, getting her comfortable with stepping over different terrains. She trotted her around barrels and worked with different training devices. They moved in a rhythm together as if they were one. This horse trusted her fully and she clearly had helped it regain its confidence. It was a beautiful sight—Amy in her element.

I let her finish the training and went to the pen that held the dam and her filly. I entered and leaned against the rails. The dam lifted her head and blew out a breath, concerned with why I'd joined them. She stepped protectively toward her foal. I remained still and after a moment of seeing no threat, mum went back to nibbling grass. The little golden filly pranced and kicked and danced around.

Walking a little farther into their pen, I squatted down on a knee, hoping Honey's curiosity may bring her to me. After a minute or two, she crept closer, her inquisitiveness pulling her toward the interesting new thing in her pen. She stopped, sniffed the air, and tested my scent. She did the same ritual until she was close enough to nibble. Stretching her short neck out, she sniffed my body. I kept my hat lowered and sure enough, she bit at it and pulled it from my head.

I laughed, and she jumped back. Surprisingly, she didn't bolt for her mum. Instead, she moved closer and snagged my shirt and tugged. I laughed again, and her scrawny legs jumped and ran back to the protection of her mum.

I heard Amy laugh behind me. Grabbing my hat, I raised up on my numb legs.

"A few more sessions like that and soon, she'll be crawling in your lap, begging to be scratched."

"She's gonna be a sweetheart when she's grown."

I walked out of the fence and tucked my hand into Amy's back pocket as we walked toward the house.

"You ready for lunch?"

"Yes ma'am."

She fixed us each a sandwich and put a bowl of fresh cut fruit on the table. We ate quickly, hungry from the work already put in.

"I need to bathe Catapult, clean that wound, muck a few stalls, then we can call it a day."

"You got it, babe."

I kissed her cheek and headed back out to get to work.

IT WAS SOMETHING ELSE TO see his bare back, ripped jeans, and sexy body in that cowboy hat as he poured a bucket of water over Catapult. I couldn't help thinking how I'd like to watch water be poured over his naked chest. I clenched my thighs from the rush of arousal tingling between my legs.

I joined him and grabbed a sponge. Together, we worked

through giving Catapult a good cleaning. After we finished the dirty job, Brock chased me back to the house and stripped me down for a shower.

He climbed in with me and instantly pinned me to the wall. His knee slid between mine and spread my legs. A sexy, shameless grin filled his face as he reached down and slid his fingers inside of me.

Our shower lasted to the point the water had gone cold. I stepped out—tired, satisfied and displaying an intoxicated grin.

His touch was magical, addictive. I couldn't get enough of him. He pawed my ass as I blow-dried my hair. I tried to flee his grasp, and it emboldened him further. He lifted me onto the counter and pressed into my naked body.

"Amy, baby..." his words filled my mouth, "you make me randy as a damn deer in rut."

I giggled and wiggled out of his grasp. "If we keep this up, we'll never make it out to our picnic."

His hungry eyes settled. "What are we packing?"

"A couple blankets, a couple beers, some berries and, how about homemade vegetable soup?"

He stroked my face and let me down off the sink. "That's perfect. What do you need me to do?"

"Get the horses ready. Saddle Dixon this time. I'll get the rest."

It worked out perfectly that I'd made a batch of soup the day before to eat on for a few days. I warmed it and poured it into a couple travel camp jars before I packed the rest and carried everything out to the horses. He had them saddled and ready. The high sun had lowered into the evening and the temperature was much cooler, making for a pleasant ride.

Brock helped me load the saddle bags and bring the horses in from the pasture. We gave them their evening feed, and I locked up the barn.

I hopped into my saddle and winked at the handsome cowboy next to me. He brought Dixon alongside to Merlin and leaned in for a kiss. Dixon jerked, and Brock caught himself before falling forward.

I smiled at his frown and kicked my heels, putting Merlin into a gallop. We made it down to the creek with the sun setting toward the hill. After the horses were tied, I laid the blanket by the bubbling creek. I unpacked the food while he opened the beers. He handed me one and I drank down the cool, refreshing liquid before setting it aside and moving behind Brock. I rubbed along his shoulders that I was sure were sore from the hard day's work.

He moaned beneath my touch. "How do you always know just what I need?"

Taking hold of my hand, he pulled me around him, onto his lap. "I loved being with you today. We should do this every Sunday."

I smiled as I met his loving gaze. I put my hands back on his shoulders, massaging him again.

"I think that can be arranged."

His hands slipped inside my shirt, rubbing along my waist and up toward my breasts. "What's the cost?"

I leaned in and whispered in his ear, "Making me call out your name."

He lowered me onto the blanket. "That, I can do."

THE SUN HAD FALLEN, AND among the dark gray, little dots of white sprinkled like glitter across the sky. I held her beautiful naked body beneath me, running my fingers gently over her stomach and the warmth I'd just been inside of. She purred beneath my touch. A tender, satisfied smile filled her face. As I looked down at her, I couldn't hold the words back any longer. I put my hand in hers and raised it to my chest.

"Do you feel that? How hard it beats for you." Her loving gaze stayed fixed on mine. "It's yours, Amy. You've had it since that first night. I was taken with you then, and I'm even more smitten now."

I kissed her fingers. She eased them out of my hand and placed her hand on my face, lowering me down to her. Tears welled up in her eyes as she kissed me passionately. I leaned my head against hers.

"I'm putty in your hands, Amy. I'd do anything to keep getting your love."

She affectionately ran her thumb along my jaw. "You're not alone in those feelings."

Her leg slid around me and I lowered myself on top of her, easing inside of her, ready to give more love to the woman who'd stolen my heart.

CHAPTER 15

here was no denying it. The seed Brock had
planted in my heart had blossomed into something
beautiful, something incredible I never imagined I'd
experience again. Each day with him was better than the last,
and he'd slowly started leaving his own things behind at my
house. My bathroom was the most obvious. Every day after
work, he'd come over and shower, help me make dinner, assist
with the horses, and every chance we got, he'd take me
beneath him and make love to me like there was no
tomorrow. The man had relentless passion, and my body
craved his intoxicating touch.

His sister's wedding was the next day and it was time I
shopped for a dress. Grams, my mother, and Heather all
thought it was such a big deal, they drove to my house to help
me shop.

"You realize it's just a dress. I didn't need all of you here to
pick it out."

I set the bread for lunch on my dining table. Heather eyed
me with a disapproving stare.

"It is a big deal. He's taking you to meet his family, Ames. That means he sees a future with you."

I took the seat next to Heather and tried to calm the whirlpool of emotions swashing in my belly.

"When are *we* going to meet him?" my mother asked.

"When she's good and ready," Grams chided.

I glanced at Grams and smiled. I understood my mother's interest. As much as I had spoken about Brock, I knew my grandmother and parents were anxious to meet him.

"You'll love him." Heather assured her. "He's one of the good ones."

I smiled appreciatively at her comment. It was true. Brock was a rare find. He was handsome, caring, understanding, and suffused with passion.

"Maybe sometime in the next couple of weeks we could all have dinner here," I said, as I grabbed bread from the bowl.

"I like that idea," my mother responded simply and with that, it was done. Now, I had to let Brock know. My nerves bunched at the thought of whether or not my father would approve and then my tension instantly settled. Of course he'd love Brock. Who didn't?

After lunch and a long ride into town, I came out of the department store dressing room with my first dress and did a little spin for them. It was red, knee-length and skin tight.

Heather's eyes sparkled. "You look hot."

Mom shook her head. "I don't think that's what you want to wear to meet his family for the first time."

I glanced in the mirror. The dress did look stunning against my tan complexion, and it formed my modest curves like a second layer of skin, but my mom was right. It wasn't appropriate to meet his family. I had no doubt Brock would love it, but I needed something that was more me and less going out on the town.

The second dress was navy blue with white polka dots, tiny shoulder sleeves, and a flowing skirt.

Heather scrunched her face. "Cute, but not you."

Grams wiggled her head. "I agree. It's not right."

I went back in for a third dress. It was a pale yellow, above the knee, heart-shaped strapless, that was form-fitted at the waist, and then flowed outward with soft chiffon fabric.

I walked out and all three of their faces lit up. "That's the dress," Grams said.

Heather and Mom nodded. "Definitely," Heather agreed.

"You look beautiful, honey." My mom's eyes welled up with tears. She'd only seen me in a dress for three occasions—homecoming, prom, and my wedding. I stopped looking at her so I wouldn't cry, too.

"Okay, I'm buying it." I scurried back into the dressing room and took another spin in front of the mirror. Butterflies danced in my belly. I was excited for Brock to see me in it.

I KNEW AMY AND A parade of women had gone shopping for a dress today. That was always something about women that I didn't understand—why around any special event you always found them in herds. I wanted to steer clear of my own house for that exact reason. There were far too many women screaming, crying, and dancing around there with the wedding being held in my backyard and only a day away. My grandfather and I had built a gazebo by the lake that would play host to the ceremony. The real party would start afterwards. A tent, tables, chairs, catering and a DJ were all being brought in. That was one thing the Baisdin's knew how to do well—celebrate. There was no doubt the reception would go well into the night.

All day, I thought about what Amy might wear. I couldn't wait to see her long legs and tight, little package in a dress. My groin knotted at the thought.

I ran a cold cloth over my bare back and grabbed my t-shirt and work gear. Unfortunately, I had to stop by my house after work. I needed fresh clothes, my button-down shirt, new jeans for the wedding, boot cleaner, and to see how my baby sister was faring.

I parked my bike where I could find a spot. There were cars and trucks covering the driveway and yard. Deliveries were being made, tents set up. It was chaos. My sister came running out of the house and waved her little hand in the air with a big grin on her face. She ran up to me, and I wrapped my arms around her short, little body and spun her around.

"How you doin', B? Ma driving you crazy yet?"

Bethany planted her bare feet back on the ground and huffed.

"I swear, if she tells me one more time how *she* wants something done, I'm going to lose it."

I laughed and patted her long, black hair as I walked inside with her. Looking around, I cringed at the mess that had become my house. Food, alcohol, flowers, shoes, clothes, and wedding supplies were scattered everywhere. I liked things neat and my sister did not. It was temporary, I reminded myself, and made a direct line for my bedroom and a shower.

When I came back out, my sister, aunt, mother, and grandmother were huddled in my kitchen talking over one another. Bethany handed me a beer when I joined them.

"We're looking forward to meeting Amy tomorrow," she said with a cheeky grin.

My mother eyed me with her big, brown, judging eyes. I tucked her short, broad-shouldered body in my arm and kissed her forehead. "Ma, listen and listen good. This is the woman I'm going to marry. Treat her well or I *will* disown you."

Bethany jumped up and down and giggled as my mom clicked her tongue against her cheek.

"Did you hear that, Ma? Brock wants to marry her?"

Damn straight, I did. The thought had crossed my mind several times in the last week. It wasn't the right time to propose yet, but I knew Amy was the woman I was going to spend the rest of my life with.

GRAMS AND MOM HAD LEFT to head back home so they weren't driving too late in the night. Heather stuck around and helped me figure out the details of hair, make-up, and shoes.

"I'm nervous to meet them tomorrow," I told her as I slid my foot into a pair of strappy wedges.

"Those are perfect. Have you ever even worn them?" She looked up at me from my barely used high-heeled wedges with knitted brows.

I laughed and lifted my foot to admire the shoe. "You know I like shoes. I just never have a good reason to wear them. Tomorrow, I do."

"You should put a loose curl in your hair and go with this lip gloss." She held it up from the small pile of make-up on my bed for me to see.

"What about eyes?"

"Go light. This brown eyeliner and," she grabbed one of my eye shadow compacts, "these shades of tan."

Thankful for Heather's fashion expertise, I gathered what I'd need for tomorrow and set it on the bathroom counter and hung the dress in the closet before meeting her downstairs in my comfy pajama pants and fitted t-shirt.

I was startled to see her holding the photo of me and Darrell.

"I know you won't like what I'm about to say, but..."

My stomach clenched. I took the photo from her hand.

"Maybe it's time to put the photo somewhere else."

I tucked the picture in my arms and swallowed. I didn't want to get angry with her. I knew why she was suggesting it, but it still pained me.

"Please don't be mad, Ames. I'm suggesting it out of respect for Brock."

Clutching the photo to my chest, I thudded across the floor, and landed on the couch with a thump. I looked down at the photo. Tears welled in my eyes, and my throat constricted as I ran my thumb along his face. It brought back excruciating memories of the way he smiled when he walked into a room and saw me and the way he held me in his arms after making love to me.

My stomach knotted uncomfortably. Thinking of Darrell that way left me feeling a strange guilt, like my thoughts alone were cheating.

Being in Brock's arms was just as incredible, if not more. He always held one firm arm around me when I slept, as though I might run away in the night and he had to keep me close to ensure I didn't. Sometimes at night, he'd wake and caress along my body, stirring me from sleep and inciting arousal he was eager to satisfy. And when I walked into a room, his eyes always sparked with adoration and attraction before he took me into his arms and kissed me senseless.

I leaned my head back on the cushion and sighed, refusing to let the tears come. I hadn't cried in over a week and wanted to keep it that way.

"Will you bring me a beer?" I asked softly.

Heather giggled. "I'll bring you two."

I set the photo on the coffee table as I tugged enthusiastically on the beer.

She sat opposite me on the couch. "Where do you have Darrell's belongings?"

"Everything is in plastic containers in the basement. I couldn't bring myself to get rid of any of it."

"What if you and Brock move into together? What would you do with Darrell's stuff then?"

I took another long swallow. I knew my eyes were wide like a deer caught in headlights. "I'm not ready for conversations like that. Whatever Brock and I have, it's too new to be looking into future plans."

Even though I wasn't ready to talk about it, the thoughts had still crept into my mind—several times.

"You should probably get ready to have those conversations, Ames. Brock's practically moved in already."

A motorcycle rumbled up the driveway outside.

Heather took a swig of beer and smiled. "Speakin' of the devil."

WHEN I OPENED THE FRONT door, I found Heather and Amy on the couch—Amy in her pajamas, a beer in her hand, and the photo of her and Darrell behind her on the coffee table. I was pretty sure I'd just left one group of emotional women for another, and I couldn't help the tension building in my shoulders and neck at the sight of Amy's troubled expression and sad eyes.

A smile lifted the corners of her mouth when she looked over at me, and my tension eased. She stood from the couch and made her way across the room. I folded her right into me and laid a deep kiss on her lips like I'd been waiting to do all day.

"Would you like a beer, too?" she asked, her eyes now glossy and soft as she looked up at me.

"Yes," I replied with a little too much enthusiasm, but I needed it after the time spent with the rowdy Baisdin women. Her ass swayed as she walked into the kitchen but I managed to pry my eyes away to join Heather in the living room. I set my bag down by the couch and leaned back into the cushions. My chest tightened after glancing at the photo. I pointed toward it before looking at Heather.

"How's she doing?"

"We were having a tough talk before you got here."

That's all Heather got to say before Amy returned and handed me a beer. I grazed her arm and then took hold and pulled her into the couch with me. Having her in my arms eased any remaining tension right out of me. I rubbed my thumb along her waist.

"How'd shopping go?" I asked before taking a drink.

Heather's face lit up and Amy's eyes sparkled. Apparently, it had gone well.

"She found the perfect dress." Heather grinned.

I was tempted to have her try it on for me after Heather left, just so I could take it off.

Heather looked at us and then set her beer on the coffee table. "I need to get going. It's getting late."

Amy stood to hug Heather. I waved good-bye and they walked out the door. Amy came back a moment later. She walked over to the couch and looked down at the photo of her and Darrell. I could see the different emotions transitioning over her face and I was about to reach out for her, but stopped when I saw her reach down. She held the frame close to her chest.

"I'll be right back," she said quietly.

She walked to the basement door, behind the stairs, and disappeared. I took several tugs of beer and waited for her to come back. Several minutes later, she still hadn't returned. I went to investigate and found her leaning over a plastic container, full of a man's belongings. She was holding a shirt and crying quietly into it.

My chest tightened uncomfortably at the sight of her distress and heartbreak, but that wasn't the only emotion I felt. To my own surprise and shame, I was jealous. She'd obviously come down to put the photo with the rest of Darrell's belongings—belongings I didn't know she still possessed—and got overwhelmed by the memories of him. I wondered if she would ever love me as much as she loved him or if she were capable.

I came up behind her and slowly took her in my arms. She leaned into my chest and quietly composed herself. "I'm so sorry. I feel like all I ever do is cry around you. I came down

151

here to put the photo with the rest of his things. It was more difficult than I expected."

I stroked her hair and tried to soothe her even though I was struggling myself. My eyes roamed over the multiple containers. It was shallow of me to feel jealous, but I couldn't help wanting to be her man, the only man. I wanted the love she held for him. I pulled my emotions together and kissed her head.

"That means a lot to me, that you would do that." I pulled her chin up so I could read her eyes. "But I don't want you to do something you aren't ready for. I don't ever want you to resent me for—"

She put her hand up to stop me.

"Brock, I would never resent you. I brought the photo down here because I wanted to. I want to move forward with you."

There was pain and concern in her eyes for me and for how I felt. As foolish as it was, I needed to see that. I needed to know she wanted me, wanted us.

I claimed her lips and pulled her tighter against me. I wanted her then, but it wasn't right, not next to his belongings. So instead, I lifted her and carried her upstairs where I laid her on the couch beneath me and stripped us out of our clothes as her eyes filled with desire.

CHAPTER 16

I let Brock rest while I went out to the barn and got the feed put out for the horses. Last night, putting the photo of Darrell and me away had been harder than I thought. As soon as I opened the containers, the memories flooded me. I touched Darrell's shirt and instantly missed him and his warm and affectionate touch. The tears flowed out of me, and I did my best to control them. I was so tired of crying, especially in front of Brock.

He'd come down to check on me and found me exactly the way I didn't want him to. I could see the internal struggle and discomfort on his face. Guilt pummeled my gut. I knew I needed to start looking forward, and that's what I was trying to do. He just caught me at a very delicate moment, but as usual, he put his feelings aside and offered me comfort. The man was too good to me. There were times I felt guilty for how good of a man he is. My broken and messed-up heart was still holding me back when he was all-in.

I truly wanted to move forward with him, but for every few steps forward, something always knocked me back a step.

Today was a day of love and celebration and I wanted to embrace it.

I headed back to the house and found Brock making breakfast. I admired his backside in his gray lounge pants. He looked over his shoulder, caught me staring, and grinned as he tilted his head for me to come to him. I think he had my body trained at this point. The slightest curve of his finger, head tilt, or whisper of words, and my body responded to his demands, willingly and hungrily.

He pawed my ass and pushed me against the counter. His large, solid frame covered me as he planted his lips on mine. When his lips parted, my head tilted toward him, still wanting more. He reached around me to grab the plate, and I pouted. He laughed, bit my lip, and pulled it between his teeth.

"Don't get me started, gorgeous. We can't be late. I have to walk Bethany down the aisle."

My eyes remained locked on his solid, chiseled torso as he carried our plates to the dining table. Memories of the way he'd loved me with that body sent a trickle of arousal over my limbs and buried itself deep within my sex. He rounded the corner and winked at me. No doubt, my heated cheeks revealed my passionate inner thoughts.

My feet woke up and followed him and our breakfast to the dining room. Just as I expected, my plate was next to his and when I tried to take the seat next to him, his strong hands nestled over my hips and gently slid me onto his lap. I giggled before his lips covered mine and snuffed out the sound.

I placed a hand on his chest and pulled away as my breath grew heavy. "Can't be late, remember?" I eyed him playfully.

His grip tightened on my ass, adjusting me over his growing erection. "I don't want to imagine how difficult it's going to be keeping my hands off you once I see you in your dress."

"Speaking of...we really do need to hurry and get ready. I want to put loose curls in my hair and that will take me a while."

His eyes sparked with apparent interest as he bit into his breakfast. "You're going to make it tough on me, aren't you?"

"Make what tough?"

"I'm going to have to fight off every single man at the wedding while also tending to my brotherly duties."

I laughed. "You don't have anything to worry about. You're the only man I want."

He stopped his fork on the way to his lips and set it down and stared at me.

"What?" I crinkled my nose.

He kissed my cheek and squeezed me against him. "It feels good to hear that, really good."

Wanting to add to his happiness, I kissed him, long and soft. We finished our breakfast while discussing the itinerary of the wedding. We had to arrive early, so I dumped our empty plates in the sink and rushed up stairs to get ready. I kicked him out of my room so I could surprise him once I was completely dressed and done-up. He got ready using the first floor bathroom.

Once my make-up was glossy and sparkling—my hair in thick, wavy curls, and my legs shiny and smooth—I donned the dress and strappy wedges. I cracked the door of my bedroom and heard him walking around downstairs. My stomach did a loop-the-loop as I crept along the floor. He heard me coming and walked toward the steps.

As soon as I heard the steps creak, my stomach jumped around in my gut. I knew she was going to look stunning, but my imagination didn't do her justice. Her long, smooth, shiny legs met my eyes first and I was instantly glued, desperately awaiting what followed. My eyes trailed up her bare thighs to a dress that had been made for Amy's slender, toned, curvy body. If any color was a perfect representation of her, it was that yellow. Her long, light-brown hair hung in waves over her shoulders. Her smile was wide and shy, anxiously awaiting my reaction.

If my hard-on and bulging eyes weren't clear enough, I didn't think stuttering over my words would be any better.

"What do you think?" She did a little spin and the bottom of her skirt lifted, baring more of her naked thighs.

A low growl escaped my lips. "Baby, you look gorgeous, like the damn radiant sun. I'm screwed."

Her face lit up and she giggled.

"Come're."

I pulled her in close to me, gripping my hands around her tight ass, and pressed my lips against her glossy, berry flavored ones. My fingers slid up the soft fabric, lifting it off her thigh and found their way to the satin panties beneath.

Her pleasured moan filled my mouth and it took every bit of my self-control not to strip us both out of our clothes. Her hands held steady on my shoulders as my other hand took hold of her thigh, hugging her leg around my waist.

I caressed between her folds, pulling eager breaths from her lips. My body tensed with arousal. I ached to be where my fingers were. A mixture of gratitude and disappointment filled me when she slowly pulled away from my kiss and touch.

"Brock..." My name escaped in a breathy whisper.

"I know, baby. We need to get going, but you feel and taste and look so damn good."

I released her leg and she adjusted her dress and the panties I had ardently brushed aside. She lifted her hand and wiped her gloss off my lips. My brain couldn't think of anything other than having that lip gloss covering several parts of my body. She seemed to sense my lascivious thoughts because she grinned and winked at me.

"Save those thoughts for later."

I licked at the remaining berry flavor on my lips. "Looking forward to it."

My hand found hers and I tugged her with me to pick my hat off the dining table. I walked her out to my Nova and opened the door for her to take the passenger seat, giving her ass a squeeze. The playful look she gave me in return spread warm appreciation through me.

I WASN'T SURE WE WERE going to make it to the wedding if I'd let him continue. And now, the way he held his hand on my bare thigh and glanced over at me with affection and desire in his eyes had my stomach dancing with excitement.

When we pulled up to his house and I saw the multitude of cars, trucks, motorcycles, business vans, and loads of people walking around, my excitement turned to trepidation. I was about to meet all of Brock's family and friends. I grew nervous, wondering if they'd like me and what kind of questions they might ask. He must have sensed my uneasiness. He gave my knee a tender squeeze, then when he parked, he leaned over to my side and kissed me.

"Don't worry about a thing. They're going to love you."

He came to my side of the car and opened the door for me. I put my hand in the crook of his bent elbow and walked with the handsomely dressed man next to me. He'd worn his black boots with dark denim jeans that fit his firm ass like a glove. Tucked into his jeans, and behind a leather belt, was a white, button-up shirt. Above that, a light caramel vest and of course, he'd worn his black cowboy hat.

"I didn't get a chance to say it before. You look handsome."

He leaned sideways and kissed my temple.

"Thanks, gorgeous."

He led me toward his house and my nerves swelled into a giant knot in my stomach. I could hear several women laughing, talking, and shouting over one another. The door swung open and a little boy dressed similar to Brock ran out, waving a garter in his little hand.

"Troy! Stop right now!" a woman bellowed from beyond the closing door.

Brock leaned down and scooped up the fair-haired little boy. He laughed and wiggled and clenched the garter in his fist.

"I'm not giving it back," he whined.

Brock poked his stomach and then quickly snatched the garter out of his hand.

"This doesn't belong to you. It belongs to Bethany and you're old enough to know by now, not to antagonize the Baisdin women. Nothing good comes of it."

At the end of his reprimand, a short, fair-haired woman with flushed pink cheeks, a curly up do and a coral, over-the-knee bridesmaid dress, lurched through the door.

"Oh, thank God, you're here. Bethany is about to lose it," she jutted out her hip and frowned at Troy, "and he isn't helping things any."

Brock let out an amused laugh, held Troy steady and turned his body toward me. "Lexa, this is my girlfriend, Amy."

Lexa's attention snapped to me. Her already pink cheeks turned a shade brighter. "I'm so sorry." She outstretched her hand. "I'm Brock's cousin, Lexa." She shook my hand and then pointed to Troy. "That's my son. He's a menace."

We both laughed and the knot in my belly loosened. She waved us in.

"Come in, come in. Have a beer while we wait for the ceremony to start."

We walked in to chaos. Bags, clothes, shoes, food, women, children, and a photographer were scattered about the open living room, kitchen, and dining room. Brock set Troy down on the floor and looked around for who I assumed was his sister. He took my hand and gave me a wink as he moved us farther into the chaos until he found the bride he was looking for.

The tiny, curvy, black-haired, young woman squealed with excitement. "Brock!" He outstretched the hand that held the garter. "Found something of yours."

Her eyes gleamed brightly. The love between Brock and his sister was obvious. I envied them in that moment.

Bethany lifted her garter out of his palm and set it on the chair next to her. "Thank you!" She looked at me with a generous smile. "You must be Amy? We've heard great things about you." She eyed Brock with a knowing look. Something secretive passed between them.

I outstretched my hand and she used it to pull me in for a hug. "If you're going to date Brock, get used to being man-handled by the whole family."

Her hug was warm and genuine. I laughed and she let me go and took hold of my hands. She studied my eyes and face, then opened our arms so she could look over my dress.

"You look beautiful, Amy. I'm so glad you came." She giggled and reeled me in for another hug.

"You're a beautiful bride. Your dress is gorgeous."

She jiggled her hips and the long, sequined, strapless, ball gown swished over the tile floor.

"Ah, I'm so excited!" she beamed.

Brock's own smile was wide as he looked down at us with pride and adoration in his eyes. His smile sagged slightly when he looked past us. I turned my head to see an older woman, who no doubt was their mother, based on her similar dark hair and features. Her large, brown eyes studied me as she neared. I held my breath as her eyes bored into mine. In my periphery, it appeared the entire room had gone still, watching us.

The woman tilted her head, judging me. The fight or flight instinct kicked in. Part of me was ready to bolt. Brock's large, comforting hands took hold of my shoulders and some of my fear settled. She glanced up at him and then a forced smile eclipsed her discerning stare.

"I'm Johann. Brock and Bethany's mother. You must be Amy?"

"It's a pleasure to meet you." I outstretched my hand and she clearly debated taking it, and then glanced at Brock, before ultimately shaking my hand.

Two women joined her, standing on each side. The woman on the left had short, shiny, black hair and was taller than Johann, yet had similar features to her and Bethany. The third woman had auburn hair, pulled back into an up do with pretty green eyes and a pleasant smile.

The taller, black-haired woman waved her hand in the air. "Don't mind Johann. It takes her a while to warm up to, well, any woman Brock shows an interest in."

Brock let out a breath. "Amy, this is my aunt, Victoria." He pointed to the woman who had spoken. "And my Aunt Susan." He pointed to the woman with auburn hair and a kind smile.

Susan eyed Johann sideways. "By marriage," she added.

Apparently, there was underlying tension between the two

women. Johann rolled her eyes and then her face lit up when she looked at Brock.

"Brock, darling."

She nearly shoved me out of the way to get to him. His expression silently scolded her and then transitioned into one of affection. He pulled her in for a hug.

Bethany leaned into my ear. "Brock's her favorite. He can do no wrong." She winked at me.

Johann's eyes narrowed at Bethany.

"What? It's true."

"All right, ladies. It's time to get in procession," Lexa announced, as she approached with Troy on her hip, a little girl by the hand, and three more young women in matching bridesmaids dresses.

Susan gave my arm a gentle squeeze. "I'll walk out with you."

Brock pulled me in close and kissed me in front of all the women of his family before Susan and Victoria escorted me out to the gazebo.

Rows of chairs filled the interior. At the end of each row sat a mason jar with coral and yellow daisies jutting out. Bows of the same colors were tied to each chair along the aisle. Mason jars with tea candles hung from the ceiling, giving a romantic ambiance to the scene and an arch with coral and yellow daises adorned the front of the gazebo, facing the lake.

I sat next to Susan and her husband, who she introduced as Johann's brother, Carl. She pointed out several other family members while we waited for the ceremony to start. I hoped she wouldn't quiz me later. Names and faces were blurring together as the memories of my wedding filled my mind. I pushed those emotions aside and focused on Bethany and her fiancé's special day. Thankfully, I was distracted by the music beginning to play.

Couples walked down the trail of jars and flowers before ascending the stairs onto the gazebo and lining up on each side of the wedding arch. Troy and the flower girl paraded down the aisle, followed by Brock and Bethany. Everyone rose when they saw them coming. Brock searched for me among the crowd. His handsome smile lifted the corners of his mouth as he kept his focus on me. Several emotions filled me in that moment and one of them stood out the most, terrifying me with the knowledge—I was falling in love with the handsome cowboy coming down the aisle.

I TRIED TO KEEP MY EYES on getting Bethany safely down the aisle so I could hand her off to her soon-to-be husband, Luke, but I couldn't pry my eyes off the most beautiful woman standing in the gazebo. Amy stood out like a stunning ray of sunshine in her yellow dress and long, shiny, golden-brown hair. When the moment came to hand Bethany off to Luke, I reluctantly peeled my eyes off Amy and gave my baby sister a kiss on the cheek, before leaving her with a man I trusted would take good care of her.

I took the empty seat next to Amy and immediately wrapped her in my arm and kissed her cheek. Her eyes lit up with something new, something I hadn't seen before. It was an incredible feeling to see adoration in her eyes. I'd been waiting for a moment like this, to know her feelings were the same as mine. I raised her chin and pressed my lips gently over hers. She leaned into my arm and chest and watched the ceremony of my sweet baby sister and her fiancé.

By the end of the ceremony, Amy wiped at the tears that welled up in her eyes. Even I felt sentimental by the display of Luke and Bethany's excitement and love. I couldn't help imagining Amy being my wife and what our lives would be like together and what our children would look like. I kissed her head and pulled her up from the chair as everyone followed the newlyweds out of the gazebo.

We took our seats at our designated table and chatted with my family while the salads were delivered and our champagne glasses were filled. I couldn't keep from touching Amy and having her body close to mine. Seeing her comfortable and enjoying her conversations with my family had my chest about to burst with pride and joy. She fit right in and everyone was eager to get to know her. Her hand squeezed my knee when she saw the way I was admiring her. Was I that obvious? Probably. This woman had me wrapped around her finger and I'd fallen worse than a school-boy crush, but to know she was feeling it too, gave me incredible gratification.

As the last of the glasses were poured, I kissed Amy's cheek and then stood to give my toast to a magnificent union. I lifted my glass and everyone followed.

"Bethany isn't just my baby sister, she's my best friend, my confidant, and a very important person in my life. I've watched her grow up into a beautiful, kind woman who deserves a man that will respect her, protect her, and make her happy. When I met Luke and saw the love he had for her, the effort he put into ensuring she was cared for and happy, even when the Baisdin temper came out..." After the laughter settled I turned to my sister and Luke, "I knew Luke was the man for you. Love like yours is special, and meant to be cherished in the best times and the hardest. I know the both of you will fulfill every promise you've made today. I couldn't be prouder of this union or happier for the both of you. Congratulations Bethany and Luke."

I tried to control the emotional knot in my chest as Bethany shed tears down her sweet face. Luke proudly nodded to me and wrapped his wife in his arms. The tables around me clapped and I sat down and admired the soft, damp eyes of the beautiful woman in front of me.

"You're an amazing man, you know that?"

I pulled her chin up to me and kissed her. "I'd like that to be us someday."

The words slipped out and there was no taking them back. My muscles clenched as I awaited her negative reaction. Different emotions transitioned over her face and then a soft smile lifted the corners of her mouth. She leaned in and kissed me. Relief filled me that she didn't clam up and avoid eye contact, yet her silence left room for questions.

CHAPTER 17

$\mathcal{I}$t was becoming clear to me how serious Brock was about our relationship. From practically moving into my house, to the silent words between him and his sister, to the hint of marriage in the future. I was falling for this man, but I couldn't help wondering if something was wrong with me. My feelings evidently were not moving at the same pace as Brock's. He was picturing our future, and I was just catching up to the present. I ate the wonderful-smelling food brought out to us, but barely noticed the flavor. The knot in my stomach grew throughout dinner, and it didn't help that Brock's mother kept a watchful eye on me as though I was going to claw out her son's heart at any moment.

I drank down the glass of wine in front of me, hoping to settle my jittery nerves. Brock too started watching me with concern in his eyes. I needed air. I excused myself and rushed to the house in search of the bathroom. Using a washcloth, I dabbed my flushed cheeks, then held onto the sink counter and took several breaths. Was I having an anxiety attack? Couldn't be. I was fine, just a little overwhelmed with the day's events and the amount of emotions in the air. After collecting myself, I used the bathroom and stepped out, surprised to find Johann standing there waiting for me.

"Sorry. I hope you weren't waiting long." The jittery nerves settled by the wine sprung back.

Her hawkish eyes narrowed in on me. "What are your intentions with my son?"

Good God, the woman was forward, aggressive even.

"I'm not sure what you mean?"

Her arms folded over her chest and she let out a breath as though my comment annoyed her.

"You know exactly what I mean. I've seen the way my son looks at you. He's in love with you. Brock is an incredible man. He deserves a woman who will give him the same kind of love he will give, and by the looks of it, you don't seem to share the same feelings he does."

Now was the time for a backbone if I ever needed one.

"I'm sorry, Johann, but we just met, and I've barely had time to get to know you. You have no idea what my feelings for Brock are, nor do I deserve to be cornered and questioned like this."

Her tongue clicked against her cheek. "You better not hurt my son." She started to add to that comment, but stopped when Lexa rounded the corner with the flower girl on her hip. Her eyes moved back and forth between us.

"Sorry to interrupt. Is the bathroom free?"

Glancing at Johann's threatening stare, I nodded. "Yeah, excuse me."

I stepped around them and stopped outside on the porch, gripped the railing and attempted to control my whirlpool of emotions. Johann glared at me as she walked past me, headed toward the wedding tent. Brock saw the interaction and intercepted his mother on his way to me.

I WAS ALREADY CONCERNED ABOUT how long Amy had been gone, then I saw my mother and Amy eye each other with heated stares across my deck, and I knew my mother had opened her big mouth and said things she shouldn't have. I'd probably scared Amy with my comment earlier; I didn't need this too.

I placed my hand on my mother's shoulder and looked into her large, brown eyes.

"What did you say to her?"

My mother stepped forward in an attempt to get me to walk with her toward the tent. She let out an annoyed breath when I didn't budge. "She's not good enough for you. I can see she doesn't share the same feelings you do. That woman will break your heart. I'm trying to protect you."

My head tilted back as I gathered my patience. "Don't try to chase her off like you have the others. Amy is different. You don't know what she's been through. She lost her husband at the same age Bethany is now. I'm the only man she's dated since her husband passed, and dammit, Ma, I'd like to keep it that way."

In the corner of my eye, I saw Lexa walk out of my house and set Lily down. Lily ran back to the tent for the cake that was now being served while Lexa spoke with Amy. Relief filled me when Amy's shoulders relaxed and she smiled.

I gave my mother a pointed look. "I mean it. Amy is here to stay. I'm serious about her. She deserves to be treated better. Give her the same respect you do Luke."

"Brock—"

I shook my head. "Don't make this an issue between us." I kissed her temple before making my way to Amy. As I reached the top of the steps, Lexa looked over at me, nodded and made for a quick exit.

One look in Amy's eyes told me she was about to flee at any moment. I knew I had to put all my efforts toward damage control.

I stepped up to the railing and leaned my ass against it. I wrapped my hands around her hips and placed her between my legs. Her eyes softened when they looked at me.

"You know when you get that pouty face the first thing I want to do is love you 'til it's gone, right?"

She laughed, and I put my hat on her head and placed my hand on her jaw, bringing her in for a kiss.

"I know today has been a lot for you to absorb, and I know my mother can seem crude, but she means well. I can see there's a lot going on inside that beautiful head of yours. Wanna talk about it?"

She leaned into my body, resting her hands on my shoulders. I was pleased to feel her body lax in my arms.

"Not right now. We're at your sister's wedding, and I don't want any of that time wasted. We should get back."

She started to move her body in that direction, and I stopped her. "I don't care that it's my sister's wedding. If something is bothering you, I want to fix it."

She smiled and kissed me. "You already have." She took my hand and pulled me back toward the tent. Whatever had been bothering her, she'd clearly made her choice about it. I accepted it for now, wanting to make the best of tonight's celebration. I pawed her ass as she walked down the steps. She leered her gaze toward me and arousal caused me to swell.

I wrapped my arm around her as we walked toward the tent. "Have I told you how good you look in my hat?"

Her beautiful, bright smile lifted her lips. "I think you might have mentioned it before, but I still like hearing it."

LEXA'S WORDS REPEATED IN MY head as I walked with Brock back to our table. She'd told me not to let Johann get under my skin. She'd shared a little about Johann and how Brock had become her anchor when her husband left, that he'd looked after all the Baisdin women. Since Brock's heartbreak,

Johann had become overly protective of him and quick to run off any woman he brought around, but with me, it was different. With me, he stood his ground and told Johann and the others to welcome me with open arms. She said it was obvious how much he cared for me.

Johann had been right about one thing, her son was an incredible man. That was one thing we could agree on, if we never agreed on anything again. Without realizing it, Brock had become the driving force of our relationship, moving us forward when I was too scared to. He always made me feel safe and wanted, and when he wasn't around, I felt a little empty without him.

When he came to ensure I was okay and was determined to put our relationship before the wedding celebration, it hit me how foolish I was being. It didn't matter my feelings were moving slower than his because they were still growing day by day, and one thing was clear—I didn't want to lose him.

We sat back at our table and nibbled the different flavored cakes from each other's plates. He put a dab of icing on my cheek and laughed before licking it off. The sensation sent goose bumps over my skin. He winked and rubbed along my inner thigh, tempting me with his sensual caress.

The DJ started the music and called for the first dance of the bride and groom. My body warmed with reverence as I watched Bethany lay her head on Luke's shoulder and slow dance with him. I wanted to slap myself for how I'd responded to Brock's comment earlier. Of course he hoped our future would look like this. He'd never been married or known unconditional love like I had. He wanted love like that with me, and instead of appreciating his heartfelt confession,

I'd smiled and given a kiss to avoid the anxious feeling it brought up.

The first chance I got, I wanted to make it right. I wanted to tell him the truth, that I'd fallen in love with him and that my fear of being vulnerable had distracted me from how much he means to me. I leaned into his chest, and he wrapped his arms around me. I could feel his love washing over me.

I reluctantly sat forward when the DJ called for him to dance with Bethany while Luke danced with his mother. My eyes were glued to Brock and Bethany laughing and chatting. Every once in a while, one of them would glance my way, which left me wondering how much they were talking about me. As entranced as I was, I didn't notice a man slip into Brock's chair.

He grazed my arm with his hand. I peeled my eyes away from Brock and Bethany to find a tall man my age with ginger-red hair and dark blue eyes staring back at me.

"I'm Tye. Brock's cousin. You wanna dance?"

I looked over at Brock to see if he'd noticed that Tye was talking with me. Of course, he did, and he gave a nod of approval our direction. With the song coming to an end and the next one starting, I got up and joined Tye on the dance floor. He kept his hands securely in the safe zones.

"Sorry I didn't get a chance to introduce myself earlier. When you came out, my mother kept your attention until the wedding started."

"It's all right. Your mother was good company. She's really nice."

"Thanks. You and Brock been together long?"

I almost laughed at the question. "No, actually we haven't."

"Oh." Clearly my response surprised him. "I would've guessed you've been together a while."

It was nice to hear we gave off that impression.

"It definitely feels like we've been together longer than we have."

Tye flicked Brock's hat with his finger. "You know what it means when a man puts his hat on a woman?"

I tilted my head, curious. "Humor me."

His eyes crinkled at the corners. "He's letting everyone know you're his."

Tye dipped me, surprising me. I giggled as he lifted me back up. He held Brock's hat in his hand and an impish grin on his face. Brock stepped up behind Tye and swiped his hat from Tye's hand and placed it back on his head.

"You plannin' on doin' something with that?" Brock met Tye's stare with his own playful, yet challenging expression.

Tye laughed. "Better keep close to this one. She's a looker." Tye turned his head and winked at me. "Thanks for the dance."

Brock tapped Tye's shoulder as he left, then scooped me up in his arms to dance with him through the next song.

"Don't take anything Tye does too serious. He's a big flirt."

I smiled, humored by the interaction between them. "I like your family. They've made me feel welcome."

Brock held me tighter. "Good, I want you to feel comfortable around them. I apologize for whatever my mother said to you. It obviously upset you."

"Don't worry about it. You were right. She does mean well. She loves you and wants to see you happy and so do I."

Brock kissed my temple and brought his lips to my ear. "I didn't mean to startle you with what I said earlier. I'm sure coming to a wedding brings up a lot of past emotions. I don't want you to feel like I'm trying to rush things between us."

I rubbed my hand along the back of his neck and raised my chin to kiss him. "You don't need to apologize. It's me who should be apologizing. This has been great coming here with you. I appreciate that you wanted me to get to know your family. I appreciate you, Brock, and I haven't done a good enough job of expressing that. And I more than appreciate you." I paused to take a breath and let the hammering in my chest settle. "I'm falling in love with you."

Brock tilted his head back to meet my eyes. For several moments, his gaze moved over my face. Different emotions transitioned over his. His eyes filled with appreciation and elation. He held me tightly around my waist and lifted me off my feet and spun me. My feet hit the floor as his lips covered mine.

When the song was ending, he clutched my hand in his and rushed me off the dance floor. He walked us out of the tent, away from the party and nosy eyes, and stopped us short before the edge of the lake. The pink and orange glow of the setting sun lit up the sky behind us.

Brock held my face gently in his hands. "Amy, you don't know how good it feels to hear you say that." His beautiful hazel-green eyes gazed down at mine. "Because I've fallen completely in love with you."

Those simple words lit up everything inside of me. I moved into his open arms, and he held me close, putting his head against mine.

"This has happened fast, but I...I don't want it to end. You make everything better," I told him.

He kissed my forehead then lifted my chin with his hand.

His eyes were glazed and filled with adoration. "I know what you mean. Before you, life was dull for me. You make everything brighter, better. I know sometimes it's hard for you to let the good in without being reminded of the pain from your past, but it means the world to me, that of all the men you could've had, you let me in."

He kissed me with unbridled passion. His hand pulled my ass against him, and I moaned when he pressed against me.

We each took a heavy breath when our lips parted. He stroked his hand across my cheek and brushed a loose curl away from my face.

"If you let me, I'll never stop loving you, I'll always be there for you. I'll always take care of you. We have something incredible, Amy. I want to keep it going. I want you to be mine."

There weren't words I could create to express my emotions in that moment. I wrapped my arms around him and held him tightly against me. I didn't want to let go, not for a second. I pressed my lips against his and loved him with my mouth. His hand lowered down my back and over my butt. He squeezed me firmly in his hand and removed what little space there was between us. A low grumble escaped his lips when I grazed his hardening erection.

"I want you now," I whispered. "I want you inside of me."

Hunger filled his eyes, and his expression grew serious. "You're going to get what you want."

He took my hand in his and walked me around the outside of the tent toward his house, avoiding contact with anyone who might interrupt his mission. We walked into his house, and he looked around, making sure no one witnessed us sneaking into his bedroom. He closed the door behind us and locked it. His lips drove needy, eager breaths from my mouth as his hands slipped beneath the skirt of my dress and yanked my panties off my hips. I kicked them away and wrestled with his belt and freed him from his jeans. His kiss came rough and eager. He pressed me against the door. I wrapped my legs around his hips and he thrust himself between my thighs.

FROM THE MOMENT I SAW her in this dress, I wanted this. I wanted to feel the soft fabric bunch between my fist and flow over us as I sunk myself deep inside her. Then, to have her tell me she was falling in love with me and wanted me now, there was nothing that could've stopped me from having her. I held her steady, one hand on her thigh, one on her back as I plunged into ecstasy. The sound of us coming together and the velvety feel of her swelling around me, tightening with each thrust, had my body and mind damn near about to explode with pleasure.

Holding her ass up with one hand, I cupped her mouth with the other as she let out an uncontrollable satisfied moan. "Shhh, baby, we don't want anyone to hear us."

Oh, hell, who was I kidding? I removed my hand from her soft lips. "Fuck it, moan all you want."

I tilted my head back, gripped her hips and slid her back and forth over me. A low groan escaped my lips as the last of my pleasure left me. I leaned the weight of my body against her, and she held tightly to my neck and shoulders.

"That was incredible," she whispered.

I lifted my head and looked into her beautiful baby-blues. The exact eyes I would be blissfully happy to look at the rest of my life. I ran my thumb across her bottom lip, then stroked her smooth cheek while still keeping us together as one.

"We're not done." I winked and carried her to my bed.

CHAPTER 18

*A*pparently, telling Brock what he meant to me gave him added stamina. When we returned to the reception, I was worried people might have noticed we'd been gone a while, but that wasn't the case. Luke, his best man, and his three groomsman were performing a choreographed dance for Bethany and all the guests. Everyone was too distracted, hooting and hollering, and recording the entertaining dance with their cell phones to notice our absence.

Brock pulled me into the crowd, and we joined in the cacophony of hoots and wails as if we'd been there all along. The choreographed dance was spectacular. I would've loved to see Brock up there too. He would've fit right in with the five cowboys clicking their boots and tipping their hats. The men's feet swept across the floor and their hips swung to the beat of the music, drawing all the ladies' eyes and the envy of the men with them. Except the man standing next to me, he was grinning from ear to ear watching me have a good time.

Between Brock's and my confession, our secret

rendezvous, and the excitement of the dance, my body was humming with pleasure. The hypnotic atmosphere continued even after the choreographed dance. The DJ kept the upbeat music playing and almost everyone hit the dance floor. Brock and I showed off our moves to the line dance, then the ladies on the dance floor took over with the Cupid Shuffle. The men lined the outside and watched us ladies shake our hips.

More liquor passed hands and more music boomed from the speakers. Bethany, her bridesmaids, and I stole the dance floor, laughing and gyrating to one song after another. Brock joined me, catching me in his embrace, and spinning me the length of his arm. My skirt lifted from the momentum and Brock's eyes lowered to my bare thighs before pulling me back to him.

He leaned his head down for me to hear his private share. "You're the most beautiful woman here tonight."

I blinked and nodded to his sister. "She's the most beautiful one here tonight."

He shook his head. "You shine like the sun."

My eyes were glued to his salacious gaze. "It's because of you."

He grinned and lifted me, holding me tightly as he spun me around. He took my hand in his. "Walk with me."

I started to follow, but Bethany caught my arm.

"Amy, can I steal you away for a moment?" She glanced at Brock for approval.

The corner of his mouth raised and he nodded.

Bethany slipped her arm into mine and guided me to the vacant gazebo.

"Luke and I will be leaving soon, so I wanted to steal you away for a few minutes."

She glanced behind us to make sure no one was going to interrupt and relaxed her hip against the wooden railing.

"I want to warn you. I know my mother will take any chance she gets to run you off, don't let her. I've never seen my brother so happy. I know it's because of you. He's completely smitten with you. I hope that when Luke and I get back from our honeymoon and get settled that we can all get together. I'd love to get to know you better and I want you to know you're welcome in our family."

I lowered my head for a moment to collect my emotions. Her words meant a lot to me. I raised my chin and looked back at her similar hazel-green eyes and sun-kissed freckled cheeks.

"Your mother did corner me, but I don't blame her. I understand why she's protective of Brock. Today, meeting your family, coming to this wedding, made me realize how much Brock means to me. I've fallen for your brother. I'm just as smitten as he is. He makes me feel incredible. It's so soon, but I feel like I already love him."

Her eyes glossed over, and her smile nearly reached each ear. She glanced behind me and that ample smile spread. I looked over my shoulder, and Brock stood on the steps, frozen in place. Bethany brushed my arm with her hand.

"I'll see you when we get back from Hawaii. I'm really glad you came today."

She slipped past Brock as he continued up the remaining steps. His eyes spoke volumes: eager, possessive, aroused, elated. He pushed me against the railing and claimed my mouth. His warm hands and whiskey-flavored lips said what his words didn't. My body tingled with sparks of electricity. His possessive body held me steady, pinning me to the railing.

I could feel his heat against my abdomen. His kiss was consuming, passionate. The world slipped away and all I could feel was his need to have me close, to have my body responding to him.

Heated lips parted from mine and that loss of warmth left my head spinning. My body begged me to reconnect, so I did. I pulled him down to me and slipped my tongue between his lips and showed him how much my body needed his touch.

He leaned his head against mine, both of us breathing heavy. "Amy, you don't know what you do to me. You're too much." His hand gripped my hip while the other rubbed along the nape of my neck. "I've wanted a woman like you for so long, but you're better than I could've imagined, than I could've dreamed of." His promise was whispered. "I'm never letting you go."

CHAPTER 19

*A*ll the emotions from the wedding carried me for days. I was sickeningly gleeful as Rick described it. But I was thankful to be walking around on cloud nine. It made it easier for me when Maisie, Dixon, and Ranger all returned to their owners throughout the week. New arrivals filled their void and kept the ranch busy.

I'd even begun training Honey on a lead rope and getting her used to the feel of a blanket on her back. Her lack of fear and naïve curiosity helped the process along. Brock and I made sure to see each other every chance we got, and most nights, he stayed over at my place. Today was Saturday and he'd planned a barbecue at his house to accommodate Bethany's request. She and Luke had returned from Hawaii on Thursday and Brock said she'd nearly begged him to plan something for all of us to get together.

I joined Jared in the barn to check on him before heading out.

He glanced over at me as he stretched the feed bucket into the air. "You look good."

I glanced down at my semi-worn jeans with a couple light rips in them, my cowgirl boots, and my green tank top with black beads across it.

"Eh." I tilted my head. "It'll do."

Jared laughed. "You look good even when you don't try to, Ames."

My stomach instantly knotted. I hadn't thought about Darrell all week and suddenly felt guilty as though I needed a reminder. Jared had called me that nickname a time or two before, but it hit home today after not having thought about Darrell in a while.

He set the empty feed bucket down. "What's wrong? You look startled."

My jittery hands filled my pockets. "Darrell used to call me that."

"I'm sorry." Jared flipped the bucket over and sat on it. "How you doing with the new guy? He treating you right?"

The corner of my mouth raised. Jared was several years younger than me, but at times, he acted like an older brother.

"He treats me *too* good." I leaned against one of the empty stalls. "I haven't thought about Darrell in a while because of Brock. When you called me that, it brought back a few memories."

"Do you miss him still?"

"I do. I used to miss him every day, and then once I met Brock, he lessened the pain and loneliness I used to feel, but I'll never stop missing Darrell entirely. I don't think you ever do when you lose someone the way I lost him."

"I've noticed a difference in you since you've started dating Brock. Your step is a lot lighter than it used to be."

I smiled. I knew what he meant. "What about you? Any

ladies in your life?"

He rubbed the stubble on his chin and tilted his head in thought. "There's a girl that has potential."

I chuckled. "Potential? That doesn't sound exciting at all. You should be much more enthusiastic when talking about a woman."

Jared's blue eyes sparked with humor. "She's more than potential, but I'm not sure I'm good enough for her."

"Good enough? Jared, don't sell yourself short. You're a really good lookin' guy, you have a degree and a good job. Heck, if I was your age, I'd be interested."

His hand rubbed the back of his neck. He stood and paced a bit then joined me at the stall. He leaned his arm against it and met my gaze. "I always thought she was out of my league. She's older than me, has a good job, and she's kind of tied up with someone right now."

My eyes widened and my stomach did a loop-the-loop. "Jared, you aren't talking about—"

"No! Ames, I'm not talking about you." His cheeks flushed. "Although, you are gorgeous and if you'd ever asked, I would've taken you to dinner in a heartbeat, but no, I'm talking about an instructor who works at the university I went to."

My rollercoaster stomach came down from one loop and rode another. "How much older is she and is she married?"

"She's twenty-five and she's going through a divorce."

"That sounds like a complicated situation that you may be walking into. How involved are you?"

He licked his bottom lip, hesitating. "We've slept together a couple times."

I leaned my head against the stall. This was a more

complicated situation than I thought. I wanted to take more time to talk with him, but I needed to get to the barbecue.

"Just be careful she isn't on the rebound. I don't want to see you develop feelings for this woman, while to her, you're just filling a void."

He nodded. Probably something he'd thought about already. I turned to head out of the barn. He gently grabbed my wrist to get my attention and then released his grip. "Those things you said. Hearing it come from you means a lot."

"I meant it. You're a good catch. Any woman would be lucky to have you. Be careful with this woman, okay?"

Jared nodded. "Thanks for the talk. Have fun tonight and Ames..."

I turned my head.

"You do look good in that outfit. Brock's a lucky man."

I laughed and rolled my eyes. "See ya Monday."

I STARTED UP THE BARBECUE, popped the top of a fresh beer, and checked my cell phone. It was a few minutes past the time Amy was supposed to have arrived. Bethany sat atop the picnic table with Luke on the bench next to her, giving me a questioning look. I shrugged. Tye and his newest fling were side by side on the opposite end and Lexa rounded the backside of the house, following Roger, a cooler in tow.

"Thank you for doing this. We needed a night away from the kids," Lexa said.

Roger dropped the cooler by the table.

"I brought beer and brats." He opened the cooler and fished out a package of meat. I took it from him and emptied it onto the grill.

"Where's Amy?" Lexa asked.

"Fashionably late," Bethany pointed to the corner of the house.

We turned our heads the same direction as Bethany's. My stomach instantly danced at the sight of her. Damn, she looked good. She might be beautiful in a dress, but when she dressed natural in jeans and a tank, she took my damn breath away. I grabbed a beer out of my cooler and popped the top. Wrapping her in my arms, I kissed her sweet lips before handing the beer to her. My hand found its way down to give her ass a squeeze and she let out a squeal of surprise. My sister and cousins laughed.

Bethany hopped off the picnic table. "Remember what I said? Get used to being man-handled." She pulled Amy in for a hug. I watched Amy's face light up and that small change in her body pleased me immensely.

"All right, give her back, B. I haven't seen her since yesterday."

I stepped behind Amy, wrapped my arms around her back and held her by the waist, leaning into her and sucking in her intoxicating citrus scent before nuzzling into her ear and

186

nibbling on it. She giggled beneath me, and Bethany rolled her eyes.

"You two are worse than us, and we're the newlyweds."

"They're in the honeymoon stage," Tye told her.

Amy's hand grazed my ass as I slipped away to check the food on the grill. She winked at me and bit her lip when I leered at her. Arousal tickled my groin, and I bit my inner cheek, shutting it down quickly.

"Damn man, she's got you whipped," Tye joked.

I took a swig of my beer and chuckled, watching Amy's sexy body walk to the picnic table with Bethany. "You don't know, Tye. *You just don't know.*"

Bethany and Amy broke out into girlish giggles. The women shooed the men away from the table and started setting it while us guys stood around the grill bullshitting.

"So, when's the proposal happenin'?" Tye asked.

I clicked my tongue against my cheek and flipped the burgers. "It's too soon. I can't rush it with Amy."

Tye shook his head. "You gotta put a ring on it before someone else does. You have the best lookin' woman here."

Luke elbowed him hard. "That's my wife you're talkin' about."

"Yeah, and she's my cousin. She loved me first, and I know you aren't blind. Amy's a fox."

I gave Tye a pointed look. "Let words like that come out of your mouth again and you're gonna have my fist buried in your face."

Tye laughed and shrugged. "Wouldn't be the first time." His eyes brightened. "We should get the girls to play football with us."

I looked over at their jeans, dresses, sandals, and boots. "I don't think they'll be up for that."

Tye looked over his date and Amy. "Maybe some strip poker," he suggested with a lecherous grin, before taking another sip of beer.

I slugged his shoulder and a mouthful of beer sprayed out of his mouth. He coughed before taking a breath. The ladies looked over at us, curious about the interaction. Bethany waved her hand in the air and spoke loud enough for us to hear.

"He probably deserved it."

"He did," Luke replied.

With his devilish grin, Tye shrugged, and took another swallow.

I pulled the grilled meat and put it onto three plates. The brats, burgers, chips, and potato salad Bethany brought flew off the three plates from the center of the table. We laughed at Tye's jokes, listened to the details of Luke and Bethany's honeymoon, and everyone wanted to know about Amy's ranch.

"Y'all are welcome to come over and ride anytime you want."

I slipped my hand beneath her hair and pulled her toward me so I could kiss her cheek. Seeing her have a good time with my family and friends strengthened my affection toward her. She glanced her baby-blues my direction and I could see the love in them. Damn, it felt incredible. I'd waited a long time to feel something as good as this and now that I had it, I sure as hell wasn't going to take it for granted. Not for a second.

"Really?" Bethany asked, excitement squeaked her voice.

"Yeah, just give me call and we'll plan a day to go riding.

I'm thinking of buying another horse, actually. One for guests to ride." She looked my direction. "Or maybe one for Brock."

Could this woman get any better?

I lifted her hand and brought it to my lips. "No, baby, I'll buy you another horse, it'll just happen to be one I like." I winked at her.

She smiled and leaned into my open arms.

"Seriously, you two are sickeningly sweet together," Lexa proclaimed.

Amy rubbed my arm that held her waist. A grin smeared her pretty face.

"So, did ya'll remember your suits? 'Cause if not, Tye is going to try to pressure you into football or poker," I said.

"Oh, I remembered." Bethany hopped off the picnic table. "They're in the car. I'll be back."

"Ours too," Lexa said.

Amy sat up. "I'll go with you. Left mine in the car too."

Emily grabbed Tye's keys and followed the girls.

BETHANY SLIPPED HER HAND INTO my arm as we walked to our vehicles. "You probably just made my brother's week by offering to get him a horse."

"I've been thinking about it for a few days. I can't always count on having a healthy horse boarding at the ranch. I figured he'd enjoy helping me pick it out since he'd probably be riding it the most."

"He won't say it in front of the guys, but he's probably ecstatic about horse shopping with you."

Lexa nodded. "No doubt he is. After you get the horse, you'll have to invite us over for a girls' night. It'll be fun to go riding, get drunk, and share some deep, dark secrets about our past relationships."

Bethany elbowed Lexa.

"What?" she bit out. Bethany nodded her head toward me.

Lexa scrunched her face. "Oh, my gosh, I'm sorry. I'm a little tipsy and—"

"It's okay. You don't have to apologize."

A knot formed in my stomach for the guilty expression on her face and for the reminder. The few hours without any kind of reminder had been fun while it lasted.

"What happened?" Emily asked, a concerned look on her face.

I stopped at Bethany and Luke's car while Bethany rummaged through the backseat for her tote and swallowed the lump in my throat. I needed to get used to having this conversation whether I wanted to or not.

"I was married once. My husband died in a farm accident."

Emily's hand went to her mouth as she sucked in a breath. "That's terrible. I'm so sorry."

Tears stung my eyes. "I'm sorry. It's not something I'm use to talking about." I looked toward the sky, trying to stop the tears.

Bethany rubbed along my arm, and Lexa embraced me, squeezing me tightly against her.

"Don't apologize for getting emotional. I can't even imagine what it would be like to lose Roger. It had to have been awful for you."

I nodded and wiped at a stray tear. "I've never really opened up about it until Brock."

"Is he the first guy you've dated since your husband?" Lexa asked, releasing me from her arms.

"Yeah."

"Oh, my God, that is so sweet. He probably feels really special."

"He does," Bethany confirmed. "He's fallen head over boots for her."

That brought a smile back to my lips. "I feel the same about him."

"You two really are adorable together," Emily said, smiling.

The front door opened. The guys billowed out, led by Tye. He whistled at us from the porch.

"Hey pretty ladies, you ready to get your toes wet?"

The ladies glanced at me.

"Yes," I called back.

The girls and I walked together, gathering our bags from each vehicle and then met the guys in the house. Swim trunks were handed to the waiting men before everyone claimed an area to change. I dropped my bag on Brock's bed and pulled out my two-piece with a cream knitted design over top of the brown fabric. Brock stretched over my shoulder and glanced in my bag.

"What are you looking for?"

"A toothbrush."

I chuckled and pulled it out to show him. "Of course I'm staying the night."

He kissed my cheek. "Good."

The corner of my mouth raised. "Were you actually worried?"

His warm arms cocooned me against him. "No, gorgeous. I needed to know if I had to stop drinking so I could drive us to your place. Wasn't sure if you had to work early."

I leaned my head back on his shoulder as his lips seared my neck between kisses. My breath left me when his warm hand slipped beneath my shirt and bra, grazing his palm over my hardening nipple.

"I'm all yours tonight," I whispered.

He sucked at my neck and then bit with just enough pressure to send a ripple of arousal through me.

"That's what I like to hear."

He lifted my shirt over my head and ran his strong, calloused hands down my bare sides. His hot breath on my ear sent anticipative chills down my spine.

"I should leave you to change, or I might not let you out of this room." He pressed his front against my back.

"Brock…"

His calescent lips left a trail of damp moisture along my collarbone. "Yes, baby?"

"You're right."

The feel of his lips lingering over my skin taunted me as he unbuttoned my jeans with ease. His fingers reached in and caressed my desperate and aching warmth below. A moan escaped my lips as his bold and greedy touch slipped in and out, rocking me to the edge of my restraint.

"Brock…oh, my Go…that feels…"

"Yes?"

"Don't stop."

His arm wrapped around me, holding my trembling legs steady.

"Amy..." His lips caressed along the tender skin of my neck. My body convulsed, the pleasure too much. "You feel like heaven in my hands."

My orgasm ripped through me, a compilation of fire and ice, exploding in different parts of my body. My knees gave out. A sound of pleasure escaped his lips as he lifted me onto the bed. The moment his exquisite fingers left me, the cold shock of his departure snapped my eyes open. His hands grasped my thighs and turned me toward him. I looked up to see his hazel-green eyes looking down at me as though I were the prey and he was ready to eat.

"Hurry up and change. I'm about to lose myself in you if you don't."

He stole one last, fleeting touch between my thighs before grabbing his swimming trunks and disappearing into the adjoining bathroom. My head collapsed onto the mattress. I laid there, catching my breath before I rose and undressed.

I STOOD OUTSIDE WITH THE rest of the group, waiting for that beautiful woman to join us. She walked out the back door a moment later and my aching blue balls damn near popped. Her tight, toned body and long, tan legs were torture. I could look but couldn't devour. Not now, anyway. It didn't take long for her to catch the attention of the other men either. My gut tightened at the way their eyes shined when they looked at her.

I glared at Tye, probably a little too dangerously. His expression soured, and he looked away from her, Roger followed. Luke intentionally ignored her entirely. Smart man. She tucked herself in my arms, and I leaned down to her ear.

"You look good enough to eat, too good."

She leaned back and giggled. I scooped her into my arms, her legs dangled over the crook of my elbow and her arms hung around my neck.

"Ready to get wet?" I winked at her.

Her cheeks grew pink and the secret that passed between us stirred my already sinful thoughts.

The cool water soothed the damp heat pooling on my skin and the aching in my groin. Her bottom hit the water when my waist did and she let out a squeal of surprise and then relaxed in my arms as the water covered her body. I released her legs and she wrapped them around my waist. I cupped her ass in my hands and held her against me. I loved the feel of her body against mine. The trust she felt with me. My Amy.

I leaned in and kissed her soft lips and then leaned back into the water, half-floating and letting her sit on my hips. Luke lifted Bethany and charged into the water. She crashed into it with him, letting out an excited squeal. Their heads popped up, and they both laughed before she shoved his head back down.

Lexa pointed at Roger. "Don't even think about it."

She dipped her toes in the water, and Roger looked past her to me. I nodded, encouraging his idea. He scooped Lexa into his arms and rushed into the lake, her legs flapped in the air before the water rushed her and left no body part dry.

We all laughed when Lexa popped to the surface and splashed water in Roger's direction. Emily took off running from Tye, expecting a similar fate. It only incited him further. He chased after her and caught her in a few steps. He lifted her and ran into the water with her. She giggled and kicked and kissed him when he didn't dunk her.

"Got any rope lying around?" Luke asked.

"Yeah, in the garage. What do ya need?"

"We should tie it to that tree over there." He pointed to a large oak tree on the edge of the lake. "It'd make for a good rope swing into the lake."

I nodded. "Yeah, give me a hand with it."

I kissed Amy before exiting the water and joining Luke in the garage. We found a good amount of rope and walked along the edge of the lake to the tree. Luke carried the ladder behind me.

I FLOATED WITH THE OTHER girls and watched Brock's muscular frame carry the rope to the large oak tree. He and Luke set the ladder up against the tree, and he used his muscles to raise himself the rest of the distance the ladder couldn't reach. Seeing his damp muscles flex in the sun reminded me of how he'd used those arms and hands not long ago. Arousal tightened my thighs at the memory.

I shook my thoughts and returned my attention to Brock straddling the large branch, securely tying the rope. He climbed down and pulled on the rope, testing its durability. Seemingly satisfied, he worked two knots into the rope—chest and hips high.

"Who wants to test it out first?"

Luke shrugged. "I will."

Brock handed him the rope and moved out of the way. Luke stepped back several feet, ran, and then swung into the air, holding tightly to the rope. His body tilted almost parallel to the lake before he let go and splashed into the water, drenching all of us around him. He rose out of the water, smiling.

I glanced over at Brock who held the rope and was taking several steps back. He gave it a good tug and then he sprinted forward and flew into the air before coming down in a big splash. I covered my face as the water landed.

He didn't come up out of the water, and my stomach knotted. I searched for him, the panic setting in and then I felt his hands on my thighs. Relief coursed through me. His head rose out of the water.

"Aww baby, you look worried."

I wrapped my legs around his hips and rested against his arms on my back. "I got concerned when you didn't come back up."

"Nothing to worry about." He caressed my cheek with his hand before kissing me. "I'm not going anywhere."

I tilted my head, already feeling angst over the words before having said them. "Nothing is guaranteed. I know that too well."

He thumbed my bottom lip. "You can't let that hold you back from living. C'mon." He took my hand, pulling me out of the water and led me to the rope dangling from the tree. He held it in one arm and me in the other. I stepped back with him, my arm around his back and then together we charged forward. My stomach lifted into my chest as his grip tightened and my feet left the ground, swept into the air. He hugged me tightly to him as gravity took hold of our bodies. The water swallowed us whole, taking with it the sights and sounds of the world. My eyes opened beneath the water and Brock filled my vision. His hands took hold of my face as his lips covered mine. He kicked and propelled us upward, raising me from the depths. Together, our bodies bobbed to the surface.

Spellbound by this man, I took a breath and then pulled his lips back to mine. I needed him like my lungs needed air.

CHAPTER 20

The next week passed by too quickly. We both had been busy at work, him more than me. He was close to finishing the current house and had a lot of final touches that needed his attention. Fortunately, it had given me the opportunity to do something very special for him.

With apparent interest in his eyes, Brock stood in my barn, caressing the neck and mane of the dark, bay thoroughbred in front of him. His eyes glistened with the same hypnotism I had when I first saw Merlin and Ransom. My lips drew back into a lengthy smile.

"He's yours. His name's Thunder."

"Amy...he's magnificent. When did you buy him?"

Thunder shoved his muzzle into Brock's hand for the treat lying in his palm.

"Yesterday, when you were busy with the inspectors. I wanted to surprise you."

"You more than surprised me. This is..." His eyes softened, filling with gratitude. "It's the best gift anyone's ever given me." He swiftly closed the distance between us and enfolded me in his solid arms. He leaned his head back and with his enthralling hazel-green eyes, he stared down at me, capturing me in his magnetism. "I love you, Amy. Do you know that? I love you, so damn much."

He kissed my lips, soft and affectionate, and then a deep rumble escaped his chest. He pushed me against the outside of Thunder's stall. His hands claimed every bare part of my skin he could access and then feverishly explored the areas that were covered. He lifted my legs and tucked them around his hips.

"I love you, Amy. Did I say that already?" He chuckled between hot, searing kisses. "Because if the words aren't sinking in, I'm going to work them in another way."

My words caught in my throat as humming pleasure seized my body. "Broc…"

His hips thrust against my pelvis. Damp heat filled my core.

"I love you, too."

His head tilted back and he stared down at me, piercing me with his intense and hungry eyes.

"Say it again."

"I love you."

His hands crept beneath the buttons of my flannel shirt. With little flicks of his fingers, they came undone. Heat swarmed inside my body like an angry nest had been ruptured.

"Again baby."

He spread my flannel open and tugged it off my shoulders.

"I love you, Brock. From the first moment I met you, you lit a flame that I thought had burned out. I love you for the man you are. The way you make me feel. I love you more each day."

His hands squeezed my ass and held me firmly against him. I kissed everywhere my lips could reach as he carried me to the saddle room. He closed the door behind us and set me on the wooden surface.

The heat of our desire rose like a storm. His kisses suffocated me, coming fierce and fast. Bottles, brushes, buckles, leather straps scattered wildly as he flung them out of the way. His hands moved fast, removing any piece of clothing in his way. He lifted his shirt and tossed it into our blurry surroundings. My hands slid over his solid chest and abdomen, admiring the ripples of muscles sculpted in perfect form.

His eyes penetrated mine, betraying his most intimate thoughts. He clasped a hand behind my back and fisted my jeans, removing them with swift precision. They dropped to the floor and my hands instantly seized his, shedding the unwanted fabric between us.

Eager hands palmed my ass and drew my body close to his. His heat pressed against my damp underwear. I could feel him grin beneath his kiss. His eyes stayed locked on mine as he spread my thighs and lowered himself to one knee. He gripped my legs and jerked my body forward, bringing me to the edge of the surface.

Every part of me tingled with anticipation as his warm hand slipped beneath my underwear.

"I hope you're not attached to these."

A quick and wicked tear filled the air. The cool air blasted the scorching heat between my legs. His tongue ran across his lips as he looked down at me.

"Hold onto something."

He spread my legs, giving himself full access. My hands gripped the edge of the wooden surface in preparation of the glorious phenomenon that was about to take place between my thighs.

THIS WOMAN DOESN'T KNOW WHAT she does to me. I'm hungry for her love, her body. I want to see her head roll back in pleasure, knowing I'm the one to drive her body wild. I held her legs steady as I devoured her. Loving a woman like this is an art, and Amy, she's my damn masterpiece.

Desperate moans repeatedly escaped her lips as she arched her body. Her orgasm whipped through her, and I didn't stop. I dragged out every last shiver until she trembled weakly, her eyes glazed, and utter satisfaction covering her beautiful face.

Her eyes sparked with renewed interest when I stood, and she saw how aroused I was. Her loving hand reached out and stroked me. I gripped the wooden counter and leaned into her heady touch. Several strokes in and I nearly lost myself, but not without having her first.

I leaned into her, opening her legs for me and plunged into

the slick heat awaiting me. My head rolled back as I slid in deeper. She felt amazing, mind-blowing. I gazed down at her sensuous stare. She leaned back, and I took one hand to her thigh and the other to grip the counter for stability.

Her moans erupted, a chorus of pleasure. I couldn't slow down, couldn't think. The friction, the sound of us coming together, it blanketed my thoughts, my senses. I couldn't get enough. I thrust deeper, harder. She called out my name and then exhilarant bliss seized my body.

I collapsed, my palms flat on the surface, holding my breathless body over hers.

"Damn, Amy, there's nothing, nothing as good as how you feel."

BROCK STROKED HIS HAND THROUGH my hair as we laid in bed after a warm shower. I traced my fingers over the outline of his ex-inspired tattoo—a black bird with a leafless tree drawn into its spread wing. I'd never seen anything like it.

"What does it mean?"

His hand continued to send soothing waves of pleasure over my skin as his fingers slipped through my loose strands.

"It's a reminder to never let the pain of my past hold me back and get in the way of living."

A humored breath left me. Ironic how well that applied to me.

"You're amazing, Brock. Truly. Your strength inspires me."

He shifted his body and raised my chin to meet his gaze. "You want to talk about strong. You lost someone you loved dearly and found a way to continue to move forward. You built a life and a business on your own. You heal wounded horses and give them a chance at life again. You're the inspiration, not me. You're beautiful, Amy, inside and out, and you are strong. Incredibly strong. Don't ever doubt that."

"I love you, so much."

His hand caressed my cheek. "I love you, gorgeous. Don't ever doubt that either."

He kissed me soft and sweet and held me close against him, running his fingers through my hair until sleep took me.

I WOKE, FEELING INCREDIBLE. I was looking down at the most beautiful woman, and her heart belonged to me. The night before meant more to me than Amy would ever know. I had what I'd been waiting the last several weeks for—her love. The moment she'd said it, I couldn't have her fast enough.

I leaned over her and caressed along her stomach until her eyes opened and a smile swelled her cheeks.

"Morning, gorgeous. Think we can get a ride in before your parents get here?"

She stretched and wrapped her arms around me, pulling me down for a kiss.

"Sure can, they aren't arriving until noon."

"Good, I'm looking forward to riding my new horse."

"You'll have to let me know how he rides. I held off so you could be the first."

I held her face in my hands and loved on her luscious lips. "You're perfect, baby. Simply perfect. The little things you do to make me feel special. I can't tell you how much that means to me."

Her soft, lengthy leg wrapped around mine, pulling me between her. There's nowhere else I wanted to be more. I slid my length across her silky folds. Her head tilted back as her body arched, welcoming me. My lips found hers, covering the sweet breathy moans escaping her lips.

"I love you, Amy."

Impassioned blue eyes seized mine. Her hand grazed my face, taking hold and locking me in place, inches from hers. The kiss came, full of heated need, before the emotional words escaped her perfect lips.

"I love you, too."

It was difficult to let her out of bed, but a stunning thoroughbred was waiting for me in a stall. A thoroughbred that I was now the proud owner of. I rushed through a shower and took breakfast to go. With it being Sunday, I held onto my eager, childlike enthusiasm and assisted Amy with feeding the horses and letting them out to the pasture. Once all the horses were cared for, I led Thunder outside the saddle room and hitched his rope and prepped him for a ride. I winked at the beautiful woman saddling Merlin next to me.

"Should we make a wager?"

A humored breath escaped her. "What did you have in mind?"

"If Thunder and I make it to the top of the hill first, you ride me tonight."

Her smile grew wide. "And if Merlin and I reach the hill first?"

"I give you a backrub and you can choose the position."

Her boot hooked into the stirrup, lifting her tall, graceful body onto the saddle. She turned Merlin toward the barn entrance as I hurried atop Thunder's saddle.

"I'm going to enjoy that backrub," she said, escaping quickly from the barn.

I pushed Thunder into a gallop, testing his limits. No matter who reached the top of the hill first, it was a win-win, but still, I had to try. A man's got to hold his own, especially in his own wager. Thunder was built well, holding his own against Merlin, but there was no beating the hours of training Amy had put in with him. As we neared the top of the hill, Thunder's speed declined. Merlin's endurance brought him and Amy to the top before us. We joined them a couple strides later.

"You know, I would have given you a backrub even if we won."

She leered her gaze at me, a lascivious grin on her face. "I would have ridden you without the wager."

My jeans tightened at the provocative words escaping those sexy, pink lips. A low grumble escaped my chest.

"Woman, you don't know what you do to me."

"Oh, I think I do, and I like it."

Watching her now, sitting atop the lustrous gray thoroughbred, her face to the breeze, the sun kissing her skin, I wanted to hold onto this moment because, little did she know, tonight I'd be asking her father for her hand in marriage.

BROCK SET THE LAST PLATE on my dining table and leaned against the chair.

"Think my introduction with your parents will go better than your introduction with my mother?"

I gave Brock a reassuring smile. "It wasn't that bad. She's just looking out for you."

Brock came around the table and pulled me into his arms, resting his hands together on my lower back. "I promise the next time you see her, she'll be a lot nicer. I've made sure of that."

I rubbed along his arched biceps. "Don't be too hard on her or she'll really hate me."

He nuzzled my nose with his. "Not a chance. If I love you, she has to."

I chuckled before leaning up to kiss him. "She doesn't have to do anything."

A vehicle pulling up the drive sounded in the distance.

"They're here," I said with a nervous grin. I took Brock's hand and led him toward the door.

"How should I address your father?"

"Call him Henry. I've told him enough about you, we're past formalities."

I swung open the door and waved at my parents and Grams as they exited the SUV. They reached us and I waved them all in.

"Mom, Dad, Grams, I'd like you to meet Brock Baisdin."

Dad outstretched his hand for Brock to take. "It's a pleasure to meet you. We've heard many great things about you."

Brock smiled appreciatively. "I can say the same about you."

A twinkle lit up my father's eyes. My mom smiled and stepped forward.

"I'm MaryAnn and this is my mother, Evelyn."

Grams pulled Brock in for a hug. Her tiny stature disappeared behind his tall, muscular frame.

"Call me Grams."

Brock let out a breath; his shoulders lowered as his nervous tension eased.

We all settled around the table and filled dinner with light conversation about the ranch, Brock's business, and everyone's current affairs. When we finished, the ladies moved into the kitchen to clean up. Brock entered and wrapped his arm around me and kissed my hair.

"Your father and I are going to take a walk out to the barn and check the horses. See you in a bit."

I stepped into the archway and watched them walk out together, feeling slightly anxious about their private time together.

Mom patted my shoulder. "Stop worrying. Your father likes him. I can tell."

I turned and met her identical baby-blues. "And what do you think of him?"

Grams placed the last dish in the dishwasher. "He's handsome."

Mom glanced over her shoulder, and I let out a humored laugh. "Yes, he is."

"You did well picking him," Grams praised.

"What about you?" I looked at my mother's unreadable expression.

Her lips eased into a pleasant curve. "He's charming and obviously adores you. I like him."

Instantly, the tension left my shoulders.

THE MOMENT I STROKED THUNDER'S MANE, MY SHOULDERS RELAXED.

"It's a fine horse Amy bought."

"It's the best gift anyone has ever given me."

"My daughter evidently cares a great deal for you."

I leaned my weight against the stall rails. "I care a great deal for her, too. More than care for her. I love her."

Henry's eyes remained focused on Thunder as he stroked his muzzle. "You know what she's been through?"

"I do, yes."

Henry's tall, lean frame adjusted. He set his elbow on the top rail and leaned his weight against it, before meeting my gaze.

"Amy's been through something that no young woman should ever have to live through. She's incredibly strong, but it took a lot for her to get where she's at now. The last thing she needs is another broken heart."

"I understand."

"Then, you won't mind me asking...what are your intentions?"

The corner of my mouth creased. "I was hoping you'd ask. I've been waiting for a woman like Amy to come into my life for years. When she finally did, it didn't take me long to realize what an incredible woman she is. It also didn't take me long to realize how much I love her and how proud I'd be to call her my wife. With your permission, I'd like to ask Amy to marry me."

The man's cool demeanor was unaffected. He tilted his

head and rubbed his hand along his chin, obviously contemplating what I'd said.

"Would you want to live here or your house?"

"Whatever would make her more comfortable, but considering how things are now, we'd likely live here. It would make more sense with the ranch."

Henry's eyes focused in on mine. "Would you want to become co-owner of the ranch?"

"If Amy wants me to, but that isn't an interest of mine, so we're clear on that."

Henry nodded. The man was evidently very intelligent and protective of his daughter. It increased my already growing respect for him.

"How soon would you want to get married?"

"I don't want to rush her. A longer engagement might be appropriate. She and I can decide that together. I want whatever makes her happy."

A smile grew from the corner of his mouth. "That's what I want, too. You have my permission. I believe you'd make my daughter happy. But I do want to make it clear for you, if you do anything to hurt my daughter, you'll have a serious problem on your hands."

I received the blessing I'd hoped for and it was sealed with a promise I expected. I reached my hand out for Henry, my future father-in-law, to shake.

"I respect you, Henry, and appreciate how important your daughter is to you. I hope I can make you proud to have me as your son-in-law."

CHAPTER 21

The morning sun filtered through Amy's bedroom window, casting a warm glow over her beautiful face and disheveled hair. Moments like this, when she was peacefully sleeping in my arms after loving her well into the night, left me with a feeling of heart-swelling joy. How did I get so lucky to end up with her? She was everything I'd ever wanted, and I couldn't wait to ask her to take my last name. I leaned across her side and swept kisses over her eyes, nose, and cheeks. She giggled as her eyes fluttered open. She held me in place so she could claim my lips.

"What are you so happy about?" she asked.

"I'm glad it's the weekend. I've been waiting all week for our trip."

"I can't believe how good you can keep a secret. I've been dying to know where you're taking me."

"The quicker you get ready, the quicker you can find out."

Amy's long, slinky legs eased off the bed. My morning wood ached the moment I caught a glimpse of her perfectly round cheeks taunting me from beneath her tiny, cotton shorts. Might as well satisfy the needy bastard. I chased her down and stripped off the blockade of fabric between me and downright filthy erotic bliss. I lifted her into the shower and met the silky wetness waiting for me.

"You're gonna have to wait just a little longer, baby."

A lecherous grin spread across her soft, pink lips. She wrapped one lengthy leg around my waist.

"It's worth it."

ANTICIPATION HAD ME WIGGLING IMPATIENTLY in the passenger seat of Brock's Nova. My eyes were glued to what was beyond the windshield as he finally took the exit to our destination. As soon as I saw the sign, I had a feeling of where he intended to take me for the weekend. I looked over at him, excitement bursting from my core.

"Are we going to the horse track?"

"Yes, baby, we are. And after the race is over, I booked us a very nice room to enjoy for the weekend."

I squeezed his hand as a squeal of excitement left me. I hadn't been to the races since I was a teenager with my parents. I couldn't wait to enjoy it all, and being there with Brock made it all the more special.

Brock pulled into the parking lot, and I nearly jumped out the moment he shifted it into park. He came around the other side and wrapped his arms around me.

"I'm glad you're this excited. I hoped you would be. C'mon, let's head in."

He took my hand and led me to the ticket window. He handed them off and we were ushered through the entrance. The place was buzzing with life. People were going every direction toward the seating stands, the restaurant, and the betting stations.

Brock gave my hand a squeeze and winked at me.

"I have a surprise for you."

He led me to the stables. We met a tall, slender, dark-haired staff member at the gate. He raised his hand and stepped toward us.

"I'm sorry, no entry through here, you have to be a VIP or staff member to go beyond this gate."

Brock nodded and smiled. "I'm here to see Alex Fernando. I'm a friend of his."

The guy's lips twitched and then the corner curved up. "Brock Baisdin?"

Brock nodded.

"Come on through."

The man lifted the lock and opened the iron gate for us to walk through. Anticipation pooled in my stomach as we neared the stables. Brock leaned down to my ear as we walked hand-in-hand past staff members, jockeys, and several attendees dressed as fancy as we were.

"I got a private tour, just for you, gorgeous. A friend of

mine still works here. We'll walk around a bit and see the horses and jockeys, then I want to find him and thank him."

I tried to contain the excitement threatening to break out in a dance. I wrapped my arm around him and stopped, so I could give him a long, appreciative kiss.

"This is awesome. Thank you."

He kissed my forehead, and we continued meandering through the stables, watching horses being prepped for the race. We rounded a corner, and Brock's pace picked up. He waved his hand at a man in a red and gold staff shirt with lustrous black, wavy hair and olive skin.

"Alex."

Alex turned from his conversation with one of the horse owner's employees. His smile widened.

"Brock. It's good to see you." They gave each other a brief pat-on-the-shoulder-type hug. "It's been a long time."

"Yeah, it's good to be back in my old stomping ground."

Alex glanced at me. Brock put his arm behind my back and motioned toward me. "Alex, this is my girlfriend, Amy."

Alex outstretched his hand. It was large and rough like Brock's—another hardworking man.

"It's a pleasure to meet you. Brock and I talked over the phone. He said you're the proud owner of the Flanders Ranch."

"I am."

"A friend of mine knows the owner of a horse you treated. I've heard nothing but good things about what you do for them horses."

My cheeks grew warm. "Thank you. I love what I do."

"These horses need special people like you." Alex looked past us. "Well, I got to run. Won't be long before the first race starts." He met Brock's gaze. "I hope you two enjoy yourselves. I upgraded your seats for ya. Couldn't get you your own box, but I think you'll be pretty happy with the location."

A grateful smile lifted the corners of Brock's mouth. "Thanks man. I really appreciate that."

"No problem. It was good to see you again."

Brock pulled our tickets from his pocket and read the seating number. He smiled wide.

"He upgraded us to *very* good seats. He put us in the VIP area. I'll have to do something to thank him later."

"That was really nice of him. How long have you been friends?"

"Nine years. We started working here in the same month when we were both twenty-one." Brock took my hand. "Want to place any bets before we head out there?"

I grinned. "Yes."

"I knew you would. C'mon, baby, let's win some money."

After reading through the booklet and getting tips from Brock, I placed three bets, then we headed to the concession stand for something quick to take with us to the stands. We settled into our seats with a great view of the finish line. I sipped on my sweet tea while Brock looked over my betting tickets.

"You went with three, huh?"

"Yeah, what did you choose?"

"Eighteen, and did a trifecta box with three, six, and eighteen. Either way, we're winning some money."

I wiggled in my seat. "They're starting."

The atmosphere of the race was perfect. The sun was high, the clouds scattered and puffy, the breeze light. The stands were full and the energy was humming. Brock and I attentively watched the starting gate. The bell chimed, and the gates released nearly a dozen horses eager to get to the finish line. Jockey colors and numbers were a jumble between lean bodies and long legs. My eyes followed the horses we'd bet on, and I squeezed Brock's hand as they gained in position.

"Look, Brock, number three is heading to the front."

Brock kissed my cheek. "Looks like you picked the right one."

As the horses crossed the finish, I sprung out of my seat. I turned to Brock, standing next to me, pride in his eyes. I leaned toward him and lowered my voice, containing my enthusiasm the best I could.

"We just won a thousand dollars!"

He placed his hand on my chin and raised my lips to his, giving me a quick kiss. "Good job, baby. You gonna pick the next one for us too?"

I laughed at his cheeky smile. "I'm not that good or lucky. I'm taking our winnings and stopping there."

"Mm hmm, we'll see."

By the end of the races, we won two-hundred and forty-nine more dollars and were now ready to check into our hotel and head out for dinner.

Brock carried my bag up the steps of the Tifton Resort just outside of the racetrack. He waved the key card in front of the scanner and the light changed from red to green. He opened the door for me to enter, and I had to remind myself to keep breathing. Sitting atop a king-size, four-poster bed with long, flowing white fabric tied to each post were dozens of rose petals. Next to the bed sat a stand with a bucket of ice holding a bottle of wine and beside it, two wine glasses.

Beyond the breathtaking rose petal-covered bed were

floor-to-ceiling windows overlooking a fountain in the middle of a small garden. Connected to the bedroom was a small kitchenette and a bathroom with a giant mirror that hinted to a luxury, whirlpool tub.

"Oh, my goodness, Brock, this is amazing. You didn't have to do all this. It must have been so expensive."

He closed the door behind us and set our bags by the door. He pulled me into his arms and looked down at me with his stunning hazel-green eyes.

"You think I care about the money? No baby! This is our weekend. I want you to enjoy every moment of it because I want you to know I'll always take care of you. I'll do anything to make you happy, because you're the woman I want to spend the rest of my life with."

His lips came down on mine, full of passion and apparent need. Need that drew eager breaths from my lips and caused x-rated thoughts to cross my mind. His hands pulled me against his hardening erection before he backed me toward the bed, pinning me between him and it.

With a groan, he pulled away in an evident attempt to regain his composure. My body begged to have his lips devouring me once again. Confused by the sudden interruption, I watched him fish his hand into his pocket and pull something out, clutching it in his fist. He placed his head against mine and rubbed his thumb along my cheek.

"I had a whole evening planned out with a dinner in the courtyard, but I can't wait a moment longer."

His eyes locked on mine, full of adoration and hope. He outstretched his palm and displayed what was in his fist—a tiny, black velvet box with a radiant cut yellow and white diamond engagement ring. He dropped to one knee before me, running his free hand along my legs, sending arousal coursing between my thighs like a whip of lightning.

"I've known you were the woman for me for some time now. It didn't take long for me to discover that my future had to have you in it. I love you more than anything in this world. Amy, there is nothing that would make me happier than if you were to be my wife."

The tears welled up in my eyes. Between the tempting arousal and unexpected shock, my body didn't know how to react. A moment of debilitating fear seized my body. The last man I loved and married, I lost. I wouldn't survive if I lost Brock, too. My hesitation must have been apparent. Disappointment filled Brock's eyes. He lowered the hand that held the ring.

"It's too soon—"

I raised my hand to stop him. "Yes." The word came out barely a whisper.

Brock's eyes widened and the hope and adoration returned.

"Yes?"

My body betrayed my mind. I couldn't believe I was saying it, but I wanted to be with this man, every ounce of me was screaming yes.

He stood and enfolded me in his arms. I buried my face in his neck, letting the warmth and comfort of his touch soothe my fears. "Yes. The answer is yes. I love you so much."

I could feel his muscles relaxing. He held me tightly against him and kissed my hair. "Damn baby, you scared me there for a second."

I pulled away, putting a small space between us so I could look at him. "I won't lie, I'm scared, but seeing the way you're looking at me now, only reminds me how much I love and need the man standing before me. I love you, Brock. I want you in my life and if that means taking this leap with you, then I'm in."

His piercing gaze penetrated me deeply. His hand stroked my cheek before his lips claimed mine. His intoxicating scent, heated body, and growing erection suffocated my senses. I leaned back onto the bed as he laid me beneath him. I inched back and his hungry eyes followed the form of my dress, down to my knees. He set the black velvet box aside and pulled the ring from it. He slid it onto my finger before bringing his warm hands to my thighs. He bit his bottom lip and slowly released it.

"I've never wanted you as much as I do now. You're gonna be my wife, Amy. I'm gonna be wearing a permanent hard-on and cheesy grin for quite some time."

My laughter was suppressed by his warm hands gliding up the inside of my thigh. The anticipation of his touch already had me warm and wet. His thumb swiped across me and the shock that smeared his face was priceless.

"When did you? All day you've been without them?"

I nodded.

A low growl escaped his lips. "Baby, that's incredibly hot. You should have told me sooner."

"You were so full of surprises this weekend. I wanted to have one for you."

His finger twirled around my clit before his hands reached for his belt buckle. "Fuck, Amy, I'm so damn aroused right now, I'm about to bust out of these jeans."

"Then, let's not waste any more time."

HER HANDS WORKED QUICKLY RELEASING me from my agony. She folded the jeans over the sides of my hips and my aching erection sprung forward. She took it in her hand and glanced up at me with those sweet, seductive eyes. *Yes, baby, please take me in your mouth*, was all I could shamelessly think. My wish was fulfilled and her glorious mouth worked me from base to tip. I groaned in pleasure when I hit the back of her throat.

Her hand worked circles as she slid me in and out. The blood left my brain, and I struggled to keep myself upright. I held one hand on her shoulder while the other clenched her beautiful, long hair in my fist.

"Amy...fu...ck...your mouth is magic."

I thickened, nearing my climax. My arousal increased when she moaned and pulled more of me between her lips. One invigorating pulse and my orgasm drowned out the world, leaving me with numbing satisfaction.

I looked down at the woman who would be my wife, the woman who gave me incredible pleasure and lifted my spirit the moment we entered the same room together. I placed my hands around her face and raised her to me.

"You're perfect. Absolutely perfect. I love you, baby. So damn much."

CHAPTER 22

Strong, calloused hands caressed warm water over my shoulders and breasts. Brock's adoring kisses trailed over my collarbone and neck as I admired the sparkling ring on my outstretched hand.

"Do you like it?" he asked, pulling more bubbles and warm water toward my exposed chest.

"I love it. It's beautiful."

He took my hand in his and rubbed his thumb along it, admiring the ring with me. "As soon as I saw it, I thought of you."

His head leaned against mine, and his kiss came soft on my hair. "I've never been so happy. You're gonna be mine, Amy, all mine."

I leaned up and turned to face his gleeful, shining eyes. "I'm already yours."

"No, baby. You're gonna take my name and I don't know why, but that means a great deal to me."

His words were emotional strings attached to my heart, tugging feverishly. I brought his hand to my lips and kissed it.

"I'm proud to take your name. You are an incredible man. I don't know what I did to deserve you, but I'm so thankful to have you."

He pulled me to his chest and kissed my forehead before placing his lips on mine. "Better put some more hot water in this tub. You're not getting out anytime soon."

His free hand slipped between my legs. My body responded eagerly, instantly warm with anticipation. I reached behind me and turned the knob to hot.

ON THE ROAD HOME, I couldn't stop looking over at my fiancée. Yeah, like a lovesick fool, I kept repeating *my fiancée* over and over in my head. I lifted her hand to my lips and kissed her soft fingers. Her eyes lit up when she smiled. Just looking at her, I wanted to pull the car over into the nearest dark, dirt road and pull her onto my lap.

"Eyes on the road." She grinned.

"It's not easy with you sitting next to me looking gorgeous."

She giggled, and I slipped my hand onto her upper thigh.

Her eyes glazed over with what I was sure was the memory of the sex we had before leaving the resort.

"What do you think about me moving in with you and selling my house?"

She looked at me, concerned. "You'd be okay with that? Selling your house?"

"Yeah, baby. It's just four walls to me. My home is wherever you are."

I hit a soft spot with that one. Amy's eyes took on a new sheen. "I think you're racking in the bonus points now."

A chuckle escaped me. "Might as well get them while I can. I know there'll be days I'll need them."

I brought her fingers to my lips again and kissed them before nibbling on them. She giggled in her seat and batted her long, beautiful lashes at me.

"We're home." I pulled the Nova into the driveway and parked it just outside the house. Our house. That was going to take some getting used to. Looking at it from the outside, I was already seeing the work I had ahead of me along with some necessary remodeling work inside. Turning it into *our* home was going to be my first priority.

THE NEXT MORNING, THE FIRST thing I did was call Heather and my parents to share the news of our engagement. Heather's excited shriek nearly burst my eardrum.

"I'm so happy for you! When's the date?"

"Last night we decided on March fifteenth. It's between our birthdays and the weather will be nice."

"Where's it going to be at?"

"We're not sure yet. We thought about the gazebo on the lake at his house, but if the house sells before the wedding, then that wouldn't be a good choice, so we're still thinking about it."

"What about your dress? When do we go shop—"

Heather's words trailed off as Jared burst through my front door. Shock swept over me instantly. He'd rarely ever come in my house and the grief-stricken expression on his face had my stomach instantly in a knot.

"What's wrong?" I asked over the sound of my thudding heartbeat.

"It's Ransom. You should come now."

I raised the phone to my ear. "I gotta go. I'll call you back."

Shoving my phone in my pocket, I quickly followed Jared out to the barn. I approached Ransom's stall and instantly froze in place. Ransom was lying on his side with blood around his nostrils. With shaky hands, I opened his gate and lowered myself next to him. Tears pooled in my eyes as I checked to see if he was breathing. When my hand pulled back from his breathless nostrils, the tears gushed from my eyes. While running my fingers through his soft mane, I laid over his neck, painfully holding back sobs.

"Should I call Andrea?"

All I could do was nod my head yes as my lip quivered and

my heart broke in two. My sob broke lose when I heard Jared tell Andrea that Ransom had passed away. I wiped my tears with my shirt as he returned to the stall. He squatted down next to me and placed a hand on my shoulder.

"I'm sorry, Ames. I know how much Ransom meant to you."

As much as I appreciated Jared's support, he wasn't the man I wanted holding me right now. "I need to call Brock and we need to get the other horses out before they get stressed."

"I'll take care of the horses. Take all the time you need."

I left the barn and immediately dialed Brock.

"What's wrong, baby?"

His voice alone soothed some of the ache in my chest.

"Jared found Ransom in the barn this morning." I swallowed back the sob threatening to escape. "He passed away."

"The guys can finish things up here. I'm on my way home."

Home. It felt so good to hear him say that.

THE ACHE IN HER VOICE brought me right back to the night she told me about Darrell's accident. Her emotional struggle all too obvious. I knew she was holding it together but inside, she was devastated. That horse was the first step she took toward healing after Darrell's accident. He was what helped build her new life. The usual twenty-five minute drive home to my fiancée was going to be twenty-five minutes too long today.

I dropped my tools in my foreman's truck and saddled my bike.

"Erik, I'm heading out. Finish things up here for me, will ya?"

"Yeah, boss. No problem. Everything all right?"

"Yeah, just need to take care of things at home."

On my drive, I started thinking of ways to ease her loss—a vacation, another horse? The guys would have to finish up the house on their own. She'd need me on the farm for the next few days, just as company, if not for anything else.

I turned onto a side road, attempting a short cut. The scenery was perfect. Tall, crooked branches arched over both sides of the road, creating a dome above me. The cool breeze dried the sweat that had lingered on my skin and the sound of my tires crunching gravel eased the tension I was holding. The idea came to me then, to take Amy on a bike trip, to a private place where I could love on her 'til the pain of Ransom's loss lessened.

As I turned the bend, my fists reflexively tightened on the bars. The sound of screeching metal tore through my ears. Instant pain seized by body as the vehicle struck my side. The bright sun was the last thing I saw before everything became dark.

CHAPTER 23

Days will pass and I will miss you.
I'll miss you every day.
I'll think of you when the wind whispers
And the sun embraces my skin.
I'll hold you close to my heart
And not forget the last words we spoke
Before we had to part.
I'll miss you until I can join you, my love.

CHAPTER 24

My pacing was causing a track in the hardwood floor. I dialed Brock again. Straight to voicemail. I palmed my face as panic dug its claws further into my chest. I didn't know what to do. My trembling hand raised the phone to dial again. It rang and I nearly dropped it in my desperate effort to answer it.

"Amy?" The fear in Bethany's voice stabbed right to my core.

"Where is he?" I asked, panicked.

"He's been in an accident."

"How bad?"

"It's bad, Amy. Get here as soon as you can."

The hard surface of the floor sent dull aching pain through my knees as they gave out beneath me. The dial tone sounded in my ears, competing with the loud thud of my heart, threatening to tear out of my chest. I couldn't, I wouldn't lose control. I swiped the phone off the floor and wiped away the tears rolling down my face. I slid into the closest pair of boots and rushed out the door.

My shaky, sweaty palm clenched my keychain in hand as I quickly cleared the distance from the entrance of the hospital to the receptionist desk.

"My fiancé, Brock Baisdin, was brought into the hospital this evening. What room is he in?"

Every excruciating second of her clicking on the keyboard only worsened my rising fear.

"He's in surgery, ma'am. You'll have to wait in the family waiting room. Second floor, room 2032."

Walking through the hospital, not knowing what condition Brock was in, brought back every agonizing memory of the day I lost Darrell. The fear of losing Brock was too much. My hand touched the wall for support. The dizziness kept me from taking a step further. My shoulder replaced my hand and I turned my body, putting my back against the wall. My knees gave way beneath me as my tears dampened the floor below.

It took several moments and a nurse asking me if I needed help for me to regain my composure and walk to the waiting room. Immediately, I saw Bethany and their mother, Johann. Bethany rushed to greet me and folded me into her arms. More tears escaped my swollen eyes.

Johann's brows pinched inward. Her emotions were apparent by the scowl on her face. Bethany released me, but I didn't want to let go. I held her hand in mine.

"Is he still in surgery?"

Bethany shook her head. "He's out. He's..."

I squeezed her hand as the knot in my stomach enlarged. "What?"

"The doctors have him in an induced coma to protect his brain from swelling. He had head trauma in the accident."

The sound that escaped me was a combination of weeping and choking on the vomit rising up my esophagus.

Bethany nudged me toward a chair. My head fell into my hands as more tears gushed like an opened floodgate. Bethany rubbed my back, trying to soothe me.

"You can go in and see him."

My breath left me the moment I walked into his hospital room. Cords were attached to different parts of his face and bare chest along with a sling on his arm. Bandages covered what were surely painful skin abrasions. The heart monitor and breathing machine sounded next to me and reminded me to let my own breath out. Through watery eyes, I reached out and tucked my hand under his large, warm hand. When he didn't respond to my touch, my heart shattered like sharp, broken shards of fragile glass.

This was my fault. I'd asked him to hurry home to me and because of my inability to handle loss, he was now suffering. I'd done this to him. My words caught below the knot in my throat. I wiped the stray tears from my cheeks as I looked at his expressionless face.

"Please forgive me."

A couple hours passed with me by his side, holding his hand in mine while listening to the sound of the heart monitor echo throughout the room. My tired eyes fought to close, but I wouldn't let them. I wanted to watch him and remember what it felt like to be held in his arms, to have his whispered words tickle my ear and the feel of his strong hands running over my skin. I wanted to remember the sound of his voice, his smell, and the way his love filled every crevice of my heart, body and soul.

"Please stay with me."

More than anything, I hoped he could hear me, that somewhere inside, he was fighting with all his strength to come back to me.

"You can't leave me. I can't bear to lose you too."

My head lifted from resting on his thigh as I heard the shuffle of feet cross the floor. Bethany's hand took hold of my shoulder. Johann and a nurse came into view.

"Mrs. Flanders?"

Focusing on his face through weary eyes, I nodded. "Yes?"

"I'm Regan. I'm the attending nurse and will be periodically stopping in to check on Mr. Baisdin throughout the night. We've done everything we can to make Mr. Baisdin comfortable. If you need anything, you can press the red button on the remote there and if you have any questions, his doctor will be in tomorrow morning."

"How long do you think he'll be like this?" Johann asked.

Regan turned to her. "At this point, it's a waiting game. The doctor will continue to monitor and run tests to ensure the swelling in his brain has gone down. If it does, he'll ease him off the medications."

"And if he doesn't get better? If the swelling doesn't go down?" she asked, her voice shaking.

"That's something Dr. Owens will be able to answer better."

Regan gave a sympathetic smile. We all knew what it meant if Brock didn't get better. As my sobs broke loose, Regan politely took his leave. Bethany cried next to me, holding me in her arms.

"I'm so sorry, Amy."

There was no consoling me.

CHAPTER 25

The next morning, I pried my tear-stained face from the hospital sheet that covered Brock as the doctor and nurse walked in. He took his time explaining all of Brock's injuries and the hope he had for Brock's recovery. He suggested I take a break and take care of myself, but I had no intention of leaving Brock's side, at least not until Bethany or Johann arrived. I didn't want Brock left alone. He needed to know we were there beside him, fighting alongside him, exactly like he would do for any of us.

Just as the doctor and nurse finished checking Brock's medication and stats, my phone rang. The battery was near dead. I was going to need my charger and a change of clothes soon. A glance at the screen told me Rick was calling about Ransom.

"Good Morning, Amy. Jared filled me in on Ransom. I'm sorry to see him go. That was a fine horse you had."

I wept against the phone, not just from the loss of Ransom, but the words I had to say next.

"Brock was in a bad accident last night. I'm at the hospital with him. It's not good, Rick."

"Jesus, Amy. What can I do?"

"Would you mind taking care of the horses for me, so I can stay here with Brock?"

"Of course. Jared already called Andrea. She'll be coming by today. Do you want us to bury Ransom here on the property?"

"Yes, please. I'll be by soon. I need to stop home for clothes and necessities."

"Do what you need to, darlin'. We have it handled here."

Johann and Bethany walked in moments after the doctor and nurse. I stopped rubbing along Brock's arm and stood to greet them.

"Any changes?" Bethany asked.

With a knot in my stomach, I shook my head.

"You look exhausted. You should go home and get some rest."

"I am going to stop home, but only to shower and get an overnight bag. I'll be back as soon as I can."

By the time I pulled up my driveway, Rick had already dug a burial spot with the backhoe. I rushed inside, wanting to avoid the scene that would be next. A quick shower and my bag packed had me ready to return to the hospital. Rick spotted me as I tossed my duffel in the truck.

"Amy."

I turned to face him, no doubt I looked worn.

"Come here, darlin'."

Rick wrapped me in his arms.

"You don't deserve this. Any of this."

It seemed my life was destined to be filled with tears and

heartbreak. My weeping left damp circles in his flannel shirt. He gently released me.

"You want to say good-bye to Ransom?"

"I said my good-bye yesterday. I can't do it again."

Rick nodded, clearly understanding my state of emotions.

"Go to your man. I'll put in some extra shifts."

"Thank you, Rick. I'll ensure you're compensated."

Rick nodded as I left.

Returning to the hospital was gut-wrenching. The stench of cleaning supplies, plastic, and death loomed around me, taunting me. I walked in to find Brock alone. Johann and Bethany had likely left to find something to eat in the hospital cafeteria. I set my bag down and took the chair next to Brock. I filled him on the activities I'd done and talked about our recent trip to the race track just like the doctor instructed me to. My conversation remained with everything in the past. Every time I imagined our future, the words caught in my throat. I had to be realistic. The future wasn't promised.

Footsteps behind me had me turning my head quickly. Brock's friend John stood in the doorway staring at Brock with utter shock on his face.

"When Bethany called, it hadn't sunk in, but now it's real."

"The doctor says we should talk to him, hearing familiar voices will help him heal. Would you like some time alone with him?"

John nodded, never taking his eyes off Brock's motionless body. I stood and pointed at the chair for him to take.

"The doctor recommended that we say his name and talk about past events he was a part of."

I waited just outside the room while John sat next to Brock. When the man's own voice grew shaky, and I heard him fighting back tears, that's when I broke down. My back slid down the wall, and my head fell into my hands. I kept my sobs quiet as John reminisced about the times they played ball together, got their first trucks, tore through the neighbor's corn fields then had to spend the next few weeks working off the losses. When John thanked Brock for being there for him when his mom died, I couldn't keep it together any longer. I stood and went to find Johann and Bethany.

I met them in the hallway, returning from lunch. Bethany's eyes enlarged when she saw me. She took hold of me, and my head fell to her shoulder as I cried. Johann ran to Brock's room, clearly concerned the worst had happened. She stepped out of the room and glared at me as I approached.

"Was that necessary? To scare me like that? Why don't you try to hold yourself together for him, at least?"

Her cheeks puffed out as she let out an angry breath. Her shoulder rubbed against mine as she stormed past us.

"I'll be back later tonight," she told Bethany. "I'd prefer it if you weren't here, Amy. I'd like some time alone with my son."

"Ma!"

"He's my son. I have every right to want time alone with him."

I squeezed Bethany's hand. "It's all right. She's right. I'll go now. You can stay."

Johann was clearly happy with my choice. I returned to Brock's room for my bag. Giving a sympathetic nod to John, I leaned over Brock and kissed him good-bye.

"I'll see you tomorrow, Brock. I love you."

"You're leaving?"

I tilted my head toward Johann. "She deserves some time alone with her son."

John looked from me to Johann and back to me again. He nodded, seeming to understand perfectly.

"I'm going to head out too. I'll walk with you."

With my bag in hand, I slipped my free arm around Bethany and said good-bye. I gave a cordial smile to Johann and then walked out with John.

"How bad is it?" he asked.

"The doctor isn't saying much more than they are making Brock as comfortable as they can, that they'll continue to monitor him for improvement, and for us to stay positive."

"Damn, that sounds bleak. How are you holding up?"

"This is the first time I haven't cried in the last twenty-four hours."

"When is the last time you ate something?"

That question had me thinking. I couldn't remember the last time I had eaten and I wasn't sure I could if I tried.

"Some time yesterday." I glanced over at his concerned expression. "Don't worry. I'm fine."

"You know Brock will fight like hell to get back to you, don't you? He loves you more than I've ever seen him love anything."

A shiver ran through my body. I stopped in my tracks and lost all composure. John put his hands in his pockets and nervously shuffled his right foot.

"I'm sorry, Amy. I didn't mean to make you cry. It's what I have to hang onto, you know? That his love for you will pull him through."

I sucked in my sobs and pulled my shoulders back. "I know. I'm sorry. I thought my days of crying were over when Brock proposed to me."

The ring on my finger suddenly caught my attention. I bit into my cheek, refusing to break into more sobs.

"Why don't I take you to get something to eat?"

"I'm okay. Really. I just want to go home and get some rest."

"All right. Take care of yourself, okay?"

I nodded to him and left him to find my truck in the parking lot. Once inside, I let out every emotion I was holding onto.

For the first time, I didn't want to go home. Home reminded me of all that I had lost. My home was cursed with death. It clung to the grounds and walls of every building. Instead, I went the opposite direction and drove to Brock's house.

Walking into his home brought with it comfort and sadness. It was filled with our memories and it made me second-guess my decision to come there. Seeing the couch and the place we laid by the fireplace reminded me of that night—the night he listened to me spill my heart. The night I realized how much he meant to me. I walked to the kitchen and pulled out two bottles of beer from the fridge. I carried them into his room, popped one, chugged it, then did the same with the second. Afterwards, I buried my face and body into the smell of him. I cried into the blanket until sleep owned me.

CHAPTER 26

As soon as I woke, my body slowly and begrudgingly sat up from the bed. I rubbed my swollen eyes and then reached for my nauseous stomach. Drinking on an empty stomach had been a bad idea. I rushed to the bathroom and threw up the contents of last night's attempt to forget my current misery.

Some mouthwash and a toothbrush solved the horrid taste in my mouth. There was no cooking breakfast after that, so I called Bethany to check on Brock.

"Any changes?"

"The doctor said they did another MRI this morning and will have the results for that soon. Other than that, the status is the same."

"I'll be on my way shortly."

"Amy."

The sound of her hesitation had me sitting back down on the bed with my stomach twisting into an even worse knot.

"What is it?"

"I'm so sorry to have to say this, please know that I tried to persuade her differently, but my mother has asked for you not to visit anymore. She feels your presence is causing stress for the family and for Brock. She...she put you on the no access list. The hospital won't let you in if you do come. She said she heard you asking Brock for forgiveness. She thinks this is somehow your fault. I'm so sorry, Amy. Believe me when I say I don't agree with her decision, but she is Brock's emergency contact and the executor of his will and there is nothing I can do."

The phone collapsed to the floor and my body followed it, sliding from the bed. I could hear Bethany's voice in the distance calling my name, but my body had gone numb. I couldn't feel anything. I stared at the wall for what seemed like several minutes. Bethany's voice faded and was followed by a dial tone and then my phone was silent. The room was silent.

I know my body was in shock and my mind was desperately trying to catch up with the atrocious information I had just been given. When it finally sunk in, that I couldn't see Brock, that I couldn't be by his side to fight with him, to help him heal, to tell him how much I loved him, I lost all control. My body shook viciously and the tears wouldn't stop. I screamed and wailed and thrashed against the side of the bed. I was losing the man I loved, once again. He was being ripped from me and there was nothing I could do. I felt helpless, alone, depressed and there was no one to give me comfort. I curled into a ball and wept until my body fell into sleep from exhaustion.

When I woke, I wasn't sure what day or time it was. I

slowly ambled to the bathroom and turned the faucet to hot. Before stripping down, my stomach churned and I hugged the bathroom toilet as I expelled what little liquid was in there. After cleaning my face, I laid in the tub, trying to control my trembling body and broken, aching heart.

Shriveled to a prune and now lying in cold water, I dried myself and grabbed whatever clothes I could find in my bag. Keeping my hands busy was all I could think to do. I moved like a thoughtless robot, cleaning Brock's house and emptying his fridge of any food that would spoil, so at least if he woke from his injuries, he'd have a clean home to come back to.

Once finished, I gathered my things and drove back to my home. My stomach growled, and I knew I needed food, but trying to eat was going to be a problem, especially with the nausea I had. When I pulled up to my house, Jared approached the truck. His eyes instantly widened as he looked me over.

"Ames, you don't look well."

I leaned forward as another wave of nausea pummeled my stomach. My head ached and objects were beginning to blur.

"Can you help me inside?"

Jared lifted me with ease and held me against him as he carried me through the door. He laid me on the couch and raised a pillow behind me.

"When's the last time you ate?"

"I don't remember," I mumbled.

"Ames, you can't do this to yourself."

I turned away from him toward the cushions. "I just want to be alone."

He stood and left my side, but he didn't leave my house. The sounds of him rummaging through my fridge and cupboards reached me. A can-opener ground metal, followed by the pouring of liquid into a bowl, then the microwave was opened, buttons pressed, and a couple minutes later, it dinged. Jared returned with a warm bowl of chicken noodle soup and crackers.

"Ames, I want you to eat this. You need it. I'll force feed you if I have to."

I sat up as the smell of comfort food reached my nostrils. Jared put the bowl in my lap, and I slowly brought the spoon to my lips. I moaned after the third spoonful. It was the same chicken noodle soup I'd always ate every time I had a cold, but today, it was arguably the best soup I'd ever eaten. Jared was right. I did need the nourishment.

"How are the horses?"

"Don't worry about them. Rick and I have everything under control. Focus on you right now."

Tears pooled in my eyes. "There's nothing else to focus on but the horses. I have nothing, Jared." I set the nearly empty bowl on the coffee table. "Johann put me on the no access list at the hospital. I can't go in and see Brock or be by his side when he needs me the most."

"Damn. What did you do to piss her off?"

"She was eavesdropping when I was alone with Brock. She knows it's my fault he was in the accident."

I wiped a stray tear off my cheek. Jared placed his hand on my shoulder and rubbed it.

"Please don't tell me you believe that garbage? His accident wasn't your fault. It's the fault of the bastard who hit him."

As much as I wanted to agree and to believe that, I couldn't. It was my phone call that put him in that situation.

I leaned toward the pillow to lie down again, and Jared pulled me back to him. "Nope, you're not going to lie here and cry." He took my hand and raised me from the couch. "We're going riding. Merlin and Thunder need exercised."

Just hearing Thunder's name stung my heart. My expression must have revealed it.

"Come on, let's at least go see Honey. That little prancer is enough to make anyone smile."

CHAPTER 27

The next several days were excruciating. I had developed a stomach virus and could barely hold down any food between stress and nausea. I laid in bed most of the day after every morning phone call to Bethany. The status never changed and Brock's MRI's were showing very little improvement. I'd cry myself to sleep after each phone call and beg for him to come back to me.

When my phone would ring, I'd stare at Heather's or my parents' picture displayed on the screen. I knew they were calling to talk about the wedding details, but I couldn't do it. I couldn't face saying the words out loud.

Each day, Jared would come in around lunch time. He'd make a sandwich for himself and then leave one for me in the fridge. Sometimes, he'd leave notes telling me how Honey was doing in an attempt to coax me outside. After a week of avoiding everyone and wallowing in my own self-pity and pain, Jared had apparently had enough. He walked up to my bedroom and stood in the door frame with his arms crossed.

"You've suffered enough, Ames. It's time to shower and

join me on the ranch. You look like shit, you smell like shit and damn it, I can't take seeing you like this anymore. I'm not the only one. Rick is worried, too."

I didn't move. I didn't have the energy or motivation. Jared's heavy footsteps padded across my floor. He was clearly on a mission. He hoisted me off the bed and carried me into the shower. With clothes on, he shoved me into it and turned on the shower head. Cold water blasted my face and chest. I screamed and cursed at him which only made his grin widen.

"I'll have some food ready for you downstairs. After that, we're going riding. Get ready, we have a lot of work to do today."

With slow movements, I made it through a shower, getting dressed and eating some of the sandwich and fruit Jared had left for me. I slid on my boots and walked out into the chilly weather. The leaves were turning beautiful hues of yellow, orange, and red sprinkled across the rebellious green. I pulled my jacket tighter around my neck, blocking the cool breeze. With my hands covered in work gloves, I joined Jared in bringing Merlin and Bella out of their stalls.

"How's she doing?"

"Real good. Rides like a dream. I'd buy her off Mr. Anderson if he'd be willing to sell her."

I stroked Bella's neck and she nuzzled my shoulder in response. Immediately, the familiar touch and smell of the horses soothed some of the ache in my chest. I laid my head against Bella's mane and reveled in the joy it brought me.

"I'll saddle them. You look like you might keel over if you have to lift anything heavy."

I didn't argue. I still wasn't feeling well and coming out for a ride was going to take a lot of energy.

Once the horses were saddled, I helped tighten straps and then climbed atop Merlin. He blew out an excited breath, ready for the freedom of the ride.

"You gonna be able to keep up? You and Merlin are both a little rusty." Jared winked and gave a playful smile.

"We'll do our best," I promised.

The ride to the creek was more relaxing than I thought it'd be. Apparently, it was something I needed. The cool breeze countered the heat of the scorching sun and swept the tension off my shoulders as did the familiarity of the ride. When we reached the creek, we stopped to let the horses drink. Jared eased himself off the saddle and walked to mine, offering his hands and arms to help me down. I rolled my eyes and huffed.

"I'm not that frail."

He gnawed his lip and grinned as he backed away, hands mercifully waving in the air.

"The ride did you good."

He looked me over as my feet went from stirrup to ground.

"I'm glad you made me come out."

Jared gave a smile over his shoulder as he walked to the creek. Leaning down, his long-sleeve shirt stretched over his solid back muscles. He cupped the water from the creek and splashed it over the bare part of his arms, cleaning off the barn dust and dirt, then wiped his hands on his jeans and lowered his sleeves.

He gaze fell on me, standing on the edge of the creek, staring into the water, getting lost in my thoughts.

"Ames, I'll drag you out of that house everyday if I have to. I understand that you're scared of losing Brock, but you can't lose yourself too. We need you—your family, the horses, Rick. I need you."

I glanced at his soft, blue eyes staring at me as though I may shatter into a million pieces at any moment and admittedly, I was close to it. The tears pooled in my eyes and the knot in my stomach was so tight, I wanted to buckle over.

"You're right. I'm terrified of losing him."

Jared rushed forward and enclosed me in his arms. The gesture was comforting, but it only brought more tears. He wasn't the man I wanted holding me and comforting me. More than anything, I wanted to feel Brock's loving arms wrapped around me, making everything okay again.

Jared's lips brushed against my ear as he whispered, trying to soothe me. The graze of his lips was subtle, but my body's reaction was not. I backed out of Jared's arms, guilt swarming in my gut like angry bees. My emotional state was clearly influencing my need for affection.

"We should get back."

"Ames, I didn't mean—"

I put my hand up to stop him. "It's me. I'm a mess and need to get myself together. Thank you for watching over me this week. You're an amazing friend. I appreciate you making me come out. I'll do my best to help you on the ranch today. Tomorrow, I promise I'll do better."

Keeping to my promise, I pushed through the nausea and constant thoughts of never seeing Brock again. I had to remind myself that I was strong, that I'd made it through the loss of one man I loved and I'd make it through it again, even if I didn't believe it at times. Grams' words continued to combat my own thoughts of self-pity and fear. *You're a strong woman, Amy. You're journey isn't over yet.* I wondered if she'd tell me to start thinking of what's next again, but I wasn't ready for that. Right now, I was focused on making it through one day at a time.

After another week of hearing no change in Brock's status, I did my best to fall into a routine, desperate to keep my mind busy. Several days into the fixed routine, I was finally holding down food and building my strength back. I started working with Thunder on the training equipment. Working with him gave me a little piece of Brock.

That night, the brisk wind whipped against my house, whispering screams into the darkness. The eerie sound of it chilled me to the bone, and my thoughts crept into the darkest parts of my own mind. Unable to keep still or sleep, I grabbed an overnight bag, a book, my boots and keys and headed to Brock's house.

As I pulled up his driveway, shock swept over me. His lights inside were on and Johann's car was parked outside. I turned off my lights and slowly crept my truck farther up the drive. Silently closing my door, I walked along the side of his house, investigating the activity inside while trying to be as inconspicuous as I could.

Vomit rose to my mouth and I swam sideways trying to catch my fall. Inside the window, I saw Brock lying on his couch, his head propped up on a pillow as Johann handed him two pills and a cup filled with something to drink. Paperwork filled her other hand which she set on the coffee table in front of him. I ran to the truck and spun gravel on my way out of his driveway.

CHAPTER 28

*J*ared approached my bed and sat on the edge. "Why do you look like you've been crying all night?"

Curled in the shape of a fetus, I remained snuggling against my pillow. "I'm not feeling well. Can you handle it on your own today?"

Jared ran his hand through his lengthy, light brown locks and let out a breath of air.

"Ames…" His tone was affectionately demanding. "Tell me what happened?"

"Brock's out of the hospital. He's out of his coma and at home. No one told me. Not Bethany or John. Clearly, no one wants me in his life. I don't even know how long he's been out of the hospital. I don't know if *he* even wants me in his life. He hasn't called."

"Maybe he just got out yesterday and hasn't had a chance to call you. The man was in a coma. I'm sure he needs to get his shit in order."

The thought had crossed my mind that he had just gotten

out. I sat up on the bed and Jared laughed at the damp strands of hair plastered to my face. He reached up to wipe them away, but stopped when he saw me flinch.

"You should jump in the shower. Heather is waiting downstairs for you. That's what I came up here to tell you."

"Heather's here?"

Jared chuckled. "Did you sleep at all last night?"

"Barely."

"Okay, shower, now. I'll throw together something for you to eat."

"You're too good to me."

Laughter rolled off his lips as he walked out of my room.

I came down the steps to find Heather in the kitchen talking with Jared. Knowing her as well as I do, her flirtations were blatantly obvious. Jared, on the other hand, didn't seem to notice or was trying not to. As I watched him from behind, putting eggs onto a plate, I realized how much the young guy I'd hired had grown into a man—a good, caring man. The memory of our conversation about the professor he was dating came to mind. I wanted to ask him about it the first chance I got. After all he'd done for me in the last two weeks, I owed it to him to make sure he was being treated right.

Heather squealed when she caught sight of me in her periphery. "Amy!" She rushed in and bear-hugged me before releasing me and scowling at me. "Why haven't you answered my calls?"

Jared turned his head and glanced at me, then Heather, and back at me again.

"Brock was in a car accident and was put in an induced coma. I didn't handle it well. I started to shut down like I did before."

Her hands flew to her mouth. "Oh, my God! Is he still in the coma?"

I shook my head. "He's out. I don't know when he got out though. Johann put me on the no access list and he hasn't called."

Heather hugged me again. "I'm so sorry."

When the tears started to pool, I looked at Jared.

"You should eat, Ames. You'll need it for work today."

Heather glanced at Jared and then back at me. "She's a little too distraught to eat. Can't you see that?"

Jared held the plate out for me. "No, she needs to eat to keep her strength up. You haven't been here the last two weeks, I have."

I took the plate from Jared's outstretched hand. He moved past us and out the front door. With the plate in hand, I walked to the dining table. "You shouldn't have snapped at him like that. He's been there for me day in and day out for the last two weeks. He's the one who's been making sure I didn't fall apart."

"I'm sorry. It seemed like he was being insensitive. If you had called, I'd know what had happened these last couple of weeks and wouldn't have snapped at him."

"I know. I'm sorry. I was drowning in my own sorrow and couldn't bring myself to answer questions. It was easy with Jared. He knew what was going on and conversation was, well, I didn't have to converse at all, really. He made me food and checked on me, then forced me back to work."

"Well, now that I'm here, he can take a break. I can stay for several days. I brought extra clothes and necessities, just in case. I got worried when you didn't return my calls. So, you really haven't heard from Brock? Why did Johann put you on the no access list?"

"Short story, she overhead me talking to Brock, and she thinks his accident is my fault. She's systematically cut me out of his life, probably like she always wanted to do. I don't know how long he's been out of the hospital or why he hasn't called."

One day prior...

THE MOMENT MY EYELIDS FLICKERED open and all my cognitive senses awakened, my first thought was Amy. Her long, light-brown hair, baby-blues and beautiful face filled my mind. I looked around for her, remembering her whispers distantly in my memory. Disappointment flooded me when I realized my fiancée was not in the hospital room with me.

The doctor came to see me and explained everything that had happened. He told me the swelling in my brain had gone down and the scans displayed normal brain activity. With a few weeks of taking it easy and physical therapy for my arm, I'd be "good as new."

After tears, hugs, and kisses from my mother and Bethany, and pats on the shoulder from John and Luke, I waited 'til we were alone and I asked my mother where Amy was. Her face turned downward.

"Don't worry about her. You need to focus on resting and getting better."

"I've been in this bed for nearly two weeks and my fiancée isn't here next to me. I want to know why. Ma, I suggest you start spitting out answers."

"Fiancée? You proposed to her?"

"Yes, I did. Don't look so shocked. I hadn't had a chance to tell you yet. Now, where is she?"

"I don't know where she is. I haven't spoken to her in almost two weeks."

"Why is that?"

"Apparently, she has more important places to be then next to her fiancé. You're better off without her, darling. She said the accident was her fault. Maybe she feels ashamed and wants to end things. Maybe she couldn't handle your accident."

With a busted cell phone and being too rattled to drive, I was at the mercy of my mother and her disturbing answers about Amy. She drove me home and doted on me, hand and foot. Having just survived a near-death experience and being broken and bruised from head to toe, I had no choice but to use her assistance. Getting around was still difficult and more than anything, I just wanted to rest, no doubt the painkillers were a cause of that.

At home and exhausted on the couch, I was near dosing off. My mother interrupted me to hand me my medications and to remind me of the paperwork I had ahead of me with my health and motorcycle insurance, as well as the accident lawyer.

My head ached just thinking about it, and it wasn't something I wanted to think about at all. The only thing on my mind was why my fiancée wasn't the one here doting on me. The sound of gravel kicking up in my driveway opened my heavy lids.

"Who is that?"

My mother walked to the front window and looked out.

"Looks like someone was turning around in the driveway. Get some rest. I'll come by tomorrow morning."

"Ma."

"Yeah?"

"Can you have Bethany call Amy for me? And find out where she is?"

"I'll see what I can do."

"You all right?"

"Fine. You mind handing me the brush there." Jared pointed to the one sitting on the stool.

I placed it in his outstretched hand. He used it to brush along Catapult's back. "Thanks for breakfast and I'm sorry

Heather snapped at you like that. She had no idea you've been the one keeping me from falling apart."

"It's nothing. I didn't take it personal."

"But you still seem irritated."

"It's nothing."

I leaned against the stall and tucked my boot into a rail. "You still dating the professor?"

Jared let out a chuckle. "No, Ames, I'm not."

"What happened?"

"You were right. I was a rebound. We had our fun, but I'm looking for something more serious than she can offer."

"I'm sorry it didn't work out."

"Don't be. I'm not."

Jared stopped brushing Catapult and met my eyes. "He still hasn't called?"

I shook my head.

"Maybe you should stop by his place."

"You think so?"

"Honestly, I don't know. This whole situation has you torn up, and I hate seeing you like this, but maybe if you had some answers, any answers, you'd be able to decide what direction you want to go."

Jared and I both lifted our heads to the sound of a vehicle coming up the drive. I rushed out of the barn and then stopped in my tracks when I saw the driver—Johann. Jared stopped next to me and glanced my direction.

"Looks like you're gonna get answers sooner than you thought. I'll be in the barn if you need me. Unless you want me to stay."

"No, I got this. I think."

I approached her SUV as she stepped out. "Johann, would you like to come inside?"

"No, Amy. I can't stay long. I came by to tell you that Brock is out of the hospital, but I'd appreciate it if you kept your distance. He's still not well and very confused. Seeing you would only stress him out further and the doctor said he needs rest and to avoid stressful situations for a while."

Her words were like bullets, cutting through my emotions and ripping them to shreds. Anger eclipsed the tears threatening to escape me.

"Why do you believe I would stress him out? He's my fiancé! I'm sure he wants me there."

"Don't you think you've done enough? He nearly died because of you. You're not good for him. If you really love him, you'll leave him alone."

Before I could get another word in, she was closing the car door in my face. She rolled down the window as she started backing the SUV out of my driveway.

"Stay away, Amy. It's what's best for him."

I stood, frozen like an ice sculpture as the wind whipped around me. What seemed like several minutes later, a strong hand took hold of my arm.

"Amy?"

I turned to Jared's sympathetic eyes locked on mine. "What happened?"

Somewhere deep inside my soul, I could feel what remaining strength I had coming undone. The tears trickled down my cheeks, chilling my skin.

"I can't, Jared. I can't handle any of it anymore. I'm so damn tired of crying."

Jared glanced at Rick's truck coming up the drive then

back at me. "Rick's coming in for his shift. Let me go over a few things with him while you go inside and talk to Heather. I'll be in shortly. And Amy…"

I looked back over my shoulder at him.

"You *are* going to be okay."

Feeling numb and broken, I entered the house to Heather cooking something that smelled delicious. Too bad my appetite had been destroyed. I shimmied out of my jacket and entered the kitchen to join her.

"You look shaken up. What's wrong?"

"I can't do it anymore. I feel like I never should have let Brock in. My life was fine. I was content. Ever since I met him, it's been heartbreak all over again. Johann just stopped by. Her visit wasn't friendly. She made it very clear that I need to stay away from Brock and he's not trying to reach me. Maybe she's right. Maybe it is over."

"What the hell are you talking about? He just proposed to you two weeks ago. You really think his accident and injuries have him second-guessing his proposal?"

I leaned my weight against the counter, my heart feeling heavy in my chest. "I honestly don't know, but I can't take this anymore. It's affecting me to the point that I've neglected the ranch, my friends, and family. Maybe I was foolish to think I could have a second chance at love. Maybe Darrell was it and I need to accept that. What if Johann is right and I'm not good for Brock?"

"This woman has your emotions so twisted your rambling non-sense. You know Brock loves you and that you two are great together. Don't let her destroy what you both have."

"I'm not sure what we have anymore."

*a*s I woke, every muscle in my body argued against moving and the headache between my temples made it even more difficult to think. In the distance, I heard movement in the kitchen.

"Amy?"

"No darling. It's your mother."

"Did Bethany get a hold of her?"

"I spoke with her."

"And?"

"I wouldn't expect her to come around, Brock."

I raised myself from the couch, the pain in my shoulder and head now throbbing. "What do you mean?"

"I told you, she can't handle your accident. She's too fragile of a woman. You're better off without her anyway. Look what she did to you."

I stood from the couch. Anger motivated my movements, eclipsing the pain. "What do you mean what she did to me?"

"I heard her next to your bedside asking you for forgiveness."

"Ma, the accident wasn't her fault. I took a shortcut home. It's the fault of the drunk bastard that hit me."

My mother approached the couch. Her face twisted in emotion. "Regardless, this woman isn't good for you. I can see that. Why can't you?"

"We're not having this conversation. Amy is the woman I love. I want her to be my wife. I'm telling you now, if you did anything to interfere with that, I will never forgive you."

I could see the Baisdin temper flare. She grabbed her purse and stormed toward the door. She turned to face me before exiting.

"Mark my words, son. That woman is going to break your heart."

I STUMBLED DOWN THE STEPS, the previous night somewhat of a blur. A muscular leg hung over the backside of my couch. I stopped suddenly, surprised to see Jared sleeping soundly. Apparently, we'd all had too much to drink the night before. Tidbits were trickling back to my memory—lots of beer along with Jared and Heather attempting to make me forget all my pain and confusion.

From behind the couch, a rough, tired voice spoke. "Mornin', Ames."

I walked to the couch and leaned over it. Empty beer bottles riddled the floor and coffee table and a half-naked Jared was sprawled out across the couch cushions. My eyes caught a glimpse of his chiseled torso, and I looked away before my body's reaction caused me anymore discomfort.

"Jeez, oh man. How much did we drink last night?"

"A lot."

Jared sat up on the couch and ran his hand through his messy bed hair as he stared at me affectionately. "We were trying to make you feel better. I think we got a little carried away."

I rubbed my throbbing temples. "No wonder I'm so groggy. You want anything for breakfast? I'm starving."

"Hell yeah, I do. I'll give ya a hand."

Jared moved around my kitchen like he knew it well, and at this point, I guess he did. He had bacon and sausage going as I flipped eggs and buttered toast. Chugging a tall glass of orange juice helped with the headache and grogginess, but it didn't settle the nausea.

"Last night was pretty fun. We should do it again."

Laughter escaped me. "I'm too old for that, my body can't seem to take it. I feel like shit."

"You kinda look it too."

He elbowed me and winked before stretching his arm up next to me to reach for plates out of the cabinet.

"I probably smell too, huh?"

He leaned toward me as he brought the plates down. "Nah, you smell pretty good actually."

"That's an improvement."

He gently placed his hand on my back, making sure I didn't move and knock the plates over in his hand as he moved past me. He set the plates down next to me, but his hand lingered.

"Ames."

I turned to face him. A nervous knot bunched in my belly at the affection in his voice.

"Yeah?"

"I have something I need to confess."

The doorbell rang and I nearly jumped out of my skin. Jared's jaw tightened. Whoever it was had interrupted something important and he evidently wasn't happy about it.

"I'll get it."

He rushed to the front door before I had a chance to respond. I assumed Rick needed something or had a question. I grabbed a plate and started filling it with food. I heard Jared's voice getting louder and then another voice, a very familiar voice, echoed into the house. A strange combination of elation and dread filled me.

I walked out of the kitchen to see Brock with an expression of fury on his face. He looked at me, then Jared's half-naked body, then back to me.

"What the hell is going on?" His eyes locked on Jared. "Why are you in Amy's house, shirtless, at seven-thirty in the morning?"

"Shit." Followed by several more *shits* filled my mind.

"Brock, it's not at all how it looks. Jared slept on the couch. Heather is upstairs. We all got tipsy last night and Jared crashed here."

"Get your shirt and get out."

"Brock!"

THE MOMENT MY MOTHER HAD walked out of my house, I struggled through taking my meds, making breakfast and a shower. Getting up and moving had been difficult, but once I got the blood pumping and food in me, things got easier. My first thought was Amy and how badly I needed to see her. Finding Jared's car outside wasn't unusual. Finding him inside Amy's house, shirtless, that lit off fireworks in my mind. And to top it off, the little shit seemed annoyed, as if *I* was interrupting something. Then, he had the nerve to say that my mother and I had done a real number on Amy. What the hell was he talking about? Whatever he was implying didn't matter right now, my patience was wearing thin and the Baisdin temper was rearing its ugly head.

I didn't give a damn if I hurt his feelings. I wanted him out and I wanted my fiancée all to myself.

I nodded toward the couch, indicating he needed to get moving. He seemed to understand the gravity of the situation and made a direct line for his things. He grabbed his shirt, jacket, and boots and shoved my sore shoulder as he made his way past me.

I rubbed my aching shoulder after closing Amy's front door. I expected her to run to me and leap into my arms, but instead she stood there with her arms crossed and too many emotions running across her face for me to understand what she was feeling.

"Did you really have to treat him like that?"

"Treat him like what? I just came out of a coma and was eager to see my fiancée, who for some reason felt she didn't need to be by my side. I thought you'd be a bit happier to see me. What I didn't expect, was to come here and find another man in your house."

One emotion became very clear on her face—rage.

"Do you honestly think I didn't want to be there? *Your mother* made sure I couldn't see you. She put me on a no access list, so I *couldn't* see you! I cried every night missing you. It tore me apart not being able to be there with you. Not being able to touch you or talk to you. *Every morning*, I called to ask if there was improvement and *every day*, I was told there was no change, but obviously that was a lie, because you had to have improved for the doctors to bring you out of the coma." The tears started falling down her red, puffy cheeks, but her anger was like soda in a shaken bottle; the pressure had become too much and now that I'd opened the wound, she was spewing.

"But did your sister or mother call me and tell me you were awake and okay? No, they couldn't even give me the smallest bit of comfort! I came to your house a couple nights ago, wanting to be close to you, to have any part of you with me, and to my shock, I found you there with your mother—safe and sound. Do you know what that did to me? Do you know what those two weeks of not knowing, of being afraid I'd lost you like I lost Darrell, did to me?"

"Amy, I'm sorry my mother put you on the no access list because she thought the accident was somehow your fault. It was a misunderstanding."

"Now you're defending her? You have no idea what I've been through. It was hell and your response is to defend her?"

"I'm not defending, I'm explaining her actions."

"Did she tell you that she stopped by too?"

"She did, yes. What she told me has me concerned."

"What did she say?"

"That I shouldn't expect you to come around."

She huffed, and I could see the anger building up again.

"That's because *she* told me not to come around again. She insisted that I stay away, that the doctors want you to avoid stress and I'll do nothing but cause you stress."

"She's being prot—" I stopped mid-sentence. No point in continuing unless I wanted to sound like I was defending my mother again. "Was she right, Amy? Were you going to stay away?"

The eyes staring back at me weren't the loving baby-blues I'd looked into over two weeks ago. The woman before me was broken. She'd been shattered and it would take time to put the pieces back together. I was ready to do that. I was ready to move in today and start loving her heart right back to me if she'd let me.

Her head lowered and the words came out barely more than a whisper. "I don't know."

She raised her head to meet my troubled expression. "I fell apart when you were injured. I know I wouldn't survive it if I lost you too. Maybe it's selfish of me, but I don't want to feel broken anymore or worry about losing you again. I don't want to be the woman that breaks a family apart. I truly don't want to hurt you, but I don't think I can be in this relationship anymore."

I'd heard the phrase "take an arrow to the heart" and, for the second time in my life, I'd felt what the phrase meant.

"Amy, baby, don't do this. Don't let your fear of losing me stop you from loving me."

I reached out to take her in my arms. If she'd let me, I could fix everything. But her body went rigid, and she put up her hand to stop me. She fought back her tears by avoiding looking at me.

"You should go."

"Dammit, Amy, don't do this! We have something amazing together. I want you in my life. I was making the commitment to spend my life with you and you want to throw that away? Do I really mean that little to you?"

The floor creaked above me. No doubt my raised voice had woke Heather. I moved closer to Amy and lowered my voice. "Amy, baby, let me fix this. If you want, I'll never ride a motorcycle again. I'll ensure my mother stays out of our lives. Please baby, don't do this."

In front of me, her body trembled and the tears she'd fought so hard to keep at bay rolled down her soft, red cheeks.

"I'll give you back the ring."

My aching shoulder was now throbbing as was the massive ache in my skull. "You think I give a damn about the ring?"

Anger filled my chest. I was quickly becoming lightheaded. I turned toward the door, needing air. I reached it and held the knob in my own trembling hand.

"Amy, if you let me walk out this door, I'm not coming back."

I waited, hoping with all my heart that she'd tell me to stay. Silence was the response I got. I opened the door to the bright sun and cool, crisp air. I walked into it and didn't look back at the woman who'd destroyed my heart.

CHAPTER 30

*S*ix weeks later...

The sun beat down on my bare back. I wiped the damp cloth across my neck, cooling my body down the best I could. The day was a warm one and I still wasn't used to the Florida heat and humidity, but the contracted job paid well, and it got me far away from Kentucky and the pain and memories I'd left behind there.

Not a day went by that I didn't think about Amy, but she'd made her choice and I had made mine. I'd taken a four-month contract to finish building five houses in a new housing development in South Florida. It was well outside of my normal territory, but a few of my employees agreed to come, and I filled in the positions of the ones who didn't come with local folks. The job had given me an opportunity to get space from my family and the woman who'd ripped my heart in two.

"You coming out for a beer tonight, Boss?"

"Might as well. Don't got shit else to do."

"All right, see ya at Stevie's at six."

"Yeah. See ya then."

I grabbed my t-shirt and lunchbox and loaded the truck. The last of us cleaned up and prepped for the next day. Back at the condo, I took a quick shower. On my way out, I checked my phone, a foolish habit I'd developed. I wouldn't answer if she called anyway.

A short drive in my truck and I was nodding at John and a few of my employees sitting at a round table by a big screen TV hanging on the wall. I joined the group and ordered a bucket of beers for the table. Pizza and beers were delivered and shortly after, we were soon emptying one bottle after another. Before long, the boys eyes were following the waitresses more than the TV screen.

With five beers in, I was running my thumb over Amy's cell phone number. Damn if I didn't miss her. At times, the more I fought it, the more painful it was, but I hadn't heard from her in a month. Apparently, she didn't want to talk to me and part of me wanted to see her happy after all she'd been through. If her happiness meant not being with me, then I was going to have to be miserable until I got over her.

"Dude, quit fucking thinking about that bitch."

I met John's gaze. "Don't call her a bitch."

"You haven't heard from her in weeks. Clearly, she's moved on. It's time you do too. Get a new piece of ass under you. Forgot about her for at least one night." John pointed to a tall blonde with breasts larger than my hands. "Her. There. She's been looking at you for a while now. Ah, see, now she's headed over here. Good. Take her home with you."

The tall blonde with a charming smile ran her hand along my back as she leaned in to speak privately.

"What's your name, handsome?"

Before leaving the bar with the woman I'd learned was Jessica, I took a condom from John's reserve. After a short drive home, we walked to my condo on the second floor. I opened the door for Jessica to enter. She gave a bright, cheeky grin and scanned the surroundings.

"Nice place. Yours?"

"For now. I'm renting it for a few months while I'm here on a job. It came furnished. Want something to drink?"

She eyed me with her big brown eyes and nodded. "Yeah, would love one."

I pulled a beer from the fridge and popped the top, then handed it to her. She smiled and shook her head. "Got anything else? I don't drink beer. I prefer liquor."

I tipped the beer bottle to my lips and took a swig.

"You like the hard stuff, huh?"

She winked. "You have no idea."

My cock jumped at the sexual insinuation.

"Lemme get you something you'd like, then."

I poured whiskey in a glass and handed it to her. In a couple swallows, she had it down. This woman clearly didn't want to waste time. She moved closer to me and set the empty glass on the counter. With her other hand, she trailed her fingers along the waistband of my jeans.

"How'd a handsome cowboy like you end up down here?"

The memory of Amy's and my fight slammed into my chest like a wrecking ball. I grabbed Jessica's hand in mine. "I don't want to think about that tonight."

She batted her long lashes at me and gave a wicked grin. "Whatever it is, cowboy, I'll help you forget."

That's just what I needed. One night to forget Amy's face, to forget the woman I'd lost, to forget the heartache I felt every damn day. I wrapped my hands around Jessica's ass and raised her legs around me. She held tight and gave kisses along my neck as I carried her to the bedroom.

I sat her on the bed and she moved her eager hands along the buttons of my shirt, undoing one after another. With my chest bare, she roamed her hands around my muscles and then reached for my belt.

"Damn, cowboy." Her hand rubbed over my erection. "It's as big as the rest of you."

I tilted my head back as she stroked me and pulled me into her mouth. My hand fisted her hair and the other held her by the neck as I moved in and out, sliding across her wet, slick tongue.

"Damn, I needed this."

Her moans and passionate need to please tightened my abs and groin as my orgasm shot right through me. For several moments, I felt free, not a care in the world. I laid down on the bed next to her, and she climbed above me. Her wet kisses trailed along my neck, chest, and abs and then lower, headed toward my cock.

"I need a minute, pretty girl."

What I needed now was a shower and to sleep. All the beers I'd had were hitting me hard and as good as my body felt, my emotions felt the opposite. My guilt was eating at my core and spreading like a disrupted ants nest.

I took hold of her hips and eased her off me. "I'm sorry, Jessica, I can't do this." I lifted my jeans over my hips and stood to look at her. I expected to be hit and hell, I'd take it with grace. I deserved it.

"What's her name?"

"Excuse me?"

"What's the woman's name that has you tore up?"

I sat back down on the bed and rubbed the headache forming between my temples. "Her name's Amy. She was my fiancée."

"Was?"

"Yeah. Was."

"What happened?"

"A drunk bastard destroyed my life. I had everything I wanted before my motorcycle accident. When I woke up from a coma, I'd lost all of it. My fiancée couldn't handle the fact that she'd nearly lost me and my mother did what she could to chase my fiancée out of my life. So, now I'm here."

My hands rubbed along my face. As nice as Jessica was being, it wasn't her I wanted next to me. It wasn't her I wanted giving pleasure to my body. Jessica stood and walked out to where her purse was sitting. She returned with a business card. She'd written a number on the back.

"If you get lonely or decide you're tired of missing her, call me. I like you, cowboy. I'd like to see you again."

I took the card and walked her out. At the door, she stopped and turned and raised herself on her toes to kiss me. The moment her lips hit mine, guilt and tension churned in my stomach. I quickly pulled away. I gave her a cordial smile and then closed the door.

"I'm a fucking idiot."

I tossed the card on the nearest stand and walked into the bedroom. Pulling my phone from my pocket, I landed on the bed. I pulled up Amy's picture and thumbed over the call button.

Anger surged through me that she'd let me walk out her door. That she'd let what we had go so easily. I tossed the phone onto the bed and headed toward the shower.

STANDING ON THE STEPS TO my front door, I watched the real estate agent place the *For Sale* sign at the end of the driveway. The front door opened behind me and Grams stepped out. She rubbed my back and smiled gingerly at me.

"You sure about this?"

"I am. I need a fresh start. There's nothing left here but painful memories."

"It'll be nice to have you close to home again. What about Rick and Jared? Are they coming too?"

"Not sure yet. They're both still thinking about it. I'll understand if they don't come. This is their home."

The real estate agent pulled out of the driveway, and I walked back inside to change. As I reached the steps, I had to rush the rest of the way to make it to the bathroom in time.

After wiping my face and brushing my teeth, I put on work clothes and met Grams downstairs.

"I can't seem to shake this stomach bug. Every time I'm over it and think I'm better, it comes back. I know it's the stress."

Grams pulled a bowl from the cabinet for the sliced fruit she had set out on the counter. A light chuckle escaped her as she poured the fruit into the bowl.

"It's not a stomach virus."

"Hmm?" I reached around her and stole a piece of fruit. "What do you mean, it's not a stomach virus?"

"Amy, dear, I've been here for four days now, and I've been watching you. It's not a stomach virus. You're pregnant."

My eyes blinked several times before I registered what she had said. I tried calculating back to my last period and I couldn't remember for sure, maybe six or eight weeks ago. "I need to go to the drugstore," is all I managed to sputter.

Sitting in the bathroom, staring at the white stick waiting for it to say my fate, was causing pins and needles to tingle all over my body. I glanced at the test. In bold letters it stated very clearly—pregnant.

My body movements were robotic. I placed the pregnancy test in the trash can and walked out to the bay window in the living room where Grams was sitting reading a book. She raised her eyes to meet mine.

"Positive, wasn't it?"

I swallowed and nodded, still in shock.

"That Brock must've been like a fertile bull to get you pregnant."

Brock.

Hearing his name sent a sting of pain right to my heart.

272

The first two weeks had been excruciating without him. I replayed our argument in my head over and over and cried myself to sleep over the guilt and how much I missed him. Figuring out what was next had been hard to do when not long ago, we were thinking about our future together.

Deciding on a fresh start felt like the right thing for me. I wanted to focus my life on what I loved to do. I wanted to leave behind the pain of the men I'd loved. I wanted to leave behind the pain of my decision to break off the engagement. There were times I regretted my decision, but at other times, I reminded myself it was what was best for both of us.

His mother had made it very clear I wasn't good for Brock, and I'd come to realize she was right. I came with heavy baggage and that baggage would always affect my relationship with him. I didn't want to spend my life fearing that I'd lose him just like I'd lost Darrell, and I didn't want him to change who he was or disown his family because of me.

Committing to my decision didn't make it any easier, though. I missed him daily and everything somehow reminded me of him. To me, moving had been the answer. Maybe I was running away from all of it, but even if I was, moving toward something was better than remaining here feeling miserable, lonely, and wondering if I'd always regret my decision. Not that it mattered much at this point. He hadn't called or tried to reach me either. I assumed he hated me, and I thought that was best in order for him to move on, but now everything, everything I had thought and planned came crashing down with one word. *Pregnant.*

"Are you going to call him?"

My thoughts scattered and my attention returned to Grams.

"No. No sense in calling him. It's too early in the pregnancy, but I do need to call the doctor."

Two days later, I sat in the hospital room getting the full work-up from the doctor. To my shock and surprise, I was an estimated nine weeks pregnant and the fetus was healthy. My body stopped trembling when the doctor told me my baby was okay and handed me my first ultrasound. Seeing the bean shape in the black and white photo suddenly seemed so real to me. A part of Brock Baisdin was growing inside of me. I sobbed in front of the doctor and panicked about the alcohol I had drank. The doctor said it wasn't enough to cause any known damage but from here on out, I was to stay away from alcohol and horseback riding.

Now more than ever, I was going to need Jared's and Rick's help. If I couldn't ride or lift heavy gear, I would need to bring on a third part-time employee. The idea of moving suddenly felt like something I should postpone.

CHAPTER 31

"Y ou're really starting to show now," Heather said behind me as I held up my shirt in front of the mirror.

"I know. Four weeks went by fast. It's time to come clean with the guys and make the call I've been dreading for the last several weeks."

"Maybe he'll take it better than you expect."

I lowered my shirt before joining her on my bed.

"I don't know how he'll react. It's been a long time since we've spoken. What if he wants full custody? What if he doesn't want to be involved at all? What if he wants to give the relationship another try?"

"Okay, twenty questions. I know it's normal to have all these worries, but Brock is an amazing man, and I know he'll want to be in his child's life however he can be."

"When you say it like that—*he's an amazing man*—you make me feel like an idiot for breaking off the engagement."

"You *are* an idiot for breaking off the engagement. You and

Brock were such a great couple. I still don't understand why you ended it."

Guilt and regret churned in my stomach. "You're right, you don't understand. Losing Darrell was hard enough. When I thought I was losing Brock too, something snapped. I couldn't do it anymore. I couldn't do the relationship, the fear of losing him. I come with a lot of emotional baggage. He deserves better."

"You think he deserves someone better than you? That mother of his brainwashed you. Made you doubt everything you two had together and intentionally sabotaged your relationship. If it wasn't for her, I think you'd still be together."

Thankfully, I didn't have to let that thought simmer too long. The sounds of boots hitting hardwood floor sounded downstairs.

Heather's brows pinched inward. "What's Jared doing here?"

"Probably coming in for lunch or something."

Heather's eyes rolled. "He's really been making himself at home around here. That doesn't bother you?"

"No, he's as good of a friend as you are. He worries about me."

Heather let out a breath of air before getting up and closing the bedroom door. She lowered her voice, barely more than a whisper. "I think he more than worries about you. You haven't noticed the way he looks at you or that he's *still* single. He shouldn't be single. He is much too hot to be single. Now he's making himself comfortable in your house. Does he still dote over you?"

I let out a chuckle. "He doesn't dote over me."

"Ah, yeah, he does, like a lovesick puppy. I think he has it bad for you, but hasn't had the right time to tell you. You better tell 'em about that bun in the oven, before he confesses his love for you."

"Shh, he's coming up stairs."

"Ames?"

The door opened and Heather stared at him gawk-eyed. "Seriously? You didn't even knock."

Jared rolled his eyes at her. "Yeah, nice to see you too." His eyes settled on me and he smiled before leaning against the frame of the doorway. "I ate the last of the turkey. I'll pick up some more. What would you like me to do with Honey and Ellie this afternoon? They both are due for work in the training ring."

"Have Honey wear a saddle and make her walk over the bars. Ellie needs to go through the whole circuit at least once."

"Got it. I'll see you both later."

Jared closed the door behind him and Heather stared at me wide-eyed. "And nothing about that was unusual to you?"

"What?"

"You're sharing food, and he entered your closed bedroom door like it's not a big deal to just waltz in on your business. What if you were naked?"

"He knows you're here, and we were just talking, and no, I don't care if he eats the food in the fridge. He replaces it. Why should he have to use a cooler when there's a fridge right here."

"Rick doesn't come in here and eat."

"That's Rick's choice, plus he eats as he works."

"Amy, I love you, but you've become foolish in your older years."

"Oh stop." I walked past her toward the door. "C'mon, I can at least lead Honey while Jared exercises Ellie and you need to get going home. You said you had a hot date tomorrow and I want to hear all about how amazing this new guy is when you call me Monday."

I waved good-bye to Heather as her SUV turned and exited my driveway. Jared walked up behind me, holding Ellie's reins.

"You wanna take her?"

"Nah, I'll walk Honey and get some quality time with her. You're doing excellent with the horses, by the way. You're training skills have really improved."

"I did learn from the best." He winked at me before adjusting Ellie's reins and stepping into the saddle. "Honey is all set. Saddle is already on her."

I watched Jared ride off into the training ring wondering if any bit of what Heather had said about Jared was true.

After several hours of work, I tucked my work gloves into my back pocket and headed for the house. My phone call to Brock couldn't wait any longer, and I'd been working up the courage to make the call for the last hour. Before leaving the barn, Jared caught up with me.

"Hey Ames, you up for having a drink tonight?"

"I'm sorry, I can't. I have some things I need to take care of."

"How about tomorrow? The new guy, Devon, works tomorrow and I'd like to take you out."

The statement took me by surprise. *Take me out.* Did he mean as a friend or something more? Damn Heather. She had my mind completely twisted.

"Yeah, tomorrow is fine."

After a shower and a quick dinner, I sat at the bay window watching the sun falling into the pink and baby-blue sky peeking out between the barren trees. I thumbed over Brock's photo nervously then took the plunge and clicked the photo. My nerves exploded as soon as it started to ring.

SITTING ACROSS THE RESTAURANT BOOTH from John, I pulled my buzzing phone from my pocket. Seeing Amy's photo and name on my screen put my stomach into a knot. I froze, wondering what the hell she wanted after all this time. She'd ripped my heart right out of my chest and didn't bother to speak to me for the next two and a half months after. Why now did she have something to say?

"Dude, what the fuck? You're staring at your phone like it's a snake about to bite you."

"It's Amy."

"Reject the call."

"I'll let it go to voicemail."

"No, dude, reject the call."

John snatched the phone out of my hand, hitting the reject

button before handing it back to me. "It doesn't matter what she's calling for. You've moved on."

Had I really? I'd gone on a few dates with Jessica and I still hadn't let things go any further than they originally had. Admittedly, I saw her more as a distraction. Just about every damn night, Amy's face still haunted me. I couldn't honestly give another woman my heart when it still belonged to Amy.

John's raised voice pulled me from my thoughts. "Dude, bring your ass back to the present. I asked you if you were seeing Jessica tomorrow?"

"Oh, yeah. Takin' her out to dinner and a movie. She wants to go to some Peruvian restaurant in town. I don't know what the hell kinda food is at a Peruvian restaurant."

"This Jessica is pretty high-maintenance from the shit you've been tellin' me. Is the pussy worth it?"

"Wouldn't know."

John about spit his beer out. "What the fuck do you mean, you don't know? You've been on how many dates with her? What are you waiting for?"

"Jesus John, my sex life is none of your damn business."

"All right, all right. Calm down, just making conversation. Let's go play some pool and get your mind off shit."

Playing pool had taken my mind off things, but now six or seven beers in and my mind was right back to Amy and the first time I'd met her. Just the thought of that night and how fucking good it felt to be inside her was making me stiff. I set the pool cue against the wall and headed for another beer from the table. My phone buzzed, and I quickly looked at the screen, hoping it was Amy again. Jessica's text popped up on my screen. Damn, the girl was needy for attention. Something Amy never was. No, with her it was always natural. I grabbed the beer and nodded to John and the other crew members who had come in late, that I was stepping outside.

"I saw your text to call you. What's up?"

"I was hoping we could get together tonight."

"I can't. I'm out with the guys."

"I can join you. I'm in the mood to go out."

"Not tonight, Jess. I'd like to keep it with the guys."

"Fine. Still on for tomorrow?"

"Yeah. Pick you up at six."

Leaning against the outside wall, I took another swig of my beer, and stared at Amy's call from earlier. I couldn't get her out of my mind. One phone call and it was as if the last ten weeks I'd spent trying to get over her were non-existent. As the memories flooded my mind, it was like my emotions were riding a carousel. I thumbed her picture and was about to click it when John walked out of the restaurant door.

"Don't do it, man." The rest of the guys billowed out behind him. "We're headed over to Flamingo's. Get your dollar bills ready."

CHAPTER 32

*J*ared pulled the chair out for me before sitting across from me. I opened Stonie's menu and perused the specials.

"What are you gonna order?" I asked Jared.

"A pizza. You wanna split it?"

"Yeah, that sounds good."

After the waitress took our order and brought our drinks, Jared leaned back in his chair and studied me.

"You seemed a little off today. You wanna talk about it?"

"You can read me too well."

"You wear your feelings on your sleeve. I can always tell when something is bothering you."

"There is something, but it's not something I want to talk about."

Jared leaned forward and rested his elbows on the table. "All right, then let's talk about the fact that you've brought on a new hire, you aren't riding as much these days, you haven't had a lick of alcohol in weeks, and you're shirts have become a lot baggier."

A little shocked, I looked at him wide-eyed. "You're way too observant."

"We pretty much live side by side five to six days a week. It wasn't difficult to notice the changes."

"All right. I'll confirm what you already seem to know. I'm pregnant."

Jared clicked his tongue and sat back in the chair again. "All right. Now that we got that out of the way. Does he know?"

I shook my head. "I tried calling him last night, and he rejected the call. He didn't call back either. I tried again tonight, and it went to voicemail. It's clear he doesn't want to speak to me."

The waitress set the pizza on the table, and Jared broke a slice off and put it on a plate for me.

"What are your plans now?"

"I don't know. I'll keep trying to get a hold of him. If he doesn't come around, it's fine, I can raise the baby on my own."

"You don't have to be alone."

Jared's eyes settled on mine and locked me in place.

"I...don't know what to say." My eyes darted from him to the pizza and back.

Jared let out a chuckle. "You don't have to say anything. I'm not asking for your hand in marriage, Ames. I'm telling you that I'll be here for you. No matter what you need."

"That means a lot to me. You've done so much for me already. I owe you so much more than a thank you."

Jared smiled and pointed to the pizza on my plate. "Dig in before it gets cold."

After answering all of Jared's pregnancy questions and a

couple games of pool, Jared walked me through the parking lot to his vehicle. He opened the passenger door to his truck and held it open for me.

"Ames."

I turned to face him, and he rubbed his brow in thought.

"About that thank you."

He let go of the truck door and moved toward me, placing his hand around the waist of my growing belly and the other to the nape of my neck. His lips came down on mine—sweet, soft and passionate.

I opened my eyes, and he looked down at me with affection. He rubbed his thumb along my cheek and smiled at me.

"I've been waiting to do that for a long time."

I lowered my head as a combination of emotions took a roller coaster ride through my stomach.

"Jared...I—"

"Ames, you don't have to say or do anything. I've seen what you've been through. I know you don't want a relationship. I know what you're afraid of, so I'm not asking for a commitment."

Both of his hands pushed my jacket aside, exposing my belly. His warms hands held me by the waist as his thumbs caressed me gently. "I meant it when I said I'd be here for you, no matter what."

In my periphery, I caught movement from another vehicle. My jaw nearly dropped when I saw the couple getting out of the car. I pinched my lip between my teeth, nervous about what they might have seen. I moved my jacket to cover my belly, and Jared eased his hands from my waist. He glanced at the couple and then back at me. He rubbed my arm and opened the truck door.

"Let me get you home."

MY PHONE BUZZED ON THE nightstand. I glanced at the clock to see it was eleven forty-five at night. Bethany's face showed behind the accept or reject buttons. I debated rejecting, but was worried it might be serious.

"You know it's late, right?"

"Brock, wake the fuck up, right now."

Her anxious voice sprung me awake. I sat up in my bed. "What is it?"

"Are you awake? Are you listening?"

"Yes, damn it. Get to the point."

"Lexa and Roger saw Amy and the guy who works on her ranch tonight."

"And?"

"He was kissing her. And Brock...Lexa thinks she might be pregnant."

I leaned my head back against the headboard, trying to calm the eruption of emotions exploding through my body.

"Lexa was positive it was Amy?"

"Yes."

"And he was kissing her?"

"Yeah, he had her between him and his truck."

"Pregnant? She has a belly?"

"Yes, Lexa said it's hard to say how far along she is. Two, maybe three months."

"Thanks for the call. I'll talk to you later."

"Wait? What? That's it? You don't have anything else to say?"

"No, B. I need to get off the phone. I have a flight to book."

I clenched the phone in my hand as I walked to the kitchen. The only thing that would bring down the Baisdin temper at this hour was a shot—or three—of whiskey. I slammed the phone on the counter and reached for the bottle. I yanked the top and swigged.

Two or three months repeated in my head. I did the math. It was either my child or Jared's. The thought of him having her like that burned a hole right through me. If it was his child, the man was going to lose his fucking head.

I took another swig. Of course, it wasn't his. Amy broke off the engagement because of her fear of losing me. She didn't want a relationship. She didn't want to live her life fearing the what ifs. The child wasn't his. It was my baby growing in her belly. There's no way in hell I was going to let another man take what's mine.

Morning came and I dragged myself to the shower before downing a couple aspirins and a bottle of water. After booking my flight the night before, I'd finished what was left of the whiskey. I had a lot to work through in one night. The information Bethany had given me was a lot to take in. I was sure this was the reason Amy tried calling me and my stupid ass was busy wining and dining a woman I had absolutely no feelings for.

I grabbed my luggage bag, left the remainder of my rent and the condo key in an envelope for the landlord, and dropped it at the front office. After packing my truck up, I drove to the worksite to let John know I'd be leaving.

He looked at me in shock. "You're going back to Kentucky for her?"

"Damn straight I am. Amy's pregnant with my child. I never should've let her cut me out of her life in the first place. My own ego and the shit from my past had me acting like a damn idiot. I should have fought for her and now another man is trying to take my place. There's no way in hell I'm letting that happen. That's my fiancée—*my* child."

"What about the work that needs done here?"

"You're fully capable of finishing without me. There isn't much left to do and the crew already knows what needs done at this point. I'll cut you an extra check for taking over. I'll try to come back before the job is done, if I can."

"All right, man. This is crazy, but do what you gotta do. Call me when you get a chance."

I tossed him the work-truck keys. "Will do. I gotta go. My flight leaves in an hour."

I WALKED INTO THE BARN, and Jared's eyes lit up when he saw me. He already had Honey saddled and ready for me to lead in the training ring.

"How ya feeling?" he asked softly.

"Not sure yet."

Jared let out a chuckle. "The fact that you haven't fired me or yelled at me is a good sign."

"I wouldn't do either. You've been incredible to me these last few months."

Jared adjusted the straps on Honey's saddle. "But?"

I took Honey's reins and smiled at Jared. "But nothing. You said you weren't asking for anything from me, and I believe you."

"I might've lied when I said that."

My brows pinched inward. "What do you mean?"

Jared turned to me and placed his fingers under my chin, gently raising my lips to his. "I'd like permission to steal kisses from these lips."

"The answer is no."

I whipped my head toward the familiar baritone of Brock's voice. With his arms crossed, he was leaning in the doorway of the barn, looking at Jared as if he was seconds away from turning my barn into a crime scene. It felt like my heart had leapt out of my chest and then clawed its way back in. My stomach did a loop-the-loop and my arm instinctively went to my waist, trying to conceal my swollen belly.

In an attempt to avoid a testosterone-fueled blood-bath I looked at Jared. "Can you give us a minute?"

Jared nodded and walked toward the barn entrance. He and Brock eyed each other with dripping animosity. Those seconds it took until Jared disappeared were agonizing. Once he was gone from sight, Brock finally eased his posture.

He looked me up and down, seeming to inspect me. I fidgeted under the stare of his intoxicating hazel-green eyes. I'd forgotten how gorgeous this man was. I didn't think it was possible for his muscles to get any bigger, but apparently, these last few months he'd spent time proving I was wrong. His massive frame nearly drowned out the light shining through the doorway behind him as he moved toward me.

I froze in place, unable to do anything but tremble under his gaze and the heated tension between us. He reached me and stood inches from my face, studying me as if he'd forgotten what I looked like.

"You're so damn gorgeous."

His hand wrapped around my neck, fisting part of my hair as his mouth claimed mine. That heated tension jolted me back to life. My body hummed with need. Arousal trickled to my core and exploded, leaving me wet and aching with want. His tongue dove in and out, pushing me to the point of begging for more. His hand wrapped around my waist, pulling me to him. My belly pressed against his waist, and he released our kiss, leaving me breathless. He glanced down at my belly and back at me, his grin wide with pride.

"That's why you called, isn't it? That's our baby that you're carrying." His hand gently rubbed along the side of my belly. My hand covered his and watched him stare at my belly as if it was the most magnificent thing he'd ever seen. I couldn't help smiling as I watched his eyes light up.

"It is, our baby."

He met my gaze and then kissed me softly. "I never should've left. I never should've let you push me away. You were scared and I get that now. You thought you'd almost lost me and it broke you and instead of comforting you, I let my ego and temper get the best of me. When you said you couldn't do this anymore, it broke me too. Amy, baby, we've both made mistakes, but I can promise you now, I'm here to stay. I'm not going anywhere. You, this baby, are my world, everything I need and want. I promised you before that I would never let you go. I'm here now to keep to that promise." His thumb grazed my lower lip before his hand took hold of my face and caressed my cheek. The warmth of his touch soothed every painful moment since the day he'd left.

"Tell me you love me. Tell me you'll be my wife."

PART III
ALL I EVER WANTED

CHAPTER 33

"Shh, you're gonna wake her."

Brock pulled my ear between his teeth and in a low, sensual voice he whispered, "It's not me who's gonna wake her. Mommy's about to get real loud, real soon."

I giggled as his tongue left a trail of wet kisses down my stomach. When his mouth reached below, I fisted the bed sheets and bit my lip between my teeth, keeping myself from moaning and screaming his name. Brock looked up at me and grinned when I came undone. He eased between my thighs and pressed his erection into me, filling me completely.

His hand held my thigh as he rocked me against him, taking me hard. His other hand rubbed my clit and my head tilted back as another orgasm swept over me.

Brock eased me down and rested his arms on each side of me. "Damn, baby, I can never get enough of you."

He placed kisses on my cheeks, lips, and chin before rolling me to my side, along with him. He rubbed his hand along my thigh as his gaze met mine.

"I love you."

His hand caressed my cheek before he pressed his lips into mine. "I love you, too. In this lifetime and the next."

The monitor on the nightstand lit up, followed by moans and then crying.

"She's awake."

"Take a shower and get cleaned up. I'll get her."

Brock grabbed his boxer briefs and left the room. I took my time enjoying the hot water cascading down my back, relaxing my tired muscles. Once out, I wrapped myself in one of Brock's flannels and put on a pair of my shorts. With my hair fastened in a bun, I slid my feet into slippers and walked down the hall to check on things. I entered Emma's room to find Brock lying in the recliner with Emma passed-out on his chest. He too was fast asleep with one protective hand laying over her back. I stood in the doorway, my heart swollen with love, watching the two most precious gifts I'd ever been given.

Two Years Later...

I WALKED TO THE BARN with our new dog in tow. Emma had repeatedly squealed, "my puppy," when she first saw the black, little, runt Labrador. Of course, I couldn't turn down my baby girl. Not with that kind of enthusiasm. Hell, I rarely turned her down for anything. Something that drove her mother absolutely crazy.

In the barn was my beautiful wife, preparing two horses, while Emma ran around discovering everything in sight.

"You about ready?"

"Yep, just need you to load the packs and we're good."

I hoisted the packs onto both horses, put myself into Thunder's saddle, and then lifted Emma from Amy's waiting hands. She wiggled in the saddle, overwhelmed with excitement for our camping trip. Little did she know, the trip was in our own back yard. Amy never did sell the property. I spent time remodeling and when I was done, she barely recognized the house. Of course, with all the new updates, she didn't want to leave. The new porch swing I installed was my final touch and I sealed the deal with that.

Jared quit working at the ranch the day after I arrived back in town. He and Amy stayed in touch, though. He now works for the same racetrack I once worked at. The last time Amy spoke to him, he said he loved his job and thanked her for her reference and training over the years. Without her, he never would have landed the job he did. I'm not thrilled that they stayed in touch, but I can't fault the man for wanting to be friends with my wife. She is an incredible woman.

After I returned and got settled back into our home, Amy shared with me everything that had happened between her and my mother. It took me six months to be able to speak to her again. Once Emma was born, I couldn't bring myself to keep her from her grandchild. The moment she set eyes on Emma, my mother's entire view of Amy changed. Suddenly, Amy was the best thing that'd ever happened to me. Funny how a tiny, little, blue-eyed girl can do that to a person.

I consider Emma my good luck charm. She has the ability to bring everyone together. She brought Amy back to me and her great-grandmother, Grams, now lives a lot closer than she used to. Grams couldn't stand the idea of being so far away from her great-grand-daughter so I thought what better solution than to move her into my old home. She's now six miles away and alternates watching Emma with my mother, so Amy and I can have time for just us every once in a while.

Looking down at the dark-haired, blue-eyed angel, attentive to everything her eyes can see, I couldn't help feeling like the luckiest man in the world. I looked over at Amy and she gave me a cheeky grin.

"What's the smirk for, gorgeous?"

"It's gonna be my last ride for a while, so I'm taking it all in."

"Last ride?"

She giggled and smiled at me. "I'm pregnant."

Thank you for reading Fire on the Farm! I hope it left an imprint on your heart like it did mine. If you loved Fire on the Farm, and would like to read another passionately beautiful story, begin the friends-to-lovers romance with Unbreak This Heart!

UNBREAK THIS HEART

Ever since that horrific night, I'd shut men completely out of my life. I'd gone from the spunky, fun, Alex DeMarco to a broken woman terrified of intimacy. Easing me back into dating, my best friend sets me up with kickboxing lessons from my charming and perfectly sculpted instructor--Carter Maxwell.

Carter's goal is to break through my emotional barrier and mold my heart just like he molds my body, but trusting men is a battle I'm not ready for. What's worse is my ex-fiancé, Todd Livingston--the man who tore my heart in two--wants me back, and as much as I'd like to deny it, the feelings are still there.

Both men want what I can't give--my body and my love--and neither are willing to give up the fight. But only one of them can unbreak this heart of mine.

"Unbreak This Heart is a one of kind story. It grabs you from the first page until the last. The chemistry between Alex and Carter is instant and hot. I love that Carter and Alex are there for each other. Together they make each other stronger / better. I appreciate all the thought that the author put into making this an incredible book. I highly recommend Unbreak This Heart!" ~ Kiki Reader Book Blog, 5-star review

Begin Unbreak This Heart at bettyshreffler.com!

Join my newsletter for new releases, book discounts, and book news - Subscribe at bettyshreffler.com

Turn the page for a Chapter 1 preview of Unbreak This Heart...

CHAPTER 1

UNBREAK THIS HEART

Alex

*T*he loud, obnoxious buzzing of my cell phone on my nightstand reminds me it's time to wake. I only fell into an exhausted sleep three hours ago. Dragging my heavy legs off the bed, I stumble to stand and make my way into the kitchen. The cool tile floor feels refreshing against my warm feet. It's the first thing every morning that jolts my body awake and reminds me I can still feel something —*anything*.

With the direction my life has gone these last several weeks, it amazes me I haven't lost everything. My boss has taken pity on me and given me many passes, but it will only last so long. I need to get my shit together. I'm trying. I swear I am but surviving an attack in your own home isn't something you recover from quickly.

Moving to a new apartment in Villa Heights was a way to cope. Every time I walked into my old apartment, I was reminded of that night. Leaving behind all of my furniture and telling my landlord to sell it or use it was an easy choice for me. The apartment had become a desolate cave, filled with despair, anger, fear, and disgust. It was no longer my home. I would've burned it down to the ground and watched it incinerate if given the chance.

The Keurig machine grinds and hisses, and I'm snapped back to the present. Pulling the mug from the base, I hold it between my narrow fingers and bask in the warmth before bringing the hot liquid to my lips. As it warms my throat, it sheds the last of the lingering night.

My hand curls around the white curtain and pulls it away from the floor to ceiling window, letting the Florida sunlight illuminate the room and fill every crevice of my apartment. After another sip, I close my eyes and concentrate on the sensation warming my skin. I need these little moments— moments where I forget the pain, the desolation, the loneliness.

Ever since the attack, I haven't dated. I had a fiancé, but the coward took off when I needed him the most. I can't blame him though. I became a broken woman. I was no longer the spritely, kinky, fun Alex I used to be.

Now I'm the workaholic, structured, paranoid, can't bring myself to love Alex. If not for my best friend, Jane I may not be here at all. Her spunk and loyalty gave me a string to hold on to—something to grasp onto in my deepest, darkest moments.

Glancing at the gym certificate on the table, I smile. After mentioning I wanted to take a self-defense class, it was Jane who left me a sparkly card on my birthday with a gift certificate for eight weeks of kickboxing and self-defense classes, all expenses paid. You see why I love her?

My first class is at nine and I don't want to be late. After a quick shower, I carefully choose something comfortable. I'm not a gym enthusiast, but I do know I'm gonna need as much flexibility as my clothes will allow. Settling on a peach racerback tank and black, knee-length, athletic, yoga pants, I wrap my chocolate hair into a ponytail, grab my bag and keys, and head out the door.

As I pull up to the gym, I'm already feeling good about the place. It has large windows across the front of the building. With the sun shining, I can see inside clearly. There's a class now, a group of women hitting and kicking bags with all their might. I take a breath, committing to my endeavor. It's now or never.

Opening the door, I'm overwhelmed with nerves. The eyes that descend on me, the smell of sweat and metal, and the symphony of grunts do nothing to calm them. A pretty girl with short, wavy, dark hair gives me a toothy grin from behind the front desk.

"Welcome to Raise the Bar. What can I do for you?"

I hand her my certificate.

"Oh great! You'll be with Carter. He's the best. He's finishing up the eight a.m. kickboxing class. If you want to take a seat and fill out this sheet, he'll be over when he's finished."

"Thanks," I reply, taking the clipboard from her hand.

Moving to the small waiting area that blocks my view of the current kickboxing class, I listen to a guy with a smooth and authoritative baritone instruct the women to stretch and drink water before telling them they did a great job this morning. Filling in my name and information, I wait for the next class participants to arrive.

My nerves etch wrinkles across my forehead when no other women show up, but several depart from the class that just ended. Stepping up to the counter, I place the completed form on it.

"Excuse me."

The sweet girl turns to me. "What can I help you with?"

"The certificate says nine. Was it printed wrong? No one else seems to be showing up."

"No, it's printed correctly," the young woman smiles kindly. "It's a certificate for private classes."

"Private classes?"

"Yeah, here's Carter now."

She points behind me, and I turn to see a magnificent specimen of a man walking toward me while he lowers what appears to be a fresh shirt. Flapping wings go into a tizzy, giving my stomach an unfamiliar sensation. I stare, a bit mesmerized by the broad shoulders, muscular arms, and the peek I saw of his chiseled chest and the tribal tattoo laced across his torso. And those abs! I've never seen someone in the flesh with an actual eight-pack.

Before I embarrass myself, I peel my eyes off him, glance back at the girl, and smile. The warmth of my flushed cheeks adds to my embarrassment. She gives me a knowing grin.

A smooth baritone breaks me from my internal anxiety attack.

"Hey, you must be my nine o'clock. I'm Carter."

Turning to face him, I accept his extended hand and give it a firm shake.

"I'm Alex."

Deep blue eyes study my face for what seems like an

eternity. Steadying my trembling knees, I give what's probably a crooked, awkward smile.

"Come on back. I'll show you around, then we can get started."

I follow like a loyal, scared puppy as he points and explains where things are and what equipment is what. He leads me into an area with padded floor mats, kickboxing bags, and equipment hanging from the low ceiling.

"Do you have a pair of good gloves?"

"No. I should've got some. I didn't think of it."

"It's all right. I have a pair you can borrow for today, but it will be better if you have your own pair to train with."

"Got it. I'll take care of that later today."

Carter smiles and that incessant flapping in my stomach startles me. His smile is too charming, too sexy. Avoiding his gaze, I find a place to drop my bag.

"When you're ready, we'll start with some stretches, then we'll move into some simple exercises of punches and kicks. I'll try not to work you too hard on your first day. I want you to come back," he chuckles, pinning me with that sexy smile.

"I kind of have to. My friend paid for these classes. I'm not going to let her waste her money, and honestly, I'm here to learn."

He moves to a stereo and hits a button. Upbeat music filters out through the speakers but not loud enough I can't hear him clearly.

"What would you like to learn, Alex? What are your goals?"

I cross my arms, unsure of what to do with them.

"I'd like to learn to defend myself."

Carter observes my body language with every one of my

movements. He's studying me and that makes me uncomfortable. Biting my lip, I rub my suddenly chilled arms.

"Have a seat. We're gonna stretch, then I'm going to help you reach your goal."

Sitting down, I outstretch my legs. Sitting in front of me, he outstretches his. I copy him as he moves one direction, then the other. He stands, and I follow his movements, stretching limb after limb, loosening my tight muscles.

"Good. You ready to start?"

When I nod, he grabs me a pair of pink gloves. With his assistance, I get them on, then he slides on a pair of punching mitts. Standing in front of me, he raises them eye level.

"What I want you to do is put your front leg forward and get a confident, steady stance, then punch with your right, left, then duck."

Repeating the words in my head—*right, left, duck*—I start swinging. My glove makes impact, then I lower my body before his left mitt hits me in the face.

"Good, again, but I want you to keep your gloves close to your chin. Protect your face."

Everything repeats in my head—*right, left, duck—keep gloves to cheeks*. I put power into my punches and make contact. He swings, and I hurry to duck, just missing the mitt to my face.

"Good," he winks. "Again."

This repetition continues several more times before he tells me to switch my leg and punch the opposite direction. Once more, I have to tell my brain where I'm supposed to hit before being able to make contact. The words repeat, and soon, I'm anticipating his swings and falling into a rhythm.

"Good." He lowers the mitts as I catch my breath.

"You're a natural, Alex, and your form isn't far off either. Take a drink, then we'll start on kicks."

After drinking water and getting my breath regulated, I return to him on the mat. He motions for me to follow him to an elongated kicking bag, sticking up from its floor anchor.

"I want you to kick this bag. Here first." He toes the bottom. "Then here." His shoe points to the middle. "Then here." Lastly, his shoe faces the top. "But when you kick, I want you to put your weight on the front pad of your foot. Let your body swivel and you'll be able to put more power into your kicks."

He demonstrates, and I stumble back, startled by the sheer force and speed of his kicks.

"Got it?"

"Yeah," I reply meekly, "I think so."

Replicating his movements, I swivel too far and my ankle dips. Strong hands catch my fall and stabilize me. "I gotcha."

The touch of his hands to my waist ignites an odd combination of sensations. I haven't been touched affectionately by a man in over a year, and my response to the graze of his hands is equally startling as it is tantalizing. Immediately, I wiggle from his grasp.

"Thanks."

My shy embarrassment appears to amuse him. Staring at me, his eyes soften.

"It's all right. It's your first day. A strong core takes time and practice. We'll get you there. You ready to try again?"

Nodding, I approach the bag. With concentration, I attack, giving it everything I have.

"Switch," I hear behind me.

Lowering my leg, I rotate my stance and begin my kicks

on the other side. He says switch two more times before our time on this bag is through.

"Great job, Alex. That was better. You have the drive to do well, and that will get you through all your training."

Silly as it is, I feel warm and fuzzy from his praise. "Thank you."

"You need a break or you ready for more?"

"A quick water break and I'll be ready."

The next thirty minutes, Carter puts me through more punch and kick practices, and I begin to think, *wax on, wax off.* He's teaching me proper form and how to keep my stance strong which makes my punches and kicks more powerful. By the end, I'm panting and wiping sweat from my brow. He tosses me a towel and nods for us to sit.

"You've done really well today, it being your first time. You had serious power in your kicks."

Little did he know who I was imagining when kicking those bags. I stumble through removing my first glove, and Carter smiles.

"Here, let me."

Strong hands that were demonstrating how to demolish a punching bag earlier are now providing a gentler touch as he pulls the wristband off my glove and eases my hand out of it. He takes my hand in his and I flinch at the unexpected touch. His observant gaze watches my response and tilts my hand back and forth for inspection.

"This is why your own set of gloves will work better. These are MMA gloves. You won't have these marks on your knuckles with your own hand wraps or kickboxing gloves."

Deep blue irises meet my gaze and lock me in his stare. Something passes between us like an unruly itch running across my skin. I quickly withdraw my hand and tear my gaze from his mesmerizing eyes.

"Any recommendations of where to buy gloves?" I ask as I remove my second glove and avoid getting locked in an awkward stare again.

It's been a very long time since I found a man attractive. I came to the conclusion love and men are a loss for me. I'm destined to live alone and be married to my work. These odd sensations coursing through me at the scent of his masculine soap and sweat, his beautiful blue eyes, and the innocent touch of his hands are unfamiliar territory for me.

"You can buy some at the shop here, on Amazon, or any MMA site. I'll walk you to the shop and help you pick out a pair if you'd like."

"That'd be great."

I'm ready to get away from him before I get any dizzier, but I genuinely need his help with picking out the right kind of gloves. He nods and a deal is struck. Taking the borrowed gloves off the floor, he wipes them out and tosses them in his duffle. Grabbing my own bag, I follow him to the store, packed full of workout gear.

He points to different gloves in different colors, and I catch myself staring at his short, milk chocolate hair, strong pronounced jaw, and the scruff lining it. His eyes though are what keep me from being able to look away. They're a deep, soft blue that give the impression of tenderness beneath the masculinity. Turning his head at the right moment, he catches me staring, and I quickly point to a pair of gloves.

"Those ones will work."

"Good choice." Pulling a green pair off the peg, he carries

my gloves to the register, leaving me tagging behind and still unable to escape his distracting presence.

"Give her my discount," he tells the clerk.

The shaggy-haired fella nods and rings up the gloves.

"You didn't have to do that."

"I do it for all my clients," Carter smiles and traps me in the pool of deep blue.

"Of course. Thank you." Embarrassed, I hide my flushed cheeks by digging my wallet out of my bag. Carter watches me as I check out. His lingering is causing a twitch in my jaw and my weight to shift from one foot to the other.

"So, I'll see you Tuesday evening then?"

"Hmm? Oh, yes, Tuesday's session. Thanks for everything today. I'll see you then."

Carter taps the counter and makes his way back into the gym. I let out a breath and stare at the clerk, almost forgetting why I was there in the first place. He hands me my bag and I dart out of the gym. Before I make it to the car, I'm dialing Jane.

"Hey, babe! What's up? How was your first sess?"

"*Jane Marie Anthony*. Private lessons? That had to have cost you a fortune!"

"Eh, don't worry about it. It's a gift from Kyle and me. You mentioned it so many times, I thought it was time to make you do it."

"And the trainer? Have you *seen* him?"

"Oh, yes. Carter," Jane laughs. "He's great. He's friends with Kyle. Kyle suggested him, and when I met him, I thought he was perfect for you."

"What do you mean *perfect* for me?" I ask, leaning my weight against my car.

"Well, you know? He's hot and single, and you're hot and single. Figure it out, babe."

"Jane, you know I can't even fathom a relationship."

"Honey, you won't know until you try. You do think he's cute though, right?"

Shuffling my foot, I let out an exasperated breath. "Yes, he's gorgeous and his eyes... Jane, he has the most beautiful eyes I've ever seen."

A tap on my shoulder sends me spiraling and falling into Carter's arms. I move like lightning to get out of his grasp and gather my exploding emotions.

Oh my God, did he just hear that?

Carter stabilizes me, then waves my water bottle in the air, grinning ear to ear. "You forgot this."

I can hear Jane giggling through the phone.

My hand grabs the water bottle as my expression no doubt reveals how mortified I am. Carter doesn't say anything about the comments I'm sure he just heard.

"Would you like to have dinner with me tomorrow night?"

Heat rises to my cheeks. I know my face is a solid, rosy red at this point.

"I can't. I'm sorry." Turning away from him, I dive into my car and leave before I embarrass myself any further.

"You seriously bolted after he asked you to dinner?"

Jane brings her freshly filled wine glass to my table and sits across from me, her long, lengthy legs wrapping around each other. She takes a sip, and I fidget at the sight of her bold, brown eyes scrutinizing me over the brim of her glass.

"Yes. I'm not ready. It's too soon." Raising my glass of wine to my lips, I pause. I hadn't expected to feel a tinge of regret at saying no to Carter. *Am I ready to date again? Have I laid my demons to rest enough to be able to give my heart and body to a man?*

"If you think any harder, you're going to form permanent wrinkles on that pretty face of yours."

I chuckle before letting the refreshing liquid soothe my edginess.

"He's the first man you've been attracted to. Why not give it a try?"

Jane's persistence is understandable. She knows me better than anyone even better than I know myself sometimes, but the thought of opening myself up emotionally and physically is terrifying. My apprehension and fear are a gap that lays between us, and she'll never be fully able to understand it.

"One step at a time. I'd like to conquer my first goal and make it through my classes. Trying to date my instructor would only make things more complicated."

"Sure, babe," Jane agrees, tapping her manicured nails on the table, "one step at a time."

I glance at her emotionless face. I know her too well not to recognize the intellectual wheels turning behind the expressionless mask.

She's not going to let this go…

Find Unbreak This Heart at bettyshreffler.com!

ALSO BY BETTY SHREFFLER

Healed Hearts Romance Collection
FIRE ON THE FARM
MY HOT BOSS
UNBREAK THIS HEART

Kings MC Series
CASTLE OF KINGS
CLIPPED WINGS
KING OF KINGS

Novellas
COUNTDOWN TO CHRISTMAS

View books at: bettyshreffler.com

ABOUT THE AUTHOR

Hi, I'm Betty Shreffler. A USA Today and International Bestselling Romance Author. I writes sexy and suspenseful stories with hot alphas and kickass heroines with twists you don't expect. I also write beautiful and sexy romances with tough women and their journeys at finding love. If I'm not writing or doing book events, you can find me creating book cover designs, snuggling with my dogs watching a movie, or enjoying the outdoors on my motorcycle.

Let's keep in touch!

Join my newsletter for new releases, book discounts, and book news - Subscribe at bettyshreffler.com!

Join my Facebook readers' group: Betty's Book Beauties and Bad Boys

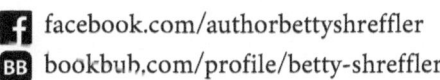

facebook.com/authorbettyshreffler
bookbub.com/profile/betty-shreffler